# The Rules of EverAfter

### KILLIAN B. BREWER

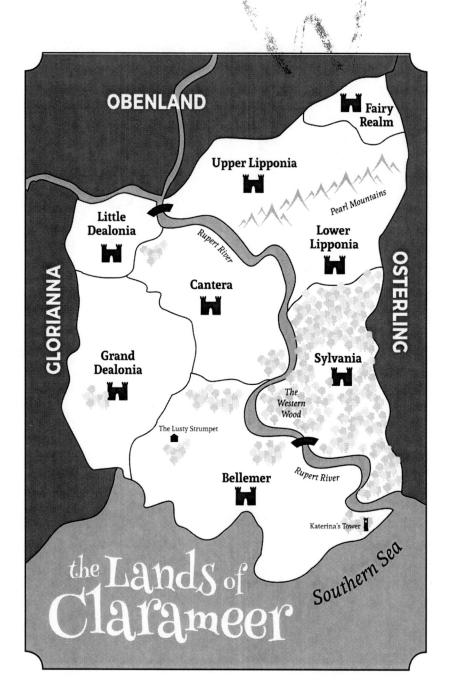

the Lands of Clarameer

# The Rules

## of EverAfter

KILLIAN B. BREWER

duet
an imprint of interlude press

*To F, my prince.*

# $\mathcal{P}$ROLOGUE

O NCE UPON A TIME, BUT ABOUT SIX MONTHS BEFORE that, Mitta, the Wednesday fairy, snuffled awake and mindlessly flipped the pink tip of her right wing to swat at a fly buzzing around her ear. She was not sure how long it had been bumbling about her head or how it had managed to get into the castle, but the humming had been irritating enough to pull her out of her hazy nap.

In the years that had passed since her ward had last done anything to warrant a blessing, Mitta found she fell far too easily into sleep at any moment of the day. Her sisters had each lucked into at least two royal children to keep an eye on, but only one in this generation had been born on a Wednesday, her day. In the first few years after her ward's birth eighteen years ago, Mitta had thought having only one child to deal with was a pleasant break. The previous generation's births had given her seven wards in the three great realms to watch over. She had almost worn her tiny wings to nubs flitting about the industrious lands of Clarameer to the south, the exotic luxuries of Osterling to the east and the quiet studiousness of Glorianna to the west to bestow blessings on births, marriages and other events. After that exhausting time, she felt she deserved an easy assignment.

However, as the years had passed, she had discovered that having just one child to watch over might have been enjoyable if he had been a more adventurous, happier child. He had been through some tough times at a young age and had needed her blessings to survive. Now, though, his life was just too quiet; she watched with envy as her six sisters popped in and out of Castle Geburtstag to tend to their wards while she sat idly in her room, feeling her wings grow weak and her once perky backside grow decidedly wider.

Slumping deeper into the light pink satin padding on the back of her chair, she heaved a deep sigh and stretched her short, chubby legs out in front of her until the amethyst-encrusted tips of her shoes peeked from the hem of her pink taffeta skirts. Stretching a little farther, she dipped the toes of her shoes into the late afternoon sun, which had begun its slow creep out of her room. A sunbeam tinted rose by the stained glass window across her room reflected off the jewels and sent tiny glitters of light dancing about on the walls. She twisted her ankle quickly back and forth to make the reflections twirl in frenzied curlicues all around her. Focusing on one particularly bright spot on the far wall, she wiggled her toes in an attempt to make it spell out her name. Yawning, she sighed. "Mitta, old girl, you are truly bored."

Picking up the copy of the *Kingdom Inquisitor* that had dropped into her lap before she had nodded off, she glanced again at the headline. "King Robert Seen at Royal Ball with Princess Emma-line! Could a Royal Wedding Unite East and West?" Below the headline was a sketch of a handsome young man dancing with a raven-haired beauty. She knew her sister Dima was behind these developments and would make sure her two brightest wards ended up together.

"Well, happily ever after to you both," Mitta snorted, as she tossed the paper onto the floor. Grabbing her silver wand from the small gilded table beside her chair, she grumbled, "Might as well check in on the boy. It's been months, and surely he must be up to something now that he is approaching marrying age."

She held the wand in front of her face and blew a quick breath through the large silver ring on the tip. A pink bubble formed on the rim of the ring and grew with each breath she huffed, until it slipped free with a slight popping sound. It floated and bounced in front of her, waiting for her to call up the image she wished to see. "Bubble, Bubble, bright and free, show the darling little Phillip to me," she chanted as she dropped the wand back onto the table.

The interior of the bubble filled with pink smoke that swirled and roiled until a hazy image began to appear. "Wow, my reception is terrible today." Mitta tapped the bubble. Inside, the image wavered but remained unclear. "Glasses, Mitta. Glasses," she said, with a roll of her eyes, and then snapped her fingers. A pair of bright pink reading glasses appeared on the tip of her button nose. She leaned closer to the bubble and tilted her head to line up the image within the frame of her lenses. "Oh, to be six hundred again and able to see without these things."

The smoke shifted, revealing the image of a slender young man who was leaning on the rails of a horse pen. His golden crown sat askew on his short brown hair and the hem of his azure doublet flapped slightly in a breeze. Phillip had grown at least two inches since Mitta had last checked in on him on his eighteenth birthday, and she was surprised to see that the gangly, knobby-kneed boy she expected had matured into a striking young man. He kicked aimlessly at the bottom rail of the fence with his left foot and cocked his head; his blue eyes stared at a shirtless, muscular man who led a stallion toward the castle stables. As the man passed, Phillip dropped his chin into his hands and sighed deeply; a far-away dreaminess clouded his eyes.

"Well, who'd have guessed that!" Mitta said with a small laugh. "Well, Philly," she said and shrugged, "it appears Thora was right, and your gate swings to that side of the pasture! I should have checked in on you more often! Guess there won't be an engagement or wedding for me to attend any time soon, unless you're really good at playing 'let's pretend.'"

Just as she reached over to pop the bubble with her fingernail, she noticed the image of a petite girl walking up to the fence beside the prince. Her long red hair fell in ringlets from under a small tiara and bounced about her shoulders. A dark purple belt cinched tight her waist, and pale violet skirts flipped around her ankles with each step. Leaning back against the wooden railing beside the prince, she glanced up at him through her lashes and smiled slightly. She said something to him, and he looked at her with a polite grin. He responded, then turned his back to the railing to lean beside her. The girl's shoulders shook as she giggled and rested her hand on his arm. He shook his head back and forth and removed her hand from his bicep. He turned to look into her eyes and said something else.

"Shoot," Mitta cursed, as she batted the bubble. "I should have upgraded these things to include audio years ago." Leaning closer to the wobbling bubble, she strained to read the young man's lips. He took the girl's hand in his own, leaned close to her face, and said something that made her blush. "Phillip, you little scamp! What did you say to her?" Watching the image of the young couple amble hand in hand toward the castle, Mitta cocked an eyebrow and smirked. "Maybe I misread this situation. I've got to show this to the girls! Finally, some progress!" .

Hastily, she poked her fingernail into the bubble, and it disappeared with another small pop. She hopped down from her chair, grunting at the tightness of her bodice. "Mitta, you need to lay off the pastries if you're finally going to be on the move again!" She brushed her hands down the front of her rosy skirts to smooth away any wrinkles and loosened the laces of her bodice.

Stepping to the gilded mirror hanging on the wall, she inspected her makeup for any smudges or streaks created by her afternoon nap. She snapped her fingers, and the glasses disappeared. She patted her pink bouffant hairdo to push a few stay hairs back into place and then turned to her chamber door.

"Dagnabbit," she spat as she looked back to the table and snapped her fingers toward her wand. It jerked up and flew across the room to her waiting hand. "Why can't you ever stick close?" she chastised the wand as she shoved it into a small loop of fabric on the side of her waist. Flinging open the chamber door, she flapped her wings and rose a few inches off the floor. With a slight lean forward, she flew quickly down the hallway to the grand chamber where she and her sisters gathered.

"Oh, girls! It's finally starting!" Mitta cried as she swept into the large, open hall. The breeze caused by her swift movement made the jewels hanging from the large chandelier in the middle of the room tinkle and the lace curtains over the tall windows flutter. She stopped abruptly as her eyes tried to adjust to the sudden darkness of the room. She could barely see her sisters sitting around the hall, all of them enthralled with the flickering images of their many wards on their magic devices.

"Geez, girls," Mitta chastised, "why are you sitting in the dark? Caught up in your kiddos' lives?" Mitta pulled her wand from her hip and flicked it toward the chandelier. The hundreds of candles on each branch flickered to life and brightened the room. Light reflected off the crystallized walls of the room and scattered tiny rainbows on the floor and on her sisters' faces. Seven carved wooden chairs, each painted a different shade, circled a mahogany table in the center of the room. Two fairies sat at the table in the chairs that matched their dresses and hair—one pale blue and the other lemon. Two other fairies, one clad in violet and one in silver, lounged on plush couches at the edges of the room. Another stood by one of the tall windows and slowly took a deep pull from a bright orange pipe, then blew the smoke into the air.

"Did you hear me? I have news! Come see!" Mitta babbled, as she swept to her pink chair and dropped her wand on the table with a careless clunk.

"What now?" Luna growled, as she shifted her eyes from a glowing yellow glass orb she held in her right hand. "Things were just getting good with Daniel and Andrew. They were having an absolute row over Daniel setting out into the kingdoms. I'm so glad I cursed Andrew with that stubborn streak! He's refusing to let his little brother go alone! What an absolute jackass he can be. These boys are drama gold! Better than anyone you girls have!"

"Yes," Fria sighed, as she dropped the large sapphire jewel she had been staring into; it landed with a plunk on the table in front of her. She pushed a stray blue hair from her face and shot a look of disgust at her sister. "I couldn't watch it anymore and had to change over to watch Princess Dinah playing with a kitten. I love when there are kittens. But you have certainly made things tough for my little Danny."

"No tougher than you did with that ridiculous curse at his birth!" Saba snorted from a couch in the corner and blew out the candle burning before her. As the last curls of violet smoke dissipated, the image in the flame of a raven-haired girl arguing with an older man faded away. "Thank goodness I came up with a way to temper that mess. You could've killed the poor boy! That would hardly have been fair."

"Pfft," Fria scoffed as she waved her sister away. "I knew you'd fix it with your last blessing, and I thought it would spice things up a bit. At least it was original. Should I have done to him what Marta did to King Rupert the Second?" Turning to the girl lounging on the other chaise, she threw her hands up. "Really Marta, you make it so easy on Mitta with those ridiculous appearance curses. Acne? Buck teeth? Receding hairlines?"

"Well, pardon me!" Marta shouted and glared at her sister. She stopped playing with her long silver braid and dropped the hand mirror she was holding onto her lap. "That," she whined, "was a perfectly reasonable curse! No one wants a bald king. It makes the crown slide off too easily! I thought it was rather creative of me to—"

"Girls!" Mitta shouted and pounded her wand on the table. "Aren't you sick of these same old arguments? I have news! Wait, where is Dima?"

"Her ward, Prince Robert, might be proposing to Princess Emmaline tonight!" Marta squealed and clapped her hands. "Dima is off to give it a little nudge! Not interfering, mind you. Just a gentle push. If she pulls her usual tricks, we'll be going to give the engagement blessings tomorrow. Before you know it, a new generation is starting! Couldn't you just spit with happiness? If they have a child on your day, Mitta, you could finally get a prince or princess who is more exciting than the one you have now!"

"No! Wait until you see!" Mitta waved her hands to call her sisters over to her side. "There has been a development on that front! I thought for sure Dima saw it too, since I think the girl is her ward. I have exciting news! Prince Phillip is courting a bride!"

"A what?" Thora asked, as she turned to the table. She took a long draw on her pipe, blew orange smoke into the air and cocked her head. As the smoke circled her head, the image of a costumed young girl dancing on a stage appeared in the haze. "Are you sure you meant bride? Huh. I mean, I'm not judging but I didn't think—"

"Yes! Look!" Mitta giggled, as she lifted her wand from the table and blew several quick breaths through the ring. A bubble quickly formed and floated before the assembled group.

"Oh, joy. Bring on the stupid bubbles," Thora said with a roll of her eyes.

"I like my bubbles. They're fun. And they look so pretty when the light reflects off them and makes little rainbows on the ground! They are certainly more fun than looking into the smoke from your nasty pipe. I swear, all that smoking has made you look ten times your two thousand years."

"Lay off my wrinkles and just get this over with. What's your little boy getting up to now?"

"He was escorting a young girl back to the castle! Just look and see!"

"Unchaperoned?" Saba gasped. "I hardly think that's appropriate! I don't think we should be looking into that bubble if we're going to see what I think we're going to see."

"Hold on," Mitta said with a confused look on her face. She leaned closer to the smoke-filled bubble but saw no image. "The bubble's blank?"

"The spell, you nitwit," Thora said, thumping her sister on the ear.

"Oops!" Mitta giggled. "Bubble, Bubble, full of joy. Show me what's up with my frisky boy!" She snapped her fingers, and her glasses appeared on her nose. "Now let's see…"

The smoke in the bubble shifted, and an image began to form. The young man sat on top of a large stack of mattresses. Beside him, the young redhead lay tucked under the coverlet, her curls splayed on the pillow. One after another, the fairy sisters exclaimed in surprise or delight as they watched the scene in the bubble unfold.

"What, by Godrick's axe, is going on here?"

"Should he be in her bedroom?"

"Oh! I can't watch this."

"Forget watching two boys fighting! A romance I can watch!"

Mitta watched as Phillip said something to the girl, stretched his arms above his head and mimed an obviously fake yawn. The girl shook her head and shrugged. Phillip reached into his sleeve and pulled out a small, green glass bottle with a shiny gold label. With a flourish, he showed it to the girl.

"What is that?"

"I know that label! That looks like a bottle of Dr. Hickenkopf's Miracle Tonic!"

"Why would he give her *that?*"

"I think that's Dima's ward, Marina. If Dima were here, she would knock your wings off!"

"Shhh!" Mitta hissed at her sisters. She slid her glasses up and leaned closer to the bubble. "Little man, what are you doing?" she mumbled, with a slight feeling of worry in her stomach.

In the bubble, the girl sat up and read the label. She smiled at the prince and nodded her head before taking the bottle from him. After removing the stopper, she placed the bottle to her lips, turned it bottom-up and took three large swallows. She handed the bottle back to Phillip and dropped her head onto the pillow. They exchanged a few words, and the girl yawned. Phillip patted her hand, crawled over the footboard and descended to the ground.

"Ha! I knew I was right! He's not interested."

"That bed is absolutely ridiculous. There must be at least twenty mattresses! Really?"

"Is that a testing bed? It looks like a testing bed."

"I haven't seen a testing bed in years! I thought they were completely out of use."

In the bubble, the image began to fade as Phillip landed on the ground and walked away from the mattresses. As he reached the door, he turned and said something.

"What did he say?"

"Where's the sound? Turn the volume up!"

"This is boring. I'm going back to watching the Sylvanian boys fight."

Mitta knitted her brows as she repeated what she read from Phillip's lips. "He said 'Sleep tight. I'm sorry.' Whatever could he mean by that? Does he think that tonic will… Oh! Oh, Phillip! Did you just… You sly thing!"

The image in the bubble faded away completely as the young man extinguished his lamp. Mitta kicked her feet and fluttered her wings and reached over to pop the bubble.

"Girls! Hold onto your wings! I have a feeling this is about to get interesting!"

# CHAPTER 1

THE CASTLE WAS SILENT, WHICH WAS USUAL FOR A TESTING night. Cauchemar, Prince Phillip's stepmother, had decreed it. The only sounds Phillip could hear as he crept down the hallway were the echoing shuffles of his feet and the pounding rhythm of his heart. He grasped his lamp tightly in one hand as he groped along the wall with the other to prevent himself from stumbling over the unevenly paved stones of the hallway floor. As he fumbled his way toward the large oaken door of the testing chamber, the acrid smoke and oil of his lamp made his nostrils sting. The lamp threw flickering shafts of light across the thick tapestries that blocked all outside light from the windows behind them. Hallways that had held so much light and carefree activity for Phillip as a child now were filled with dread as he thought about what lay waiting for him in the chamber beyond.

*How different these halls are at night.* Phillip tripped over something in his path. "Ouch! You'd think after so many times making this trip, I could do it blindfolded. Curse you, Stepmother, and curse your tapestries. Well, might as well get this over with," Phillip mumbled, as he reached out and grabbed the large iron handle of the testing chamber door. He shoved his hip against the wood and let the weight of the door drag him into the chamber.

The room was not completely dark, as he had come to expect from his previous late-night visits. A small lamp burned atop the tall night table that stood beside the stack of mattresses in the center of the otherwise empty room. Beside the lamp sat a half-empty carafe of water, a large silver chalice and an enormous leather-bound book with the word "Kings!" inscribed in gold lettering down its spine. The combined light of Phillip's lamp and the one on the table lessened the gloominess of the room considerably, and he could see the large tapestries blocking every window. As Cauchemar had decreed, neither light nor sound would disturb the girl who waited somewhere atop the enormous bed.

The testing bed sat majestically in the center of the room in which his beloved mother had died several years before. Only Phillip, King Henry, Cauchemar and the royal scribe, Peter, had been in attendance at her death. The room had been gloomy then as well, since the lamps had been dimmed on his mother's final night. She had lain in her bed and spoken to those in the room with a feeble voice.

"Peter," the queen had wheezed, "you've been like a brother to my son. You must take down my final words and share them with the kingdom." Turning to face her husband and son, she had gasped with her final breaths, "You must both guard your hearts. I see… I know…" Pointing at her son, she had said "Phillip, come out from behind your father and take my hand, my little love."

Phillip had sat on the edge of the bed and taken his mother's frail hand in his own. Tears rolled down his cheeks as he leaned close to hear her words.

"Hear me now," she whispered. "Choose your partner wisely, my son. As the birthday fairy said, you must find the one who keeps a vigilant watch in the night. There is danger if you do not." Then, she looked at Phillip's father and said, "Henry, you must…" Gasping for breath she pointed at the other woman and sighed.

"Cauchemar... she... marriage..." Then his mother shook her head, closed her eyes and left them.

Within hours of the queen's death, Cauchemar had taken the pages Peter had written, tossed them into a fire and announced her interpretation of the queen's final words. She had gathered the kingdom's citizens below the walls of the castle. With her long silver hair piled into elaborate braids about her head and her burgundy velvet gown laced high up on her neck, she stepped to the edge of the wall and spoke. "Queen Marie was beloved by you all, but by none more than me. Though we share no blood, my mother was the Mistress of Magic in her father's castle and eventually his third wife. She raised me and King Rupert's two daughters together like sisters and we spent many a happy day playing together in the fields of Cantera." Pausing to take a deep breath, she lowered her head and pretended to wipe a tear from her cheek. A murmur of sympathy rumbled through the crowd below.

Raising her head to look at the people, she continued her speech. "Though she wished for me to join her here as the Mistress of Magic for Bellemer, my life took a different path serving our step-sister, Evelyn, as her Mistress of Magic. After barely escaping the tragic events in Cantera, I rushed to Marie's side to comfort her through the loss of our stepsister. As she quickly grew ill from a rain plague, I knew I had to remain here to care for her and to help care for her son, Prince Phillip, and her husband, King Henry."

Holding a blank parchment above her head, she raised her voice. "Even with her dying words, written here, she spoke of the future, and I understand her words. She demanded that I take her place by Henry's side as his new wife and help rule this fair kingdom. My first act as your future queen will be to honor her other dying wish and guard the young prince's heart."

Grabbing Prince Phillip by the shoulders, she shoved him to the edge of the wall for all of the citizens to see. "This young man is her legacy and your future. But Marie reminded me of his birth-day fairy curse and the great tragedy that will befall the kingdom should he marry a false bride." She paused for the crowd to gasp and murmur. "So, I have declared the return of a royalty test for any young girl hoping to lay claim to his heart and his throne. I know such tests have fallen out of fashion, but we shall find the one who keeps a vigilant watch in the night. This kingdom and the prince will thrive!" The crowd cheered her loudly, but Phillip rested his head on his father's arm and sobbed heavily.

Within days, his father had fallen for Cauchemar's interpretation of Marie's final words, and his marriage to Cauchemar was formal-ized. Phillip had a new stepmother, and the kingdom had a new queen. Cauchemar refused to use his mother's chambers and demanded her own bedroom be redecorated as the new queen's chamber. She decreed that Marie's room would be used for the testing of any princesses who sought to marry Phillip. Shortly thereafter, all signs of his mother had been removed from Marie's room and the testing bed erected. All were forbidden to enter, and the room sat untouched until Phillip reached the age of marriage.

Phillip carefully pulled the door closed behind him and took a deep breath. Even though he had been in this room several times since the first night a girl was placed here, Phillip still missed his mother deeply each time he entered. Her spirit seemed to linger in every darkened corner.

*Oh, Mother, I wish you were here to guide me now.* Phillip paused to look at the stack of mattresses in front of him. The bed itself consisted of twenty thick, downy mattresses piled high within a large wooden frame and covered with a brocade coverlet in the Bellemer royal blue. The footboard had been built with slats to create a ladder to the top of the pile and featured a seahorse carved into the last board. Phillip searched for the small hole beneath the bottom mattress where Cauchemar had shoved the pea. Though the test seemed absurd to him, Phillip had learned not to question his stepmother's ways. He reached in to feel the tiny nuisance, but was distracted by the fall of a long, dark braid over the edge of the top mattress. The braid stopped around the third mattress down and swung slightly back and forth. Hoping not to waken the sleeping girl above, Phillip crept carefully and silently toward the end of the bed. *Thank Gingerfair, she's asleep already. I better extinguish her lamp before she burns down the castle.* He set his lamp on the floor and began his climb up the footboard. As he neared the top, he could hear her speaking softly to herself and he froze on the spot.

"Seventy-six, seventy-seven, seventy-eight…"

Phillip's foot slipped slightly on the highly polished railing of the footboard and he slammed into the frame with a loud thud.

"Who's there?" the girl screamed, as she peeked over the foot of the bed.

"It's just me, Prince Phillip," he said as he popped his head up over the footboard, his hand shielding his eyes. "Are you dressed for a visitor?"

When she saw the prince, a large grin spread across her face, and she said, "Oh, Prince Phillip! Honestly! You scared me! What are you doing here? They said I wouldn't see you until after the test!" Leaning forward on the bed, she fluttered her eyelashes at the prince and giggled, "You can uncover your eyes, silly. I'm dressed. Did you come to kiss me goodnight?"

Stifling a yawn at the girl's clumsy flirting, Phillip shook his finger at her and said, "Now, now. Not until you've passed the test and we're legally wed. I'm just here to make sure you're comfortable, my lady. But I'm afraid you have me at a disadvantage, for I don't know your name."

"Gwendolyn," the girl said, batting her large brown eyes and smoothing the bright yellow fabric of her nightgown down her sides. "But you can call me Gwen. It'll be your pet name for me when I pass this audition—I mean test—and we're wed."

"Yes. I like that name. Gwen it is then." Phillip finished his climb up the footboard and crawled onto the bed beside her. "You should be sleeping, though. What were you counting?"

"Stones on the wall. Honestly! I can't seem to find sleep anywhere." Pointing at a sheaf of papers discarded beside the pillows, she said, "I tried reading the *Inquisitor*, but it's just story after story about my cousin Robert's wedding to Princess Emmaline. That just made me think about our wedding, which made me more nervous. Also, not to complain, but you'd think a bed this tall would be all one could ask for in comfort, but it's terribly lumpy. Honestly." The girl pushed down on the mattresses with her fist.

"That's unfortunate," Phillip said with a slight frown. "You'll need your rest tonight so you'll be prepared for the test tomorrow. Don't let my stepmother see that. She has banned the *Inquisitor* from the kingdom. She says it's just garbage."

"Oh. I'm sorry." Gwen blushed and stuffed the paper under the coverlet. "Maybe it's nerves that are keeping me awake? I'm so worried about this silly test. I hope it isn't regal history. That's my worst subject. All those Ruperts and Henrys and Georges, and who killed what monster with what sword. Honestly, it's mind numbing! I was hoping it would be singing, since I'm an excellent singer, but that doesn't really prove my royalty does it?"

"No, singing would never please *my* stepmother," Phillip said. "She's actually forbidden song in the kingdom. She says art distracts the people from their labors and from keeping the kingdom well stocked with food and wine. She removed all the beautiful tapestries from the rest of the palace and hid them away here, so that no one would waste time staring at them." Phillip paused to pick at a thread that was sticking up from the coverlet near his foot.

"They are beautiful," Gwen said. "It's a shame to hide them in here. We Dealonians are renowned for our hardworking nature, but we still take time to enjoy life's entertainments. Your subjects would have such fun looking at them."

"Fun," Phillip snorted and pulled the thread loose from the coverlet with a jerk of his hand. "Fun is not a word my stepmother even knows. She even banished the kingdom's scribe so he couldn't produce distracting stories and songs. He was the only friend I had. I miss him terribly."

Phillip wasn't sure why he was telling this to Gwen or what had made him think of Peter. Gwen had no need to know anything about his kingdom, since he knew she would be gone by the morning. Still, she was the first princess to show any interest in anything besides marriage. And although he had hoped to be in and out of the room as quickly as with the other princesses, he had to admit it was nice to talk to someone his own age. Phillip's lower lip began to tremble as he thought about the day his friend had been sent beyond the castle walls. To distract himself, he began to pull at another thread.

"He sounds perfectly lovely," Gwen said, reaching over and placing her hand on top of Phillip's to stop him from picking at the loose thread. "Tell me more about him?"

Phillip glanced up at Gwen to see her staring at him with kindness and expectation in her eyes. Swallowing a lump of guilt that was rising in his throat, he said, "Peter and I used to explore these rooms as children, and he would make up the best stories. But now I don't have time for friends or exploring. My days are spent preparing to be a husband and a king."

"Oh." Gwen sighed and dropped her eyes, "that's so sad. My kingdom is filled with art, and my father made sure I was trained. I sing, dance, act and even sew my own gowns. I spent all of my days learning to be a cultured woman, though I'd never seen the world outside of our castle until I traveled here. It was so exciting to see strange trees and lands and people and their funny little houses. Dealonia is nothing but mile after mile of farmland. Bellemer is so much more interesting! The views from the cliffs and the windswept beaches are so beautiful." As her excitement grew, Gwen began to wave her hands about, making the lacy sleeves of her nightgown flap about her arms. "And the Southern Sea! I cannot wait until you take me to dip my toes in the Southern Sea. It made me realize just how boring my life's been! I would love to learn something more practical than singing and dancing, but I'll do that when I'm your queen! I'll bring art back to your kingdom, and you'll teach me the joys of exploring. I can see from the tapestries that your family loves adventure!"

Phillip glanced at the tapestry closest to the bed, which depicted his father slaying a dragon. With a shrug he said, "These are just propaganda. My father didn't slay a dragon. He could barely swat a fly. Adventure would be nice, I guess, but my stepmother says there is too much danger in the world for a future king. I'm forbidden to go near the sea. I'm forbidden to go beyond the castle walls until after the wedding, though I sneak out to the stables occasionally and walk the walls to look down on the sea." Realizing he was telling her more than he intended, Phillip steered the conversation back to the test. "Of course, there'll be the traditional stag hunt on the day after we're wed, followed by a banquet where we eat my first kill. It's been a tradition in the kingdom for hundreds of years. No one has bothered to teach me how to hunt, but I'll figure something out. At least I'll finally leave these walls for a day. But after the hunt, I'll be back to just roaming these halls and waiting to be king."

"But you'll have me to do it with, if I can pass the test and become your queen! We'll sing and dance and explore your king-dom together. Phillip, we will have so much fun and have each other for company! Oh, and I can give you some tips on archery if you wish." Gwen mimed pulling back the string on a bow and released an imaginary arrow into the air. "I once played the role of Gingerfair the Huntress in an evening of folly for my parents. I was quite convincing with my bow. Of course, I have to pass the test first. I'm so worried about what the test could be!" Gwen dropped her head and stared at her fingers as she twisted the rings she wore on one hand. "Honestly."

"Well, worrying won't help. If you're a true princess, then you'll pass the test with ease." Phillip bit his lips to keep from giggling as he said the words. He couldn't help but remember the disappointment and embarrassment of the last "princesses" as they were roused from sleep to discover they'd failed his stepmother's test. He felt bad for ruining their reputations as royalty, but he couldn't let any silly girl's bloodline force him into a marriage, no matter what his mother's dying words had been.

"I don't understand why a test is necessary, anyway! I didn't think any kingdom used tests anymore. I have my letters of patent and my father's word. Isn't that enough?"

"Well," Phillip said, as his mind raced for an explanation, "it would be, were it not for the warnings of our royal soothsayer."

"Oooh! A soothsayer." Gwendolyn squealed and slid closer to Phillip. She placed her small hand on his arm and leaned closer to his face. "Tell me more!"

"Yes," Phillip said, as he took her hand off his arm. "A soothsayer proclaimed that if I married a false bride, the kingdom would be destroyed. So my stepmother proclaimed that all girls be tested. Her proclamations are practically law." He kept close enough to the truth to hide his lies. It was his birthday curse and not a prophecy, but a soothsayer *had* once visited the kingdom. All he had proclaimed was that the trees would bear no fruit; then, when the orchards had produced a bountiful harvest the next spring, he was promptly tossed into the moat. Also, Cauchemar's proclamations were law. Since her marriage to King Henry, she marched around the halls of the castle daily, terrorizing the peasants and mice alike with rants and threats of horrible violence. No one questioned her words, for it had been rumored for years that she held a great magical power beyond anyone's knowledge.

"Oh, that's amazing," Gwen said, her eyes widening. "My soothsayer only said that sleep would be my downfall. What kind of proclamation is that? I mean, honestly."

"Maybe he meant if you don't sleep tonight you'll fail the test?" Phillip looked up at the ceiling to keep himself from laughing.

"Oh, no," Gwen pouted, flopping onto her back, her chestnut braid whipping behind her. "Now I'm even more worried, and it'll be even harder to sleep! Couldn't you give me a little hint as to what it might be? Why hasn't any girl passed?"

*If you only knew.* Phillip grabbed the regal history book from the tall nightstand and dropped it on the bed beside Gwen, where it landed with a heavy thud. "Try reading? It usually makes me sleepy."

"I've read so much my eyes are crossing. That will only make me more nervous," Gwen whined as she turned over onto her stomach and buried her face in the coverlet.

"Well," Phillip said, as he reached into his sleeve and pulled out the green glass bottle, "I might have something that could help you."

Gwen sat up and turned to face Phillip. She scrunched up her brows as she looked at the bottle. "What is that?"

"This is Dr. Hickenkopf's Miracle Tonic. I bought it from a travelling doctor. He said it will cure whatever ails you." Phillip showed the bottle to Gwen. The girl's eyes widened as she read the words on the gold label. Phillip quickly pulled the bottle away and started to tuck it back into his sleeve. "But I don't know if I should share it with you. It was very expensive."

"Oh, please let me have some!" Gwen begged, as she reached toward the bottle in Phillip's hand. "Surely it will help me sleep!"

"I don't know."

"Not even for your future bride?"

"Oh, okay," Phillip said with a dramatic sigh. "But don't tell anyone, or everyone will want some. Here," he said and handed the bottle to Gwen.

She giggled as she let her hand brush against his while taking it. She read the label again before removing the cork stopper. She took three quick swallows. As she brought the bottle down, she wiped the sleeve of her nightgown across her lips.

"That should do the trick," Phillip said as he took back the bottle, corked it and tucked it back into his sleeve. As he inched toward the foot of the bed, Phillip said, "It's late, and I should leave you. Now, close your eyes and get some rest." He climbed over the footboard and quickly made his way down the slats. When he reached the bottom, he dropped softly to the ground.

"Prince Phillip?"

"Yes?"

"I hope I pass tomorrow, and we're wed. You have very kind eyes."

"We shall see," Phillip said, feeling a stab of guilt. He swallowed down the feeling as he leaned over to pick up his abandoned lamp. He slipped his hand quietly beneath the bottom mattress to check on the placement of the pea. He knew the pea would now be of no consequence, and leaving it would save him the trouble of slipping it back into place in the morning. Of the four girls previously tested, most had been almost asleep when he had sneaked in or they had been knocked out by the tonic, so he'd never had to remove the pesky legume.

"Prince Phillip?"

"Yes?" he sighed as he leaned against the mattresses. *This girl has some staying power.*

"Could I sing for you? It always calms my nerves when I sing. Maybe a lullaby will help me sleep?"

"I think that would be lovely."

"*T'was a stormy night on the swampy moor, when a handsome knight came to the castle door,*" Gwen began to sing softly. Her voice was quite beautiful as she trilled her way through the familiar old tune. His own mother had often sung it to him as a child, when he had been frightened awake by a nightmare or a storm off the sea. This was the first time he had heard music in the castle since before his mother's death. Gwen's voice began fading as Phillip heard her nestle deeper into the mattresses. As he tiptoed across the chamber to the door, he heard the girl whisper the last line of the song.

"*And true love someday shall be.* I mean, honestly."

Phillip grabbed the door handle and stopped to look back toward her sleeping figure. She snored softly, and her right foot twitched beneath the heavy coverlet. He grinned and whispered, "Sleep tight."

Her voice had touched a part of Phillip he had long forgotten, and he half regretted the scene he knew would come in the morning. She really did have a lovely voice and was nowhere near as snobbish as the last few girls. She had even made him long to join in her innocent excitement. In a different situation, he was sure they could've been close friends. Marriage to a woman, however, would not happen in his lifetime, even if she were this entertaining.

"But what must be, must be," Phillip said with a shrug, as he pulled the heavy door closed behind him. Groping his way down the hall toward his own bed, he hummed the lullaby Gwen had sung. "*And true love someday shall be.*"

# CHAPTER 2

"*A*ND TRUE LOVE SOMEDAY SHALL BE,*" KATERINA SANG, AS she leaned as far as she could out of the tower window without tipping out completely and falling to the ground many feet below. If she leaned just far enough and tilted her head to just the right angle, she could watch the final beams of sunlight flicker away over the Pearl Mountains in the distant northwest. Those few little sparkles of orange and purple were worth the risk of a tumble to her death. She had not felt the warmth of the sun's kiss for several years now, so she resigned herself to watching it slip away over the hills like a long-lost love. Awake at sunset and asleep at dawn had been the rhythm of her life for as many years as she could remember. Yet, she imagined, any day now her handsome prince would be outlined in the glow of that sunset on his way to rescue her from this high prison.

"Really, Katerina?" she said to herself as she tossed her long blonde hair over her shoulder and began crawling back into the window. "You're not a princess. You're the simple-minded niece of an old witch. No prince will come for you, no matter what the stories may imply." She heaved a deep sigh, her hand slipped from the window frame, and she fell against the sill with a sharp cry of pain.

"Careful!" a voice shouted from below and shook her from her thoughts. "You're in danger of falling! A girl as pretty as you must always be careful of falling. Any man who sees your beauty should be careful too!"

"Peter!" she cried and leaned out the window again to look down on the young man below. He stared up at her with a large grin. The wind blew his mousy brown hair about, and the light from the lantern in his hand danced across his features. He had his usual leather satchel slung across his shoulder, and she knew from watching him scribble away on previous nights that he kept a small charcoal pencil behind his ear. Katerina smiled back to him as she waved his admonition away. "You need not worry about that! I'm a bird. Living in this perch has made me at home in the air!"

"Though your singing is beautiful, my lady, you're not a bird," he said with a slight laugh. "You're a graceful cat, dancing along the window's edge after being curled on the sill for a long nap. Why else do you think I call you Kitty?"

"Well, I am certainly more kitten than lady, no matter how many times you may call me one." Katerina laughed as she sat down on the ledge and pulled her bare feet up under her red skirts. She leaned back against the window frame and stared up at the darkening sky. "Oh, Peter, I'm so glad you came again tonight. It gets so lonely in this tower with just my thoughts and my aunt's shelves full of jars."

She leaned over and looked down at the boy, remembering the first night he had appeared below her tower six months before. She had been watching the sunset as usual when he startled her out of her daydreams by calling up to her and asking for directions to the nearest inn. She nearly fell out of the window from fright, since no other person had ever approached her tower. As much as she could tell from so high up and in the fading light, he was a handsome, if somewhat short, boy. His shoulders were broad, and his smile was filled with kindness. Despite his appealing looks, she had hidden from him, remembering her aunt's warnings not to speak to strangers.

To her surprise, the next sunset found him standing beneath her tower again. Every day for the next week he had called out to her, until she finally swallowed her fear and said, "Hello."

After they exchanged names, she had no idea what to say to a boy, so she asked him to tell her a story. He laughed, bowed and began weaving her a tale. As he was reaching the end of the story, he stopped and promised to return the next night to finish. He had continued to return almost every night, talking with her and telling her a continuing string of stories, until his voice, body and movements were as familiar and beautiful to her as the stars and the moon. She could tell by his simple gray tunic that he was not a high-born man, but his ease with words both formal and fantastic showed he had some exposure to courtly life. Though she knew little of his life, Katerina had come to live for the escape from loneliness his words provided.

"I was just looking to see how much sun was left in the sky so I could measure the time until you came!" she called down to him.

"I came at sunset, just as you asked, though I don't see why I can't come earlier in the day. Perhaps in the sunlight I could find a way to climb this tower and see your beautiful face even closer. Maybe even ask you to pay for your stories with a kiss?"

"No!" Katerina yelled. "You must never try to come into this tower. You should stay down there and just tell me your stories. I shudder to think what my aunt would do if she caught you here or even knew I had a visitor! I am risking far too much even speaking to you! My aunt is not a very nice woman."

"I am not afraid of some silly old woman," Peter said, with a wave of his hand and a smirk. "I have been planning to hide in the bushes so I can see how she gets inside. Then I will take care of her and take you away!"

"My aunt is not some silly old woman! Do you think some silly old woman could construct a tower with no door and yet still come and go? My aunt is a…"

"Your aunt is a crazy old Gloriannan loon! What kind of woman would lock her niece away from the world? What kind of woman forbids a girl to see sunlight? What kind of aunt—"

"I know!" Katerina interrupted his rant. "We've been through all of this before. I've questioned it all too, but she has her reasons."

"Nonsense! I'll just punch her in the nose!" Peter set his lantern on the ground, lifted his arms in a fighting stance and threw a few punches into the fading light. "I'm not just a man of words, I'm a man of action!" He danced around in small circles, swinging into the night. With a sharp jab, he hit a low-hanging branch of a nearby sapling, knocking it away from his face. The branch sprang back and whipped across his face, knocking the boy backwards onto his rump.

"Oh, Peter." Katerina giggled, as she watched him pick himself up. "I prefer a man of words to a man of action! The quill is a mighty weapon that holds magic untold, or so my aunt says."

"If only that were true, I'd simply write a door into these walls, and we could run away."

"But you *can* do magic! You take my mind out of this tower with every word! Just tell me a story!"

"What'll it be tonight? Trolls? Knights? A princess in disguise?"

"I'd like to hear the story of how a boy who lives in these woods in such plain clothes knows such fancy words."

"No," Peter said, as he dropped his chin to his chest. "That's a story I won't tell."

"Very well," she said and sighed. "Why not continue the one from the other night? I think you left off with the pretty girl in a glass coffin."

"Ah, yes! One of my masterpieces!" Peter smiled, as he puffed out his chest. He sat down on a large rock at the base of the tower and scratched his head. After pulling a small sheaf of parchment from his satchel, he thumbed through the pages. "Where was I? Ah, yes. So Francine had already eaten the poison rumberry, right?"

Katerina strained to see the young man's face in the glow of his lantern as the last of the sun's rays dipped behind the distant mountains. Realizing she had glimpsed her last of him for the night, she slipped from the window's ledge to the floor, crossed her arms on the windowsill and rested her chin on her hands. She beamed at the sound of Peter's excited voice rising from the darkness below and let her mind wander into the world his words created. Suddenly, a loud rumbling in the center of the room and a small plume of burgundy smoke rising from the floor pulled her attention toward the interior of the tower.

"Oh no!" she gasped. She stood up and leaned out the window. "Peter, hide!" she hissed. "My aunt is back! She must not see you!"

"Let her find me! I'll force her to let me take you away!"

"Peter! This is no time for joking! Put out your lantern and hide, please. Then sneak away as quietly as you can. Come back tomorrow at sunset. She rarely comes home two days in a row."

"But I will make her—"

"Please!" she begged. "You don't understand—"

"Katerina?" a woman's voice called from the smoke filling the center of the room. "Sweetheart, who are you talking to?"

Katerina watched Peter step behind a hedgerow before she turned to face the plume of smoke. "No one," she answered, as she fanned the wisps away from her face. "Just repeating my lessons like you taught me to do." Katerina began chanting in a sing-song voice, "'Legs crossed at the ankles and eyes turned down. A queen guards her words and what's under her gown. An iron fist in a velvet glove will bring a queen her kingdom's love. Music and art are nothing but waste. Hard working peasants bring good food to taste.' I think I have almost all your rules memorized."

Cauchemar stepped from the dissipating smoke, flipped her burgundy skirts behind her and crossed the tower toward the girl. Her silver hair was piled on top of her head in a complicated arrangement of braids and curls that had always reminded Katerina of a rumberry tree after it had lost all its leaves. Her mouth was drawn in its usual tight bow of disapproval and her gray eyes squinted as if in constant pain. Cauchemar wore happiness as uncomfortably as a dress two sizes too small. Katerina thought her aunt had probably been a strikingly beautiful woman in her youth, but years of annoyance and condescension had weathered her face into its current array of wrinkles and lines, like an apple left on the windowsill too long. Though she was never cruel to Katerina, she never seemed to be completely pleased with anything Katerina said or did.

"Katerina, I've told you a hundred times, you must call me Auntie! When I rescued you from your dying mother's arms, she begged me to raise you as my own child."

"I'm sorry, Auntie," Katerina mumbled, as she turned her head away and rolled her eyes. "That's the one rule I forget."

"That isn't the only rule you forgot," Cauchemar snapped. She grabbed the girl's arm and dragged her away from the window to the far side of the room. Pushing her down onto a small wooden chair, she said, "I told you to stay away from that window until the last of the sun has disappeared. You know you must keep your skin as pale as the moon."

"But Cauch—Auntie, I only moved to the window so I wouldn't choke on the smoke your entrance brings."

"Yes, that's a side effect I never could seem to eradicate," Cauchemar said, as she walked over to the large cabinet full of jars in the corner of the room. Her tall, thin frame barely cast a shadow, and the pile of gray braids on her head bounced slightly with each step. Scanning the labels, she reached for a nearly empty jar and pulled it from the shelf. "But never you mind. We must drill your lessons especially hard tonight! The time has come for you to take your rightful place on a throne! The last of those silly girls has failed my test! Just in time, too, as I was almost out of these little treats, and there won't be another harvest for a year at least." Cauchemar twirled the jar in her hand, making the one remaining pea in the bottom of the jar bounce around inside. Reading the label, she cackled and said "Oh, Sleeping Heavenly Peas! Best investment I ever made. Certainly a better deal than those beans the troll king offered me. Beanstalks that grow into the sky? What on earth would you do with one of them?"

"Grow beans too high to be stolen?" Katerina said, as she crossed from the chair and flopped onto her bed. She spread her red woolen skirts around her and picked at a loose thread.

"Pish. He claimed they would lead to riches. From beans? Who needs riches when you have a throne?" Cauchemar put the jar back on the shelf and began running her long slender finger along the labels of the other jars. "Who needs beans when you can send silly little girls to sleep with a few measly peas? Who needs to worry about food when a whole kingdom waits on you hand and foot? Now, hurry and gather your things. I just need a few items from my supplies, and we'll be ready to go."

"Gather my things? Ready to go where? Am I leaving the tower?" Katerina gasped as she leaped up from the bed.

"Keep up, child. I said it's time to take your place on the throne. You can't very well do that from in here, now can you? We're headed to my other home."

"But Auntie, I'm not a princess. I've no claim to a throne. How can I just take one?"

"Well, of course you can't just take it. That would require an entire army. I have power, but not like that. I said 'take your *place* on a throne.' You, my dear, have a power greater than an army of ten thousand men."

"Magic?"

"No. You have an aunt with ambition who has planned well for you. Though, I admit, magic has helped."

"I still don't understand," Katerina said, as she crossed the tower to the window. Leaning out, she saw Peter's lantern flickering behind the row of bushes. Glancing over her shoulder to check that Cauchemar was still caught up in her jars, she motioned to Peter to dim the lantern. Then she pointed at her ear, signaling him to listen carefully.

"Do I have to spell everything out for you?" Cauchemar groused, as she turned from the shelves toward the girl. "All beauty and no brains, I think, just like your..." she mumbled as she crossed to the window.

"I'm sorry, Auntie. It's just, I spend so much time memorizing your rules that it crowds other things out of my brain. Please, come sit with me here on the window sill and explain it all to me. I'm frightened to be out in the world. I feel so safe here in my tower; I might feel better if I knew where I was going and why."

"Oh, very well. A little night air will do me some good. Scoot over," Cauchemar said, as she bumped the girl to the side with her hip and sat on the sill. "Where do I start?"

"Follow your rule. 'Skip the prattle and endless natter. Make them get right to the heart of the matter.'"

"Very good, child!" Cauchemar beamed and patted the girl on the knee. "Fine. There is a young prince that is seeking... well, no… not seeking… let's say *in need* of a bride. You'll be that bride."

"But why would he marry me? He's never met me. I'm not even a princess."

"What have I told you!" The old woman slapped the girl lightly on the hand. "You *are* a princess. I've trained you to be a princess. You must believe you are a princess and, most importantly, *say* you are a princess."

"And if I just show up, he will believe me and marry me?"

"No. Of course not," Cauchemar said, rolling her eyes. "But I have laid the groundwork for that. You'll pass the test."

"A test?" Katerina cried out. "I haven't studied for any test."

"But you have, my dear. All you must do is stay awake all night, as I have had you do for these past two years."

Katerina looked at her aunt, her brow wrinkling. "That makes no sense."

Cauchemar grunted and leaned her head against the windowsill. "There is an old legend that a true princess is so sensitive she can feel a pea beneath twenty mattresses, and the lump of the pea will cause her pain enough to keep her awake all night." She chuckled and waved the thought away with a bony hand. "It's an absurd notion, but these royals are so inbred they will believe anything. I've made sure every girl who attempted the test has failed, thanks to my sleep-inducing peas! But you'll remain awake on top of an ordinary pea. The next glorious morning you'll be declared a true princess and marry Prince Phillip. No army needed. Just one simple pea."

"How do you know this is the test?"

"Because I set the whole thing up. By Godrick the Golden, you're a dimwit sometimes. I'm married to his father, King Henry. He knows I am a wise woman and, thanks to my interpretation of his former wife's dying words, he follows my advice." Cauchemar closed her eyes and sighed with self-satisfaction.

Taking advantage of her aunt's closed eyes, Katerina leaned out the window and looked for Peter's lantern before saying, "King Henry and Prince Phillip of Bellemer? I know them from the *Who's Who of Clarameer Royals* book you made me read. But if you're already married to the king, why do you need me? You have your throne, and we could live there at ease without me marrying some stranger prince."

Cauchemar opened her eyes and stared at Katerina in disgust. "My dear, do you know what happens to the second wife of a king when he dies? She gets tossed out of the main gate on her widowed derrière. The child of the first wife takes the throne and has no need of an old woman he has never loved."

"But not if her niece is married to the new king?"

"Well, not if her niece is the new queen and something happens to the new king."

"That's an awful thought. And surely direct blood relations will claim the throne."

"No, my dear, you will already be carrying the next king in your womb." Cauchemar reached over and patted Katerina's stomach. "The poor widowed mother will be pitied and adored by the peasants and get to keep her throne. She will need her beloved Auntie at her side as a guide."

"But how could you wish death on the prince?" Katerina asked, inching herself slowly away from her aunt's hand. "That is heartless, and you have no guarantee he won't live a long and happy life. Unless…" Katerina frowned.

"Yes, it is morbid but necessary. The day after your wedding there is to be a great hunt where your new husband must kill a stag and bring it home to share with his new bride at a feast. Your future husband has no skill with a bow, but he will draw his arrow and aim for the stag." Cauchemar raised her arms as if pulling back the string of a bow, and aimed at a candle sitting on a bookshelf across the room. She released her imaginary arrow and Katerina jumped as the candle suddenly toppled over and was extinguished. "*His* shot will mysteriously go astray and land right in the chest of his dear old daddy. As he stands there in shock, the stag will defend himself from attack with a well-placed antler right to the young prince's chest."

Katerina gasped as she covered her eyes. "That is terrible."

"As I said, morbid but necessary. But you will then be the queen of the kingdom and mother of the heir. There is a reason this must take place *after* your wedding night. It's easy as can be. See, no army needed. Just a pea, two beds and an aunt with a plan."

"No," Katerina screamed. She bolted from the window sill and ran toward her bed. "I will not help you kill two men just so you can claim a throne."

"Why, you ungrateful little twit," Cauchemar shrieked, as she rose from the window in a rush with smoke and fire dancing around her shoulders. "I could have left you for dead, screaming into the night on your dying mother's breast. And this is the thanks I receive?"

"No, Auntie!" Katerina cried, as she dropped beside her bed and cowered. "Please. I cannot allow you to kill a poor innocent prince."

"Fine," Cauchemar said coldly, as her face fell stone still. The smoke and fire about her head dissipated as she walked slowly to the rows of shelves on the far wall. "Then I shall go back to the kingdom and never return. You shall remain in this tower all by yourself. If starvation does not take you first, then I am sure you can find something on these shelves to end it all when the boredom drives you mad." Tossing a jar onto the bed beside the girl, she spat, "That one would do nicely."

Katerina picked up the jar and read the label aloud. "Pushing Up Daisy Root." She shifted her eyes from the jar to her aunt's back, then sobbed and stood slowly. While turning to the open window and wondering if she could survive the leap, Katerina noticed the faint flicker of Peter's lantern still in the bushes. Pushing her shoulders back and wiping the tears from her cheeks, she said, "I see I have no choice. I'll go to Bellemer and marry Prince Phillip. The southern kingdom is where I'll be."

Cauchemar turned back to the girl and smiled. "I knew you'd see the wisdom of my plan. Now gather your prettiest things, and let's begin your lessons. Tomorrow, after you have slept, we shall depart. I brought you a satchel for your dresses, but you need not pack much. I have already gathered most of what you'll need. Once you are queen, you will have any dress you want." She turned to the shelf again and grabbed a glass container. "I need a few provisions from my jars. Stork Tears: to guarantee a baby. Dragon Saliva: to put a little fire in that boy's heart for your wedding."

"My wedding," Katerina mumbled and she looked down to the ground. She could just make out the bobbing light of Peter's lantern as he ran off into the woods. She could only hope he had heard and understood her pleas. She stumbled to the bed to find her satchel.

"Her wedding! It's what every girl dreams of." Cauchemar purred, grabbed another jar and dropped it into the bag at her feet.

Katerina dropped onto her bed and buried her face in her hands. "I don't remember *this* dream."

# CHAPTER 3

"SEVENTY-EIGHT. SEVENTY-NINE. EIGHTY," DANIEL SAID as he stepped up to the stump in the middle of the path. Dropping the reins he held, he turned to his horse and said, "How about that, Rosemary? Eighty steps from the fence to the stump. Of course, that knowledge gains me absolutely nothing, but at least I know." He opened a saddle bag, retrieved a folded map and dropped it by the stump.

Sitting on the stump, he adjusted the laces of his soft leather boot, then ran his fingers through his wavy black hair. He pulled down on the hem of his forest green doublet and smoothed a wrinkle in his dark brown leggings. He picked up the map and unfolded it.

"Now, let's see where we are." He placed his finger on his castle in the forests of Sylvania to the east then dragged it up the border with Osterling to the lands in the north. "First we went north into the mountains of Upper and Lower Lipponia. Then we came back south along the Rupert River beside the troll king's wall around Cantera." Daniel pointed to the kingdom in the center of the map through which James had drawn a large red line. "Clearly, we won't be going in there. So if we crossed the river back there on this bridge, we must be near the beaches of Bellemer. About here, I think." Daniel placed his finger on the map and showed it to the horse. "Next we will head west into Dealonia's farmland to see Emmaline and Robert. I have to apologize for missing her wedding. That covers all of Clarameer, I guess. If I don't have my answer by then, we'll just keep heading west to visit my mother's people in Glorianna. Does that sound like a good plan, Rosemary?"

The horse leaned its head over and nuzzled at his neck. "I know. I told James I would wait by that gate, but this is as good a place as any. Go on. Find something to eat." As the horse ambled away, Daniel dropped the map, stretched his legs out in front of him and leaned his head back, letting the sunlight warm his face. "It's only eighty steps away."

In the two years since his eighteenth birthday and the onset of his insomnia curse, Daniel had counted the paces between landmarks all over the kingdoms of Clarameer. He no longer counted steps just to induce sleep, but as second nature. Often he would arrive at a spot with a number in his head, completely unaware he had been counting along the way.

Daniel had not started out counting paces but had counted sheep, much as any sleepless person would do. But the sheep grew monotonous, and he began switching it up. After counting the stones in the walls of his bedchamber several times, he counted the number of times his heart would beat in an hour. Then he began counting the stars he could see out of his window. Realizing there were many stars he couldn't see from his bed, he was struck with the idea of attempting to sleep in the courtyard with an entire sky's worth of stars over his head. He approached his brother the next day with the idea. Andrew sat on his throne beneath a green and brown banner embroidered with the acorns of the Sylvanian royal family crest. Though he would not be officially king until he married, Andrew had taken to sitting on the throne and wearing his deceased father's crown in an exercise he called "practicing."

"Don't be ridiculous, Danny," Prince Andrew had scoffed, waving Daniel away. He shifted on his throne until he could see his reflection better in the shiny silver breastplate of the guard standing beside him; he smoothed his black hair over his ear. With a wink at his reflection, he said, "I will not have a member of this family lying about the courtyard like some stable boy. It's unbecoming of your status as the younger brother and next in line to the throne of the best-looking prince in the kingdoms. What if you caught the rain plague and died? Mother would have my head on a platter. And, after all, it would be a crime for a face this handsome to be separated from a body this strong. Staying safely in your warm bed is really doing a service to all the single ladies of Clarameer."

"But, Andy," Daniel protested, "there hasn't been a plague in the kingdoms for years. And I don't sleep! What does it matter where I sit awake? Who knows? Some fresh air might actually lead me to sleep. It's one thing we haven't tried. James said he'll join me. It'll be fun for us, and I'm so bored."

"See, that is exactly my point," Andrew said, with a roll of his eyes. "That orphan twit you call your squire is nothing but a glorified stable hand. Of course he'd be at home sleeping on the stones of our courtyard. He's a cast-off of the woods! That's where Mother found him all those years ago when she was out riding. If she hadn't taken pity on him, he would have died out there or been taken in by a family more suited to his birth. Frankly, it's a bit of an embarrassment that Mother lets him run around this castle with you as if he were one of us. We know nothing of where he came from. He is a pinecone that fell from a tree, for all we know."

"Andrew, shut up," Daniel grumbled, as he took a step toward the throne. The guards crossed their spears to prevent him from approaching any closer. "I will not have you talking badly about James. So what if he is an orphan? He is the best man in this kingdom and the most devoted to me. Goodness is not some magical component of royal blood, as you so clearly show."

"Yes, you like having him follow you around, don't you? You can fawn and moon over him all you want, and he can't refuse a prince, now can he?" Turning to the guard on his left, Andrew giggled and said, "I think my little brother would like his little knight to hop in his saddle."

"You're lucky you have those guards, or I would knock that crown right off your empty head."

"Oooh! Someone is getting grumpy. Maybe baby brother needs a nap."

"Very funny. You know what, brother?" Daniel said, as an idea began to grow. With a smirk, he looked up at his brother. "You're right. I'm not going to spend the night in the courtyard."

"Of course you aren't."

"No. I'm going to spend the night outside these castle walls."

"Yes. You are going to spend the night… wait… what?"

"I'm heading out into the kingdoms. I'll never find the cure for this curse just sitting around this castle being the consolation prince. As soon as you find a bride, you will be crowned king, and I'll have even less to do than I do now. I can't stand it anymore; I need to find something to do with my time. I've been waiting for answers to come to me, but maybe they're waiting for me somewhere out there."

"Daniel, calm down. Mother will never go for that. It's not safe out there for a prince alone. You're just being silly. Your job is to sit around staying safe in case something happens to me, not larking about the kingdoms trying to get yourself killed."

"I can defend myself. It's amazing how much sword practice you can fit in when you don't sleep."

"You'll get lost."

"I've memorized maps of the kingdoms."

"You know nothing about life outside these walls."

"I know things. Lots of things. I've read every book in that tiny collection our tutor calls a library. What I don't know, I will learn in the world. You know, the more I think about it, I can't believe I haven't set out before now. The only things I really have are some knowledge, plenty of curiosity and endless time. So why shouldn't I put them to good use?"

"But what if you're captured? I'm not paying a ransom for a silly boy who is off on an even sillier jaunt."

"I'll dress like a commoner. No one will know I'm a member of this family. Look, I'll take James with me. He'll protect me."

"Oh, I'm sure. I feel so much better knowing you'll be protected by the dimwit pinecone knight."

"I'm going."

"I may not officially be king yet, but without my blessing you're not going anywhere!"

"Watch me," Daniel said with a smirk, as he turned and began walking out of the throne room.

"Daniel!" Andrew rose quickly with his golden crown slipping askew on his head. "You come back here! If you take one more step, I'll—I'll—I'll tell mother!"

Now, as Daniel sat on the stump and thought back to that day, the whole argument seemed like a dream. At least, it seemed like what he vaguely remembered a dream was. That was one of the many drawbacks to never sleeping—no dreams.

Daniel recalled the day he and James began their journey. Luckily, his mother had been much more level-headed and open to his plans than his stubborn brother. She instantly gathered her ladies-in-waiting to pack clothing and provisions for him and James. She refused to let him go dressed as a commoner, though.

"You'll see, my baby boy," she cooed, as she pushed an errant curl from his forehead, "your royal blood and the respect it brings can protect you more than the heaviest shield, and it can open more doors than the shiniest of keys."

Early the next morning, the stablemen had brought the two best horses for Daniel and James. The horses were draped in Daniel's green and brown family colors, and someone had woven ribbons into their manes. Flowers and bunting covered the courtyard walls, and all of the castle staff had gathered at the gates to see them off. Daniel was moved to see many of the older women dab their eyes with handkerchiefs. As he walked to the horses, Daniel had to pull James away from two of his mother's prettiest ladies-in-waiting, Rosemary and Lillianne.

"Wait for me, girls," James had said to the girls with a wink. "I will name these two horses in your honor so I will think of you on our entire trip."

"Come along, Sir Heartbreaker," Daniel called to James with a laugh. "The setting sun waits for no man's heart." They mounted the horses and rode over to the decorated platform where his mother and brother stood to see them off.

"Sir Pinecone," Prince Andrew said, "you bring him back alive and sleeping or you don't come back at all. And you, little brother, try to find a sense of humor out there somewhere."

Daniel ignored his brother as best he could and leaned over in his saddle to kiss his mother's cheek. Queen Rhea's gilded crown of oak leaves and acorns sat gracefully atop her jet black hair and glittered in the bright afternoon sun as she leaned over the railing to accept Daniel's kiss. Although she held her smile in a perfect imitation of calm, the queen's green eyes revealed the true fear and sorrow she was feeling. Daniel had learned at an early age that the best way to know his mother's feelings was to look into her eyes. She had informed him that his own eyes revealed his secrets as well. Daniel and his sister, Emmaline, had taken after their Gloriannan mother in both looks and temperament—darker skin and hair but a light, studious and careful nature for which Glorianna and its many universities were known. His brother was much more like his Clarameeran father—fair skinned and light eyed, but as feisty, temperamental, and changeable as the citizens and landscape of their homeland.

Queen Rhea leaned over and pinned a small green ribbon with an acorn pendant on his doublet. Patting his breast where the token hung, she said, "You are going into the other kingdoms within the realm of Clarameer as a representative of your family and your kingdom. You will show the other kingdoms who we *really* are. You are my kind and loving child. My curious and wise child. My honest and brave child. You will show them. Now, go. Find the things you need—adventure, answers, purpose, love." With those final words, she had kissed his cheek and turned away to hide her tears.

"Still looking, Mother," Daniel sighed as he leaned forward on the stump and rested his elbows on his knees. He stared at the sand underneath his foot, so different from the rich soil in the many forests of Sylvania, his home. He loved the vast woods that covered his kingdom and the peaceful citizens who lived in their shade, but he knew that life held more for him than staring at trees. He nudged the toe of his boot into the sandy path and drew the outline of a crown, but then quickly scuffed it away. The sound of an approaching horse drew his attention to the horizon, where he saw James galloping toward him on his horse, Lillianne.

James sat high and handsome in the saddle, his blond hair flouncing about his ears with each gallop of the black horse. He wore a simple brown surcoat adorned with a forest green panel on the chest that displayed the acorns that were Daniel's family sigil. The sword he wore strapped across his back bounced against his broad shoulders, and two pastel ribbons tied around his muscled upper arm fluttered behind him. The ribbons were tokens of devotion from ladies-in-waiting who had come to dote on James since puberty and constant battle training had turned his awkward, gangly frame into an ideal of manliness. Seeing James gallop toward him with the sunlight behind him, Daniel could understand why the girls had given him the ribbons and their hearts. If being raised together had not made Daniel see James as a brother, he might have been tempted to give a ribbon himself. Daniel, of course, wore no ribbons, for the ladies had quickly discerned that they were of no interest to him.

"Your Highness," James called out as he pulled the horse's reins and skidded to a stop a few feet from Daniel. "My scouting was useful! I've found the answer!"

"James," Daniel chided, as he stood and walked toward his knight, "I've told you for months now to just call me Daniel. Out here, I have no crown and I have no kingdom. Out here, we're brothers of the road."

"Sorry," James said, as he dropped to the path. "Old habits, you know. And I know that someday things will go back to the way they were. You'll sleep, and I'll stand guard. You'll rule a kingdom, and I'll wage your battles. I can't get in the habit of calling you brother when someday you'll be 'Your Highness' again."

"Well, that day doesn't seem to be any closer now than when we set out. Don't know if you noticed, but I'm still awake. Still alone. Still without a clue. Though I hope you know, no matter what the future holds, you will always be more brother to me than that pompous twit who is my blood brother."

"Once he is king, he could have you thrown in a dungeon for saying that."

"He'd have to get tired of hearing his own voice to notice I'd said it."

"Your High… um, Daniel. You can't give up hope. We've barely covered half the kingdoms of Clarameer."

"I guess." Daniel shrugged and held his hand out to James. The knight grabbed his hand and pulled him up. "I just thought I would find the answer sooner. Speaking of which, what have you've found?"

"I've found the way to make you sleep!" James said and puffed out his chest.

"Again?" Daniel asked, with a roll of his eyes. "What is it this time? I still haven't quite recovered from your last 'answer.'"

"Look, I thought that tonic would work. The old man on the wagon said Dr. Hickenkopf's Miracle Tonic would cure whatever ails you. It grows hair! It cures poxes! I watched it make a lame boy walk! I thought for sure it would make you sleep."

"James, it didn't make me sleep and it gave me the worst case of tumbly tummy I've ever had!" Daniel laughed as he grabbed at his stomach. "You are here to protect me, remember? I appreciate your helping me end the curse, but I don't want to end it by going to my grave."

"Okay, but this one is for sure going to work, and there is zero chance of death."

"Go on." Daniel crossed the path toward the woods where Rosemary had wandered off. He clicked his tongue to call her and grabbed at the reins hanging from her neck. James grabbed his own horse's reins and followed behind him, stumbling slightly as his boots sank into the sandy soil of the path.

"A little way ahead," James said and pointed in the direction he had come from, "I found the castle of the ruler of this kingdom. King Henry, I think? We're in Bellemer now, right? The castle sits on the cliffs right above the sea. Seahorses were drawn on everything."

"Yes. A seahorse is the sigil of Bellemer. That would be King Henry's castle. I've heard it is a beautiful place, with views of the Southern Sea from every window. Full of music and art and laughter. They say King Henry is the jolliest man in Clarameer."

"Then maybe I got the wrong place," James said, then cocked his head and thought. "It's small and plain, and there was definitely no one singing. They had almost no guards on duty, so I was able to ride right in."

"That's not very wise. Did they learn nothing from the fall of Cantera?"

"Right! But I just rode right in. I thought maybe they had an inn, or maybe I could find a steward and get us some food and a place to stay tonight. That's why I put on the surcoat with your sigil. I know how you royals like to entertain each other."

"One of the perks," Daniel said as he began brushing his hand down Rosemary's side, knocking the dust from her flank.

"Exactly. But I couldn't find anyone who would even look up at me. Everyone was moping around talking about another princess failing the test. Every time I tried to speak, they told me to be quiet and pointed at signs that said 'raise your crops and not your voice.' They were working away like crazy mice, almost as if they were scared to stop and speak."

"Odd," Daniel said. His interest piqued, he stopped grooming the horse and turned to look at his friend. "You said a princess failed a test?"

"I have no idea what they meant." James shrugged. "But they were obviously focused on this princess guest, so I think they will be excited to have a prince like you, too. Finally, an old woman who was feeding chickens said the whole royal family was probably in the main hall seeing off the fake princess. So I just wandered around the castle trying to find the main hall or someone who would talk to me. And that's when I found it."

"Found what?"

"The answer to your no-sleeping curse. I just opened a door and there it was. It was really lucky that I stumbled across it."

"Yes?"

"It's huge." James stretched his arm high above his head, the ribbons on his bicep fluttering in the light breeze. "And right in the middle of the room. And there was nothing else in there. Which was weird. But it was so dark, I knew it would be perfect for you."

"James, what *is* it?"

"Oh. Sorry. A bed."

"A bed?" Daniel scowled.

"Not just any bed. A huge bed. I mean, it's taller than I am. There were at least twenty mattresses on it. And I thought, 'that looks so comfortable, I bet anyone could sleep there.' And then I knew."

"You think a very tall bed will reverse my curse?" Daniel laughed and went back to grooming the horse's side.

"Wait until you see it! It has to work. I mean, I was tempted to crawl up and have a nap myself."

"I guess it's worth a try. We need somewhere for you and the horses to rest tonight, anyway. Did you make arrangements?"

"No. I was so excited I rushed right back here to find you. It gets even sandier up ahead, so Lillianne was going slow."

"Well, it's almost dark. Lead the way, and if we don't find anyone tonight, I'll just present myself tomorrow and express my gratitude then. If my map is correct and this is King Henry's kingdom, we should be welcomed. My father always said he was a fair and gentle man. He's got a son about our age, I think. I bet this princess was to be his future bride." Daniel picked up the map and tucked it back in the saddlebag. He grabbed his saddle horn and slung himself into the seat. Grabbing the reins, he turned his horse. "Anyway, maybe we can meet this fake princess that everyone is so up in arms about and learn more about this test."

"That could be exciting! I wonder what kind of test it is. I hope it involves swords."

"From the few pictures I have seen in the *Inquisitor*, the prince is a handsome man, so I'm sure princesses are vying to marry him. I guess they want to make sure they get a true one. Well, at least it'll be something different. Let's go."

Daniel knew the bed probably wouldn't help. A birthday fairy curse could never be broken by something as simple as a bed. He knew from all he had read that strong magic required an even stronger response. However, humoring James's ideas was the least he could do in gratitude for James coming with him on this journey. He turned to his knight and said, "Lead the way, brother."

James swung himself back up into his saddle and turned his horse toward the south. "Just follow me."

Daniel gently bumped his horse with his heels. *Who knows? Maybe it will work and I will dream again tonight. Or maybe I will find one of the things Mother told me to look for.*

As Rosemary began her trot toward the distant castle, Daniel began counting their steps.

*One. Adventure. Two. Answers. Three. Purpose. Four. Love.*

# CHAPTER 4

K ATERINA'S EARS RANG AND HER HEAD SPUN AS SHE
materialized in the queen's bedchamber beside her aunt.
As the last wisps of burgundy smoke whirled around her
face, she dropped to her knees and covered over her mouth, trying
her best to keep her last meal from making a reappearance. She
was not sure what had just happened. One minute, she had been
standing in the tower she had called home for the last eighteen
years, and the next, she was spinning blindly in complete darkness
before feeling her feet land softly on the stones of this room. She
assumed she had traveled this way at least once before, when
Cauchemar had brought her into the tower, but that had been so
long ago she couldn't remember it. After this dizzying experience,
she wondered how she could have forgotten it, though.

"Up on your feet, girl," Cauchemar chastised, as she grabbed
Katerina by her elbow and yanked her to her feet. "That feeling
will pass and eventually it won't affect you at all."

"It feels like that tingle of fear I get in my stomach when I look
down from my window, mixed with…"

"The sensation you get after eating a bad frogberry?"

"Exactly! Oh, I don't like this. I don't ever want to do that again!"

"Well, if you stick to the things I have been teaching you, you'll
never have to leave these walls. You'll have an entire kingdom

waiting on you hand and foot, and you'll eat lobsters, not frog-berries. Now let's get you into something more suitable to meet your future husband."

"I need to sit down a little longer," Katerina moaned, as she dropped onto the bed behind her.

"Nonsense. You'll be able to sit all you want once there's a throne underneath your little backside. Up! Up!" She dragged the girl to her feet again and pulled her across the room to a large mirror and armoire. Opening the cabinet door, she pulled out a frothy, rose-colored dress and flung it over her shoulder toward Katerina, who caught the dress just before it landed at her feet.

"It's so lovely!" Katerina cried, as she pulled the dress up to her shoulders and let it float down to her ankles. Looking at her reflection, she grinned, spun on her toes, and flared the skirt out around her legs. "If I put my hair up and wear this dress, I'll be lovelier than Gingerfair the Beloved herself! Peter will never be able to resist me in this!" Her hand flew to her mouth as she realized she had said the wrong name.

"Phillip, you dolt. His name is Phillip."

"Right! Phillip! I think I'm still a little foggy from the way we got here."

"Well, snap out of it, girl. Now go back there and get dressed." Cauchemar yawned as she pointed to a dressing screen in the corner. The girl carried the dress behind the screen and began to change into the new outfit. "I think maybe I should do all the talking until you're totally over our trip. Can't have you calling the prince the wrong name. You just stand there and look lovely."

"I hope the prince will think I am beautiful," Katerina said, as she walked from behind the screen and stopped in front of the mirror. She smoothed her skirts out and adjusted the neckline of her bodice until the dress sat perfectly. Looking up, she caught her reflection in the mirror and gasped. "Auntie! Look at me! I look like a real princess!"

"Shhh! You *are* a real princess," Cauchemar snapped, as she flicked the girl lightly on the ear. "In the name of Godrick the Golden, please remember what I've taught you, or you'll ruin this entire plan. Now let me get a good look at you." She spun the girl around and ran her eyes up and down her frame. "Not that it matters, but here," she said, as she slid the ruffles of the dress from Katerina's shoulders down onto her upper arms. "Out here in the kingdoms, it's in fashion to put a little more skin on display."

"Doesn't it get cold in the winter?" Katerina scrunched up her nose as she looked down at her chest.

"By winter, my dear, you'll be in furs."

Katerina looked back at her reflection. She had to admit, the dress made her look more like a woman and less like the girl she was used to seeing in the mirror in the tower. Though she had no interest in marrying Prince Phillip, she needed time alone with him to warn him of Cauchemar's plans. She also hoped he might be able to help her find Peter. "In this dress, the prince will have to find me desirable!"

"Eh," Cauchemar mumbled, with a roll of her eyes, "I wouldn't bet on it."

"What?"

"I said 'you can bet on it.' You look ravishing, my dear. Now let's go present you to the king." Cauchemar opened the door of her chamber and swept into the hall. Katerina followed as they hurried through the hallways of the castle. Though she couldn't decide if it was from her recent magical travel or the twisting of the many hallways, her head spun with each step. She had never been out of the few rooms atop her tower; the size of the castle made her stomach flutter with excitement and a touch of fear. Her eyes darted, as she tried to take in each inch of the castle halls. *Look at all the doors. How wonderful to be somewhere with doors!*

The farther they walked, though, the more Katerina noticed the castle was much less adorned than she had expected from Peter's tales and her own dreams of a royal home. The walls were simple stone with little or no decoration other than the occasional patch of moss or an iron sconce holding a flickering torch.

"It's not very fancy."

"You should have seen it before I was crowned and did a major cleanup. It was just awful. Tapestries and paintings everywhere. Gold, silver, brass. Crystals and jewels on everything. Gaudy, flashy things everywhere. And seashells and seahorses on everything. Yes. You are the ocean-front kingdom. We get it."

"It sounds lovely."

"Distracting. That's what it was. My stepsister was a true Canteran, easily distracted by any shiny thing that passed her eye. The Canterans know plenty about enjoying life's riches, but nothing about maintaining order and rule. That's the danger of growing up in a kingdom with so many pleasures at every turn. My stepsister had absolutely no sense of how to rule and even less sense of style."

"Prince Phillip's mother?"

"Yes. Terrible woman. Spent her time singing, dreaming, wasting away her days. And she let the peasants get away with utter laziness. Instead of working the fishing boats and nets as they should, they dallied with her festivals, concerts and plays."

"I'm sure they loved her."

"Katerina! What is Rule Number Seventeen?"

"No matter what devotion a subject offers, a queen knows love won't fill her coffers."

"Correct. With King Henry following his silly wife's advice, the peasants were loving and singing and dancing this kingdom right into poverty. Even worse, they were beginning to think themselves worthy of the same things we members of the royalty enjoy. That is a path to anarchy. I got here just in time to set things back as they should be. That nitwit child of hers is just as lost in dreams as she was. Which is why it is so important for you take his place."

"About that…" Katerina mumbled, as she stopped and stared at her feet. "Do we really have to do what you said in the tower? Couldn't I just marry him and promise to keep you here?"

Cauchemar stopped before a pair of tall doors and took a deep breath. "Remind me to give you some of my Prick Up Your Ears of Corn, because you clearly aren't listening. I said the boy is just like his mother. If he ever takes that throne, he'll lose this kingdom to the first fool who walks in with a sword. Now look pretty, and let me do the talking." Plastering a large smile across her face, she pushed the doors open and swept into the room beyond. "Henry, my love! I have solved our problem!"

Katerina's mouth dropped open as she followed her aunt into the throne room. She had never seen a room so large. Long wooden tables lined with chairs stretched along either side of the room from the doorway to the opposite end. Five chandeliers, each with at least fifty candles, hung over both tables and spread light throughout the room. A dark blue carpet flowed between the tables from her feet to a raised platform at the opposite end of the room, where sat three large, but rather plain, chairs that she assumed were thrones. Over the thrones hung an azure banner embroidered with a large silver seahorse. A portly older man with just a dusting of white hair at his temples rose slightly from the center chair as they entered the room. Under a simple golden crown, his face had the weary look of a dog anticipating the kick he knows will come from the cruelest of masters.

"Cauchemar, you've returned," King Henry said with the slightest hint of weary disappointment. "I've been looking for you ever since that imposter princess left. Someday you must tell me where you sneak off to. A hiding place like that would be handy."

Katerina's attention was drawn away from the king by a loud, short laugh from the young man sitting beside the king. He sat with one leg thrown carelessly over the arm of his chair and twirled his crown on his finger. He stared at the ceiling and bounced his leg, which was clad in silver leggings tucked into a knee-high leather boot, against the side of his throne; the silver embellishments on his blue doublet glimmered in the candlelight with each bounce. From what she could see of his body in his carefree position, he was tall and lean. His nose was small and almost feminine, but his strong jaw flexed as he pouted his lips and blew his loose, brown bangs from his forehead. Katerina assumed this was her intended groom and was surprised by how handsome he was. He turned his attention from the ceiling and locked his clear blue eyes on hers. A shiver crawled down her spine as he smiled and mouthed, "Hello." She smiled back before dropping her eyes to the floor.

"Pop," the young man laughed, "I know every inch of this castle and there isn't a nook or cranny my dear stepmother could stuff herself into where we couldn't hear her ordering someone around."

"Ignoring you," Cauchemar sing-songed, as she approached the king's throne and shot an icy glare at the young man.

"Well, it must be quite the secret spot if you've kept a young girl tucked away in there, too," Phillip said and gestured toward Katerina.

"Who do we have here?" King Henry asked and leaned forward to see the girl better.

"This is the answer to Phillip's marriage problem."

"I don't have a marriage problem. I'm not married. No problem."

Katerina couldn't help but giggle at the prince's joking tone.

"Son," King Henry chastised, "you know you can't take the throne until you're married. Also, you're being rude to a guest. Cauchemar, where did you find such a lovely young girl?"

"King Henry. Prince Phillip," Cauchemar said with a wave of her arm toward the girl, "may I present my niece, Katerina. Daughter of King Francis and Queen Evelyn of Cantera."

Katerina jerked her head toward her aunt. This was an even more fabulous story than Katerina had expected. She was not sure she could convince people she was a princess, much less the missing daughter of the murdered royal family of the old central kingdom. As she opened her mouth to protest, she was interrupted.

"Cantera!" Phillip gasped, as he stood from his throne. "There is no central kingdom anymore. And you of all people know there were no royal survivors of the troll king's attack."

"Phillip," Cauchemar said and sighed, "I can explain."

"No," Phillip raised his voice and stepped toward Katerina. "I think it's cruel of you to try to pass off some girl as the child of your dead stepsister. If my mother were here, she would have you thrown in the dungeon for trying to use the memory of Queen Evelyn in this way."

"Phillip!" Cauchemar interrupted. "If you will let me tell the story. Henry, you know I was serving as Mistress of Magic for Francis and Evelyn when Thrigor, the troll king, invaded."

King Henry sighed and nodded. "One of the saddest days in Clarameer's history. Phillip, your mother lost a third of her family that day. Including a niece named Katerina."

"Yes. He captured my stepsister, her husband, and her son and he had them all killed. But purely by coincidence, I had taken Princess Katerina out of the castle for a walk in the woods. It's the only reason either of us survived."

"How did you get over the giant wall once the troll king raised it?" King Henry asked and shifted on his throne.

"Again, luck was on my side. We were standing just beyond the point where the wall rose. Everyone assumed Katerina was killed in the coup, and I realized that if I let anyone know otherwise, Thrigor might come after the poor girl. So I hid her away and have raised her like my own child ever since. That is where I have been sneaking off to all these years. I had to tend to my lovely niece."

"Isn't that convenient for you? A girl you claim is a long-lost princess and who is practically your daughter could be sitting on the throne of this kingdom and making sure you can take all you want even longer. And it just now occurred to you to bring her out of hiding?" Phillip scoffed as he flopped onto his throne.

"Phillip," King Henry said quietly, hoping to avoid Cauchemar's wrath. "There is no need to be rude to your stepmother in front of a stranger."

"A stranger. Exactly. Pop, she is trying to pull one over on us!" Phillip raised his voice. "We don't have any proof this girl is Queen Evelyn's daughter. We don't know who she is. A secret princess rescued from a slaughter? That sounds like one of the fantasy stories Peter wrote before she ran him off!"

Katerina's ears pricked up at the mention of the name Peter. She gasped, "Phillip, do you know—"

Phillip ignored her and continued his tirade; his angry voice echoed off the high ceilings of the hall. "This could be the girl my mother warned about on her deathbed. This could be the false bride. Just some peasant girl she shoved into a pretty dress. Peter used to tell me stories about girls who claimed to be the lost princess!"

Cauchemar grabbed Katerina by the shoulders and pulled her to her chest. "Phillip, I will not stand here and let you insult this poor girl like that. She has been through enough in her life without you calling her names. This is precisely why I did not bring her here sooner. But since every other available girl in the realms has failed the test—"

Phillip jumped up from his throne with an excited smile. "The test!"

"Yes. The test. Since you are basically out of options, I thought it was time to bring her out of hiding. She will pass the test for sure, and you can marry her and claim your father's throne. I know you think I do not care for you, Phillip, but I really do want to see you married and on your wedding day hunt with your father."

"See, Phillip," King Henry said, "you need not worry about a false bride. The test will prove her true or not, and all will be well."

"Yes," Phillip said with a smirk, "and when—I mean, *if* she fails the test, then I don't marry her."

"Exactly." King Henry sighed. "Now can we please stop making a scene in front of this lovely girl and get some food. Katerina, I'm sure you must be starved after your travel here."

"More than anything, your highness," Katerina said with a small curtsy, "I could use a little nap. The trip here was so exciting, it seems to have tired me out."

"You're easily tired?" Phillip asked as he jumped down from the dais and walked over to the girl. "Well, lucky for you we have the most comfortable beds in all the kingdoms! Why don't I take you on a little tour of the castle grounds?" The prince offered his bent elbow to Katerina and cocked his head in her direction.

Katerina rested her hand on the prince's outstretched arm and let him turn her toward the doors. Glancing back over her shoulder at Cauchemar, she shrugged.

"Katerina, right?" Phillip asked.

She nodded in assent and they began walking out into the hallway. "You can call me Kitty if you'd prefer."

"Kitty? Huh. That's cute."

The girl blushed and dropped her chin again. "A friend gave that nickname to me. A friend I'd like to talk to you about."

"Well, Kitty, you'll have to forgive my anger and the terrible things I said earlier. I just fear for my kingdom's safety if I marry a false bride."

"I have a few fears to discuss with you, too," Katerina said quietly.

"Katerina," her aunt interrupted and grabbed the girl's shoulder. "No need to bend the prince's ears with silly girlish fears. Henry, are you coming as well? I think you should get to know your future daughter-in-law."

"Coming, dear." The king stood to follow them. "You are certainly confident of this girl's chances."

"Yes. I am. And so no one will question her virtue, I think you two need a chaperone."

"I've never needed an escort with the other girls." Phillip stopped and looked at Cauchemar.

"Well, those weren't true princesses, now, were they? But Katerina is the real deal."

"If she passes the test."

"She'll pass."

"We'll see," Phillip mumbled. Looking at the pretty girl on his arm, he said, "So, Kitty, would you like to walk along the walls and see the ocean? A good brisk walk in the salty air will help make sure you are good and tired before bed." He reached over and slid the ruffles of her dress off her upper arms onto her shoulders. "These frilly things look better up here, and besides, you might get chilly."

# CHAPTER 5

"NICE AND QUIET," PHILLIP WHISPERED TO HIMSELF AS he inched along the wall toward the testing chamber door. Looking up and down each side of the hallway, he checked to make sure he was alone before grabbing the iron handle on the chamber door. "Just slip in, put the tonic in the water carafe and slip right back out. Kitty sleeps, you escape again, and no one is any the wiser."

Phillip felt uneasy as he gently pushed the door open just enough to slip through. He did not like having to alter his usual manner of dealing with his intended brides, and he knew putting something into someone's water was very wrong. However, Cauchemar had refused to leave Katerina's side, and he was at a loss for what to do. Phillip assumed she would escort her so-called niece into the chamber and even sit with her all night, so he would not be able to offer the tonic while saying goodnight. "Stupid woman. I wouldn't put it past you to have given the girl a potion to make sure she stays awake."

As he slipped into the room, Phillip was surprised to find it not completely dark. A small lamp burned on the tall table beside the head of the bed; the light from the flame danced off the cut-crystal edges of a water carafe and scattered flickers of light around the chamber. *Of course. Pierre must have lit the lamp when he brought in the water. Not that I need any light. I know this path all too well now. Well, on with the business at hand.*

Phillip crossed the room on his tiptoes. *Why am I sneaking? The future love of my life is not in the bed. Still, no need to alert anyone that I am in here or the jig is up.* By the time he reached the footboard, his eyes had adjusted to the dim light of the lamp. He grasped a rung and began his climb to the top of the stack of mattresses. As he neared the top rung, a snuffling sound from the darkened corner near the doorway made his ears prick up. Freezing on the spot, he squinted to see if someone was coming.

*Relax—probably just a rat.* Phillip pulled himself up the final rungs. As his head came level with the mattresses, he could see that the water carafe was empty. *Great, I will have to get the carafe, fill it and sneak back in here. I don't have time for all that.* With a sigh of frustration, he lifted his leg over onto the mattresses. As he put down his hand to begin his crawl to the table, it landed on something under the dark blue coverlet. Jerking his hand back, he gasped.

Phillip slid his eyes up the lump under the bedding: it was clearly the outline of a body. Fully expecting to find some lazy stable boy or serving girl had crept into the barely-used room for a clandestine nap, Philip smiled to himself as he inched forward. While he would never cause trouble for the sleeper by reporting the nap, he could certainly have a little fun scaring the poor person to death.

As he reached the pillows, Phillip gasped again as he came face to face with a stranger. Phillip leaned closer to the man's face to see his features better in the dim light of the flickering lamp. The man's black wavy hair surrounded sharp cheekbones and a strong jaw lightly dusted with dark stubble. The tan of his skin showed someone who had spent many days in the Clarameer sun and possibly had Gloriannan heritage. Beneath his dark eyebrows, the man's eyes were closed in what appeared to be a deep sleep, and dark lashes lay on his cheek. *By Godrick's sword, he's beautiful.*

A twitch at the corner of the man's mouth drew Philip's gaze to the deep pink fullness of his lips. Phillip held his breath as he stared at the man's mouth and listened to the steady rise and fall of the other man's breathing. With his eyes tracing the outline of the man's slightly parted lips, Philip was taken with an overwhelming desire to place his lips there. Shaking his head to clear the thought, Phillip said aloud, "What are you doing?"

The other man's eyes flew open and he stared at Phillip with eyes as green as the Southern Sea. The man's eyes darted about Phillip's face until he eased into a smile. "I was trying to sleep."

"Oh!" Phillip gasped and jerked back. "I'm sorry. I didn't mean to… I didn't realize that… I'll just go out and let you—Wait a minute! This is my kingdom and my bed! By Gingerfair's girdle, who are you, and what are you doing in my bed?"

"As I said, I was trying to sleep." The other man pulled his arms up his side, leaned on his elbows and pushed his upper body slightly erect. "But it's hard to sleep with someone staring at you. And I didn't realize this was your bed. Trust me, I was raised to always ask a man's permission before I crawl into his bed. Had I known *you* might be in it, I would certainly have asked if I could climb in." The man winked.

Phillip felt the blood rush to his face and turned away from the light. Though he wasn't sure exactly what the man meant, it made his heart race. He sat back and asked, "Who *are* you?"

"I'm just a wandering soul who was hoping to finally get a good night's sleep." The man stretched his arms above his head and then dropped them back to his sides. "I saw this big, comfortable bed and couldn't help myself. I thought at last I would get the rest I so desire."

"This bed is not about your desires."

The man threw his head back and laughed loudly. "Oh, you're a quick one! I knew from your picture that you were a handsome man, but no one told me you were funny too."

Phillip stared at the man, unsure if he what he had just heard was a compliment. "What? I wasn't trying to be funny." Phillip tilted his head in thought until he realized how the man had interpreted his words. "Oh, no! I didn't mean *that*. I meant that this bed has a special purpose. It's not here for any random stranger to just wander in and climb into and—Did you say you've seen my picture?"

"Of course. You're Prince Phillip of Bellemer. I saw a sketch of you in the *Kingdom Inquisitor*. Though it really didn't do you justice."

"I was in the *Inquisitor*?" Phillip said, as his eyes widened. "My stepmother doesn't allow that newspaper in the castle. She says it's full of nonsense."

"She's right," the man said with a chuckle. Phillip watched the corners of the man's eyes wrinkle as he laughed, making his rugged face seem friendlier. "But it has helped me keep up with some of the news of the kingdoms while I have been on my wanderings."

"You've been out in the kingdoms?" Phillip asked. He shifted up onto his knees and leaned forward. "What's it like out there?"

"Surely you've been out in the kingdoms," the man said with a look of surprise. "You're a royal. You can go anywhere!"

Phillip dropped his head and frowned as he traced the maze of stitching on the bed's coverlet. "No," he mumbled. "My stepmother won't let me. She says it isn't safe out there for a future king."

"She won't let you read the *Inquisitor*. She won't let you out in the kingdoms." The man placed his hand under Phillip's chin and lifted his head to look into his eyes. Phillip's stomach fluttered at the warmth of the man's touch. "Who is this woman that she can have this much control over you? Your mother, you said?"

"She's not my mother. She's my father's wife." Phillip shrugged and pulled away from the man's hand. "She's awfully bossy. As a matter of fact, she's why this stupid bed is here."

"Yes," the man said, "you said this bed has a special purpose. I can only think of a couple of purposes for a bed and none require it to be this tall." The man cocked his eyebrow upward.

"You mean you haven't heard about it? I figured everyone knew." Phillip sighed and flopped back onto the bed. He lay still until an uncomfortable lump in the mattress under his back made him shift. "My stepmother is determined to find me a bride. This bed has something to do with that, but I really can't talk about it. It's a secret. Especially since I don't even know your name."

"You can call me Daniel," the man said, as he pushed the coverlet off his body and began climbing past Phillip toward the end of the bed. "If this bed has such a special purpose, I guess I'd better get out of it."

As Daniel crawled past him, Phillip felt a sudden urge to keep him there a little longer. "Wait," Phillip pleaded. He reached out and grabbed Daniel's wrist. With a gentle tug, Phillip pulled him back onto the bed beside him. "Don't get down yet. Tell me about the kingdoms, please."

Daniel looked down at Phillip's hand on his wrist and back up at Phillip's face. Phillip quickly pulled his hand away. Daniel took Phillip's hand and set it back on his wrist. "You can keep me from falling out of the bed. There is a big lump right there," Daniel said as he pushed down on the mattress. "This bed is weird." After pulling on the bottom of his doublet to adjust it over his leggings, Daniel snuggled down into the mattress. He turned onto his side to face Phillip.

"Ignore the bed," Phillip said as he lay down beside Daniel, rested his head on his arm and stared into Daniel's eyes. "Tell me about the kingdoms."

"Okay. What do you want to know?"

"Everything!" Phillip said, his voice cracking with excitement.

"Well, Clarameer is much bigger than you would think. I haven't covered much of it yet. But what I have seen is absolutely beautiful."

*As beautiful as you?* Phillip watched Daniel's face light up with the joy of telling of his travels. He could easily imagine Daniel riding across the kingdoms on a white steed with his wavy hair blowing in the wind. As Daniel continued his tale, Phillip could barely follow his words, as he was yet again transfixed by the movement of Daniel's lips and the soothing timbre of his voice. Phillip closed his eyes and let himself be lost in Daniel's words.

"Phillip, are you listening?"

Phillip opened his eyes to find Daniel sitting up in the bed and looking at him expectantly.

"Why don't you do it?" Daniel asked.

Phillip's mind raced as he sat up and tried to figure out what Daniel was asking him. "Why don't I what?"

"Go out into the kingdoms, silly. Who cares what your stepmother says? I've been out there, and if it's safe enough for me, then— "

"I could never do that alone." Phillip pounded his fist into the mattress. "I wouldn't know how to begin."

"I didn't mean go alone," Daniel explained. "You need a companion to travel with you."

Phillip could feel his heart race in his chest again as he contemplated what Daniel was suggesting. "Daniel, are you asking me to— "

Phillip was interrupted by a loud clatter from the darkened corner of the room. He turned to see a tall, muscular man with blond hair stumble out of the darkness and into the faint light of the bedside lamp. Phillip could see the man wore a dark green surcoat with acorns embroidered on the chest; a sword in a jeweled scabbard hung on his belt. The knight's mouth was agape in mid-yawn, and he shook his head. He drew his sword from the scabbard and called up to the top of the bed, "Your Highness? Are you all right? I must have dozed off."

"Your Highness?" Phillip asked. "I thought you were some type of explorer! I'll ask you again. Who are you?"

"James," the man said as he leaned over the mattress and spoke to the other man below, "I'm fine. Put your sword away. It appears I have found the owner of this ridiculous bed." The man turned to face Phillip again. "I guess there is no hiding it now. I am Prince Daniel of Sylvania. That man down there is my guardian and travelling companion, Sir James. Pleased to make your acquaintance!" Daniel sat up in the bed and stuck his hand out to Phillip.

Phillip took Daniel's hand and shook it meekly. "Well, you already know I'm Prince Phillip. No one told me we should be expecting a visit from the neighboring kingdom, so I'll ask you one more time. What are you doing in this bed?"

"Can we climb down to the ground to discuss this? Maybe it's the height, but something is making me a little dizzy." Daniel threw his leg over the footboard and steadied himself on the first rung. He held his hand out to Phillip and called down to the floor, "James! Put your sword away and come help Prince Phillip and me down!"

Phillip looked at Daniel's outstretched hand and felt a little dizzy himself. Realizing their time alone was over, he grabbed the edge of the coverlet and flung it toward the head of the bed in frustration. "I can get down fine on my own," Philip mumbled, as he grabbed the lamp from the table and followed Daniel to the foot of the bed. Both men crawled down the footboard and dropped to the floor.

"James, take the lamp from Prince Phillip and see if you can find a torch or a candle. This is truly the darkest room I've ever seen."

"There is a torch by the door," Phillip said, as he handed the lamp to the knight.

Phillip squinted when the torch flooded the room with sudden brightness. In the full light of the torch, he could see more of Daniel. The other prince stood nearly the same height as Phillip and wore a doublet of emerald green and brown, the colors of Sylvania's royal family. The fabric fell gracefully from his broad shoulders to his narrow hips, where Daniel rested his hands; he stood with his legs spread in an air of confident grace. Phillip stared at the man's kind face and waited for him to speak.

"Well, no wonder," Daniel said, as he looked about the room. "With these tapestries hanging over all the windows, you'll never get any light in here. You should take these down." He walked to the side of the room and began tugging gently on a tapestry.

"No!" Phillip cried out. "Please don't touch those. Now will you please tell me what you are doing here?"

"Sorry," Daniel said, as he let the tapestry fall back against the stone wall. "I already told you. I'm just a wandering soul looking for a good night's rest. James was here earlier and found the bed. He thought it might be a good place for me to sleep. We tried to ask someone for a place to stay but everyone is so busy talking about some girl that we couldn't get anyone to help us. We finally just gave up and came in here to sleep."

"Oh, *her.*" Phillip shrugged. "She's not important. But I still don't know why you're here in my kingdom unannounced."

"Well, you know my brother Andrew will be king in Sylvania," Daniel leaned back against the stack of mattresses. "Unless something happens to him, there isn't a lot for me to do. I didn't much care for the life of sitting around he had planned for me, so I set out into the kingdoms in search of a purpose of my own. Also I have a little problem with—"

"Excuse me, sire," James interrupted the prince. "Someone's coming."

Phillip turned to the doorway just as Cauchemar swept into the room, her burgundy gown flaring out behind her as she took quick, broad steps. Katerina followed, head demurely dropped and hands folded in front of her waist. A few paces behind, King Henry huffed and puffed as he tried to keep up with his wife's eager pace.

"Oh, good!" Cauchemar said, not noticing the men standing in the room. "Someone came ahead and lit the torches." With a sweep of her arm, she gestured toward the room and the bed. "So this, Katerina, is where you will be sleeping tonight. As you can see the bed is… Phillip?" She stopped abruptly, causing Katerina and King Henry to bump into her from behind. "Careful, you clods! Phillip, love, what are you doing in here? You know no one is supposed to be in this chamber on the night before the test. Who are these men and what are you up to?"

"I just came in to light the torches and make sure everything was ready for Katerina," Phillip said as he stepped closer to Daniel. "I found him in the bed."

Daniel stepped forward and bowed to Cauchemar and the king. "King Henry. Queen Cauchemar. I am Prince Daniel of Sylvania. You will have to forgive my arriving unannounced. I had hoped to present myself formally to you this morning, but your young prince here has kept me distracted."

"Yes," Cauchemar sneered, "he can be quite the distraction. But what are you doing here in this room?"

"Oh, I simply came in here thinking this large bed might be a good spot to sleep," Daniel replied, pointing his thumb over his shoulder toward the testing bed.

"You what?" Cauchemar raised her voice slightly. "No one is supposed to sleep in the bed unless they are here for the test!"

"Then we're fine," Daniel said with a chuckle. "I didn't break your rules because I didn't sleep a bit. You'd think a bed that large and soft would be the perfect way to fall into sleep, but not for me."

Phillip's eyes grew wide as he looked over at the other prince; the seed of a plan was taking root in his mind. "Did you say you didn't sleep?"

"Not a wink."

Cauchemar stormed over to Daniel and grabbed him by the collar of his doublet. "You need to learn not to wander into places where you don't belong."

Phillip watched as Daniel tried to pull himself away from her grasp and shot a befuddled look at James. James put one hand on the hilt of his sword. Phillip held his breath until Daniel tugged himself free from Cauchemar's hands and waved James off. Phillip was impressed with the lack of fear Daniel showed. *This might actually work.*

"Cauchemar!" King Henry chastised as he stepped to Phillip's side. "My sweet, take your hands off that boy! He is a member of the royal family of Sylvania. His departed father and I were great friends and his mother is a vision of beauty. I will not have it whispered about the kingdoms that we do not know how to be good hosts to other royals. It's been hard enough to convince the other kingdoms to send their daughters here, what with princesses failing this test left and right. We don't need to be known for offending princes too."

"Daniel?" Phillip asked, a small grin growing on his face. His heart began to beat faster as the seed of the plan sprouted. "Did you say you spent the night in *that* bed and did not sleep?"

"No, I did not sleep," Daniel said to Phillip. Turning back to King Henry, he said, "I'm sorry if I have caused a problem. I'm sure this young lady can still sleep here."

Cauchemar turned to the door and began to scream into the hallway, "Someone get me some clean sheets for this bed!" Turning back to the room, she walked over to Katerina and stroked her arm. "Don't you worry, my pet. You will still stay in this room tonight, and the test will proceed as planned."

"It's fine if I need to stay somewhere else," Katerina said with a look of relief on her face. "Daniel was here first. He should have the room."

Phillip shifted his gaze between Katerina and Daniel as he became surer of what he should do next. "Not a wink?" Phillip asked Daniel and his grin widened into a full smile.

"I told you, not at all," Daniel replied, with an exasperated look. "Why do you keep asking me that?"

As Phillip began to answer, a commotion in the hallway drew the attention of the group.

"Out of my way. I need to see Kitty!"

"That sounded like Peter," Katerina said, as she craned her neck around Cauchemar's body to see into the hallway.

"Kitty?" Peter burst into the testing chamber, his sides heaving. As he slid to a stop on the stone floor, a few leaves that clung to his simple tunic fluttered down, and he wiped a streak of mud from his cheek. "I ran the whole way from the tower! I'm so glad I found you! Phillip, I cannot let this charade go on anymore! Your life is in danger!"

"Peter?" Phillip cried out, as he rushed to his friend and pulled him into a hug. "Oh, Peter! It is so good to see you! I didn't think I would ever— Wait!" Phillip pushed Peter back and looked at him in confusion. "Did you call her Kitty? How do you know—?"

"Phillip," Peter replied, "it is good to see you, too, but that isn't important right now. I have to tell you about—"

"Young man, you were banished from this kingdom!" Cauchemar yelled; the veins in her forehead distended in anger. "Guards! Come seize this lying little traitor and throw him off the castle walls! We will not have you in here filling the prince's head with your silly stories!"

"Cauchemar, let the boy speak," King Henry said and crossed the room to Peter's side. "Peter what is this you are going on about?"

"I heard it all. Outside the tower in the woods." Peter paused as he gasped for breath. Pointing at Cauchemar, he continued, "She plans to have Phillip marry Katerina."

"Of course, if Princess Katerina passes the test, Phillip will marry her," King Henry replied. "But I don't understand what you are trying to say. What are you talking about—a tower in the woods?"

"The tower in the woods where this woman has kept Katerina locked away." Peter grabbed Phillip's shoulders and looked imploringly into his eyes. "Please believe me. I overheard her telling Katerina her plans." Peter turned to King Henry and continued, "She wants to take over your kingdom and needs to get you both out of the way to do so. She's been training Katerina to pass whatever this test is, and has coached her how to pretend to be a princess."

Phillip looked over to see Katerina drop her head in shame and step behind Cauchemar. Cauchemar rolled her eyes at Phillip and shook her head. Though he was shocked by Peter's words, Phillip remained calm as he glanced at Daniel and James standing by the testing bed and considered his plan.

Peter continued, "Do you understand me? Why aren't you upset? She intends to have you both murdered at the marriage hunt. She has enchanted the bow used at the hunt to make sure it will miss the stag and hit you, King Henry, and enchanted the stag to gore Prince Phillip. She banished me, but she is the murderous traitor!"

"Cauchemar?" King Henry roared. "Is this true?"

Cauchemar cackled. "Peter, your stories keep getting worse and worse. This is just downright ridiculous. Enchanted stags? Enchanted bows? This is almost as ridiculous as your vicious lie that I murdered Queen Marie. I was too kind in having you banished. I should've had you hanged. Someone call the guards to dispose of this babbling idiot!"

"Phillip, listen to me," Peter pleaded. "I'm not making this up. You cannot marry Katerina. You can't let this evil woman ruin your life and your kingdom."

"Peter," Phillip said, displaying his widest grin, "calm down."

"Calm down? I just told you this woman wants to kill you!"

"And Father and I will deal with that. But right now I have a different matter to attend to. You don't need to worry about marriage hurting my kingdom. I'm not marrying Katerina." Phillip patted Peter on the shoulder before turning and strolling back toward his father and the testing bed.

"When she passes the test you will," Cauchemar said from behind him. "I've had quite enough of this nonsense. Now someone haul off this lying boy and get me some clean—"

"No," Phillip interrupted her. "I have to follow the rules. Someone else has already passed your test, so I cannot marry Katerina. I'm going to marry someone else."

"You're what? Who?" King Henry asked.

"The one who didn't sleep in that bed." Pointing across the room at the other prince, Phillip said with a smile, "Prince Daniel." Phillip crossed his arms and leaned back against the stack of mattresses.

"What?" Daniel turned to Phillip with a look of shock.

"Silly boy!" Cauchemar said with a laugh. "You cannot marry another prince!"

"You heard what Daniel said. He didn't sleep." Phillip pushed himself away from the bed and crossed to drape his arm on Daniel's shoulders. "He passed the test. Those are the rules. *Your* rules. And as you always say, we have to follow the rules."

"Phillip," Daniel said, "I'm confused."

"*The rules*," Cauchemar growled, irritation growing in her voice, "are that you will marry a princess, you little pest. This," she gestured toward Daniel, "is not a princess."

"Well, I don't like that rule," Phillip sniffed. "So when I am king I will just have to change it." Though he tried to keep his face as calm and confident as he could, Phillip was sure everyone could hear his heart pounding. He glanced at the others, seeking a reaction, but they all stood with their mouths agape.

Cauchemar broke the silence. "When you are king? Ha!" She threw her head back and cackled. "You could never be a king. You don't have the nerve it takes to rule a kingdom!"

"Maybe I do. Maybe I don't," Phillip said with a shrug. He looked over to see his father staring at him. Was he going too far? Glancing over to see Daniel's face, he felt a sudden surge of courage bubble up from his chest. "But now that I have someone who passed the test, we can find out. Maybe Daniel will be the one with the nerve, and we can rule together."

"Phillip," Daniel asked, "what test did I take? Me marry you? Can someone explain—"

"This is absurd!" Cauchemar scoffed, her face growing red.

"What is absurd," Phillip said, as he stalked over and poked his finger into Cauchemar's chest, "is that we have let you run this kingdom!" Phillip pushed against her chest as he spat out his words, his determination growing with each push. "I think it's time I changed a few things around here."

"You will kindly take your hand off—"

"Daniel," Phillip called over his shoulder "do you like art and music?"

The other prince stared at him. "Um...Yes?"

"Well, I think you and I should bring some of it back," Phillip said and dropped his hand. "Take things back to the way they were when my mother was here." Squaring his shoulders, he leaned into Cauchemar's face. "That includes making this a castle without you in it!"

"Your mother!" Cauchemar suddenly screamed as she shoved Phillip back toward Daniel and the bed. "I did this kingdom a favor by ridding it of your mother, and it would be better off without you!"

Phillip gasped as flames grew around Cauchemar's neck and shoulders, in time with her growing anger. Feeling his newfound courage evaporate, he cowered from the heat of her rage. He could hear the others gasp and back away, as the flames sent long shadows across the floor. Phillip's knees trembled. He backed into someone. Air softly brushed his ear as Daniel whispered, "Steady, now."

Cauchemar flung her arms above her head. "Your little storyteller friend was right. I did intend to kill you and rule this kingdom as my own!" Her eyes flashed as she whipped her head in Phillip's direction and yelled, "And I would've ruled it the way it should be ruled!" Grabbing Katerina's arm, she yanked the girl to her side. "This halfwit could rule this kingdom better than you!"

"Auntie, calm down! You are hurting me!" Katerina pleaded. She tugged her arm from the other woman's grasp. Phillip could smell singed hair as the flames dancing around Cauchemar's head licked at Katerina's face. He could feel Daniel, James and his father step forward behind him, but felt himself frozen.

"Cauchemar! Unhand that girl!" King Henry yelled and stepped between Phillip and the raging woman.

"You want to change all the rules when you are king? Well, you cannot be king until this one is dead!" Cauchemar screamed as she pointed at King Henry. "We shall see about that!" Flinging her arm toward the king, Cauchemar shot a wave of brilliant blue light across the room at the old man. King Henry lifted his arm in fright; his jaw dropped open. As the light hit him, he toppled to the floor, his arm frozen in front of him and his face seized in fear.

Phillip's breath caught in his throat as he looked down at where his father had fallen at his feet. The king did not move; his eyes stared blankly. "You killed my father!" Phillip screamed. He dropped to the ground and grabbed his father's frozen body.

"Not exactly," Cauchemar howled. "He isn't really dead and he isn't really alive. If he can't die, you can't take his place. So you will never sit your incompetent ass on his throne! Try changing the rules now!"

"Father!" Phillip wrapped his arms around his father's shoulders and lifted him slightly. He could hear the other men bustling around him toward the raging woman. He shook his father a bit. Tears rolled down his cheek as he searched for any sign of life in his father's face.

"James!" Daniel cried out. He ran toward Cauchemar and pulled his sword from its sheath. "Attack her now!"

"Kitty! Get Kitty!" Peter cried out, as he and James charged at the women.

As Daniel reached out to grab the girl, Cauchemar snatched her to her chest and screamed. "You will never have me—or her!" A cloud of dark burgundy smoke billowed around the pair. Daniel's fingers grasped empty air.

"Kitty?" Peter began to wail as he fanned the smoke away from his face and looked frantically about the room. "Where is Kitty?"

"Father! Father!" Phillip screamed as he rocked his father back and forth in his arms. Looking around the room with tears and panic in his eyes, he pleaded, "Daniel! Peter! Someone help me! Oh, Father. I'm sorry. I'm so sorry. Someone help!"

Daniel turned to James. "What kind of castle did you bring me to?"

# CHAPTER 6

IN CANTERA, QUEEN EVELYN'S CHAMBER HAD STOOD EMPTY and unnoticed for almost twenty years, but time needed no audience to take its toll on the scattered belongings within. The lace curtains hanging in the windows had aged into the yellow of an old woman's teeth. Moths had eaten at the red damask that barely clung to the canopy railing around the top of the bed, like the last desperate strands of oily hair hanging on an old man's head. The heavy velvet bed covers were mottled and bruised by sunlight sucking away at the oxblood dyes that had once made it as plush as a new rose petal. On the vanity across from the bed, pink and yellow perfume bottles had toppled over; their precious oils had long since evaporated into the room. No trace of the sweet perfumes could be sensed over the musk of dust and neglect.

The lace curtains fluttered as the first wisps of burgundy smoke seeped from the rafters above and the stones below. The fireplace that had lain cold and dark suddenly burst forth with flames. The cobwebs along its edges hissed as they curled away from the heat and disappeared. The burgundy smoke grew thicker and thicker as it crept from each darkened corner. A crack loud as thunder broke the silence of the chamber, and the figures of two women appeared.

"Peter?" Katerina screamed, as she clawed her way into clearer air. Her shoe caught on the jagged edge of a stone in the floor and sent her toppling forward. On the cold, hard floor, she put her head down between her arms and vomited.

"You will not find that babbling dolt here, child," Cauchemar growled. She waved the last traces of smoke away from her face. "He has interfered in our lives for the last time. As for how you know his name and how he came to know my plans, well, those are the secrets of a young girl's heart, I guess. But I *will* know them, and any others you may be hiding in your heart, if I have to reach in and pull them out whole. Now get up, you simpering twit, and clean that dreck from your face."

Katerina stayed on her hands and knees and stared at the stones beneath her hands. She gagged, then sobbed. "What did you do?" she bellowed, as she jerked her face over her shoulder toward the woman. "Where are we?" she screamed. "Where are Peter and Phillip? What did you do to King Henry? Answer me!"

"Well," Cauchemar purred, as she raised her eyebrows and crossed her arms across her chest, "it appears the little kitten has decided she can roar."

"Tell me! Tell me now!"

Cauchemar knelt beside the sobbing girl and rested her hand softly on the top of her head. "My dear," she cooed, then grabbed a clump of the girl's blonde hair and pulled it sharply upward. Katerina whimpered as the woman pulled her to her feet by her hair and then spun her around to stand eye to eye. "That mouth has caused enough damage, and if you are wise you will keep it shut!"

"You're hurting me!" Katerina reached up to push the woman's hands away from her hair.

"I'm hurting you? *I* am hurting *you*? What about the pain you have caused me? You lied to me, child! I protected you from this cruel world in my warm little tower. I asked nothing of you in return, except to learn the lessons I taught you and prepare for the life I'd planned for you! And now those plans are as tattered as the curtains on this bed. You have deceived me and ruined everything." Cauchemar dropped the girl's hair and turned to study her reflection in the vanity mirror. Looking at the items scattered along the top, she ran her finger across the bristles of a dusty silver hairbrush. "Your pain is nothing compared to my disappointment."

"Then why didn't you just leave me there?"

"Leave you?" Cauchemar grabbed the hairbrush and spun to face the girl. Shaking the brush toward Katerina, she bellowed, "How could I leave you? You are like a daughter to me. I have sacrificed and lived my life merely for you for all these years! Leave you. Ha! Had I known that it would lead to this, I would have left you in this very room years ago!"

"This room?" Katerina sniffled. She stared at her aunt in confusion.

"Yes. This is your mother's room." Dropping the brush onto the floor, she turned and spread out her arms. "Welcome home, princess."

"Home? My mother?"

Cauchemar walked slowly across the room, the train of her gown dragging a trail in the thick dust. Paying no attention to the girl's questions, she pulled a torch from the wall beside the chamber door and snapped her fingers at its tip. A bright flame flared and illuminated the room. She carried the torch to the wall across from the bed and stared at the portrait that appeared in the flickering light of the flames. Katerina rose from the floor, walked up behind her aunt and looked over her shoulder at the image of four smiling faces. A bearded young man with blond hair and a golden crown draped his arm across the shoulders of a beautiful young woman whose crown adorned long, curling blonde locks, which spilled over her shoulders. A little boy with white-blond hair leaned on the woman's knee. All three stared lovingly at the baby in the woman's arms. Katerina squinted to see the image in the dim light; she noticed that the woman looked a lot like herself.

"The first painting of you." Cauchemar turned to walk back toward door to put the torch into a mount on the wall.

Katerina stood silently staring until the image faded as the torch moved farther away. She crossed the room and sat on the stool in front of the vanity. Looking at her reflection, she pulled her curls forward and let them drop over her shoulders like the woman in the painting. "That woman looks like me."

"She should. She's your mother."

"That's my family?"

"Was."

"I still don't understand," Katerina said, as she shifted her gaze to the eyes of her aunt's reflection.

"Little girl, you're not the only one with secrets in her heart. The story I told King Henry about your royal heritage was not a complete lie. You're in the castle of the queen of Cantera, where you were born. Well, it *was* her castle until the invasion of the troll king, Thrigor. I was here when it happened."

"Yes, you said you were walking with me in the woods."

"Well, that part was a little untrue. Here," Cauchemar said as she reached over and ran her fingers along the mirror. "See."

The glass began to wobble and hum. Katerina watched as her reflection faded and the reflected room grew bright. The tattered furnishings around the room in the mirror were suddenly whole and clean. The white lace curtains fluttered lazily in the windows, and sunlight streamed into the room. The woman from the painting rushed into the mirrored room holding a baby and dragging a boy behind her. Katerina turned around to look at the room. It was the same dilapidated room with no one but Cauchemar behind her.

Cauchemar grabbed her head and turned her face back to the mirror. "These are reflections of the past. Watch your mother."

Katerina watched the woman in the mirror as she flitted about the room in a panic. Dropping the little boy's hand, she ran to a large trunk at the foot of the bed and flung it open with her one free hand. She dropped to her knees and put the baby in the open trunk. Grabbing the little boy's hand again, she lifted him into the trunk and urged him to sit down. She raced to the door and pushed it shut. As she reached for the key, the door flung open, knocking the young woman to the floor. Katerina gasped as Cauchemar stalked in. However, this was not the Cauchemar she knew; her face lacked the familiar wrinkles and lines, and her now-silver hair was a cascade of raven curls. The blonde woman jumped up and flung her arms around the other woman. Katerina noticed that the Cauchemar in the mirror did not hug back. The two women hurried to the bed and began a frenzied conversation, with the young queen pointing at the children in the trunk again and again. The young queen dropped to her knees before Cauchemar and clasped her hands in front of her face in a pleading motion.

"What is she saying?" Katerina kept her eyes glued to the images in the mirror.

"She was begging. She begged me to take you and your brother out of the castle. It was really quite pathetic. She thought she could hide you both in that silly trunk, and you would survive the attack."

In the mirror, young Cauchemar nodded her head in assent and reached her hand out to the boy cowering inside the trunk. He shook his head and wriggled lower into the trunk. The young queen pulled the boy out onto the floor in front of her. Wiping tears from her eyes, she kissed his cheek and pushed him gently toward the other woman. Cauchemar drew him tightly to her side. The queen reached into the trunk and pulled the baby out and up to her breast. She placed her forehead against the baby's face; her shoulders shook with sobs. She kissed the baby's cheek, then handed her over to Cauchemar's outstretched arms. As Katerina watched the woman sob, she touched her own cheek, on the spot where the queen had kissed her baby.

A single tear rolled down Katerina's cheek as she turned to look at Cauchemar in the room behind her. "She gave us to you?"

"She knew I could get you out. My powers were still young and new, so I didn't know if I could carry her as well. We had little time." Cauchemar shrugged and stepped forward to place her hands on Katerina's shoulders. "So I did what I could."

Katerina turned back to the mirror to see the room fill with burgundy smoke. The smoke surrounded Cauchemar, the boy and the baby in her arms, until it was too thick for Katerina to see them anymore. The young queen took a few steps backwards until the backs of her knees hit the trunk, making the lid slam shut. She flopped down onto the trunk lid and blew a kiss toward the billowing smoke, then dropped her head into her hands and sobbed. A bright flash enveloped the room as the smoke suddenly disappeared, taking Cauchemar and the children with it.

"She just gave us to you?"

"She saved your lives. *I* saved your lives."

Katerina stared at the woman in the mirror. She could no longer see her face, because the woman had buried it in her hands. She began to yell to the woman to show her face again, but realized the image could not hear her. Katerina reached out to touch the mirror above her mother's hair. As if reacting to the touch, the woman in the mirror suddenly jerked her head up and stared toward the door. Raising her arms defensively, she opened her mouth in what Katerina could only assume was a scream of terror. The young queen began crawling backwards over the trunk and toward the head of the bed. Katerina gasped in horror as she watched her mother scramble up the headboard. Suddenly, Cauchemar's hand appeared on the mirror and swiped across the image. The mirror shuddered and hummed again until Katerina was staring at nothing but the reflection of her own tear- and vomit-stained face and the dilapidated room behind her.

"Trust me, child. You don't want to see what happened next."

"Mother." Katerina sobbed and dropped her head to her chest.

"Come now, dear. No point in mourning a woman you hardly even knew."

"But she gave us to you? Why?"

"Stupid woman trusted her dear, dear stepsister. Little did she realize that I was the one who let the attackers into the castle."

"You what?"

"I served up a meal of those wonderful little sleeping-peas that the troll king had given me. It was a feast to celebrate your first birthday. The guards all slept, and Thrigor just walked right in. It was really quite beautiful in its simplicity, if a little bloodier than I had expected."

"But she was your sister."

"Stepsister. And the bonds of sisterhood meant nothing to her when your grandfather died. She and your father shoved my mother off the throne, and I went from being the child of a queen to being someone the family barely tolerated. My mother was sent to live in your tower in the woods, and your parents would not give me a title, offering me the pathetic position of Mistress of Magic. They showed no mercy to my mother or me so, I showed none in return, besides saving her children. When Thrigor first appeared to me and suggested his plans, it became perfectly clear to me what I should do. I knew my other stepsister in Bellemer had a son about your age. I would raise you, marry you to him and take over Bellemer. Thrigor and I would unite Cantera and Bellemer and eventually begin a campaign to take over the other five kingdoms of Clarameer. We would rule the entire land together. So I stashed you safely away in my little tower retreat, sealed all the doors and set out to take care of my other stepsister."

Katerina raised her head and stared at her aunt in horror. "But my brother—"

"Well, he didn't really fit in my plan, now did he? And I couldn't have some boy who could claim the Canteran throne just lolling about the kingdoms, now could I?"

"So you killed him?"

Cauchemar's temples pulsed and her eyes flashed as her anger flared. "I am not a killer! How could you think such a thing! No. I simply dropped him in the woods of Sylvania and let nature take its course. There are many creatures not known to man in those woods. Creatures that would find a squalling little boy to be quite the feast. Everything was going perfectly to plan, until that absurd little boy of my stepsister's turned out to prefer men. And then your little scribbling friend ruined it completely. All my hard work ruined by stupid little boys."

"I'm glad you failed!" Katerina screamed. She slammed her fists onto the top of the vanity, causing one of the perfume bottles to roll off and shatter on the stone floor. "You're a horrible woman! I should avenge my mother and kill you myself!"

Flames burst out around Cauchemar's head as she lunged at the girl and grabbed her arm. "I'd like to see you try. You'd best remember, young lady, that you're only alive because of *this* horrible woman. And that's a state I could change with a snap of my fingers."

Katerina jerked her arm away from her aunt's grasp and stood up to face her eye-to-eye. "Fine. Kill me. I don't care. At least I know your plan has failed and Peter, Phillip and Bellemer are safe from you now!"

Leaning her face closer to Katerina's, Cauchemar hissed, "Little girl, that was one plan." As she leaned forward, the flames dancing about her head singed Katerina's face, causing the girl to lean back against the vanity table. "I promised Thrigor a kingdom. True, I cannot deliver on that now, so it's time for plan B. I can't give him a kingdom, but I can give him a princess. Now pick up that brush and fix your hair. It's time you met your future husband." As the flames died down, Cauchemar spun on her heel and stomped to the chamber door. "I will be back for you in a few moments. You will keep your mouth shut, smile and look pretty. Do you understand?"

"And if I refuse?"

"Then you will see what true misery is in this castle's dungeons, until you change your mind." Cauchemar slammed the door behind her with a loud thud.

Katerina dropped onto the stool to face the mirror again. Gazing blankly at her reflection, she grabbed a silver brush from the tabletop and began to slowly drag it through her tangled hair. "Oh, Peter. Find me, please." Looking up into the dark rafters of the room, she called out, "Mother? Help?"

# CHAPTER 7

D ANIEL STOOD IN THE HALLWAY BEFORE THE KING'S
bedchamber door and shifted uneasily from one foot
to the other. He knew he needed to enter and offer his
support, but wasn't sure Prince Phillip would want to see him.
While he was certain Phillip and he had made a connection while
chatting in that absurdly tall bed, Daniel was utterly confused by
Phillip's sudden suggestion of marriage, the fantastic tales of the
scribe and the madness that ensued with Phillip's stepmother.
Perhaps somehow his presence in the bed had ignited the whole
mess. For all he knew, Phillip could very well run into his embrace,
ignore him completely, or even order him out of the kingdom. A
guard stood on either side of the door and Daniel approached them
cautiously, eying the glittering swords hanging on each man's hip.

"Excuse me," he said; his voice quivered slightly.

The guard on the left shifted his eyes to Daniel and stared.

"Um, is Prince Phillip inside?" Daniel regretted the question as
soon as he asked. Everyone knew the other prince had not left his
father's side in the two days since the events in the testing chamber.

The man grunted in response.

"Do you think I could—"

"Doctor's in now," the other guard said and stepped in front
of the door.

"Oh," Daniel lowered his head and stared at his feet. "I'll just wait over here."

As he turned to cross the hallway, Daniel heard the door open. An old man in gray robes with a large golden chain around his neck stepped into the hall. His long beard fell almost to his knees, and he shuffled forward with a slight hunch in his back. He paused in front of Daniel and lifted his head. The man's eyes were ringed red from tears.

"Doctor, how is he?"

"No change. Still staring blindly into nothingness. There is nothing I can do. Frogberry juice and boar's fur are no match for magic. My books tell me nothing about handling this."

"I see," Daniel muttered. "But I meant the prince."

"Ah." The old man sighed and turned to walk away. "No change there either. If he doesn't eat soon, I fear we will lose the whole royal line in one week. Such a tragedy."

"Surely you can make him—"

"My boy," said the old man, who then paused and looked back over his shoulder, "grief is its own special illness. It simply must run its course. It would take a medicine far stronger than mine to change that."

"But he has to eat. Maybe I can convince him."

Throwing his hands up, the old man muttered, "You're welcome to try. Maybe you have a stronger magic than I have." As the old man shuffled away down the hall, Daniel thought he heard the old man say something else.

"I'm sorry? What was that?"

"I said, you're the only person he has asked about, anyway. Boys," he said to the guards, "let the man in."

The two guards stepped away from the door. Daniel stepped forward and pushed the door open.

"Phillip?" Daniel called into the darkened bedroom. "Are you in here? May I come in?" He peered around the door to look into the room. It was dark except for the light from a large fire roaring in the fireplace. Heavy velvet curtains hung over the windows, and plush carpets covered the floor. A canopied bed sat in the center of the room; Phillip sat on the edge of the bed holding his father's hand. The king lay with one arm frozen outstretched as when Cauchemar had flung her spell at him. The king's eyes were wide open, and his mouth stood agape. Tears streamed down Phillip's face as he stared into his father's eyes. He still wore the same blue doublet and white breeches he had been wearing when Cauchemar hit King Henry with the blast of light, though the knees of the breeches were stained from kneeling at the king's bedside. The dark circles under Phillip's eyes and the sallow tone of his skin led Daniel to believe Phillip had not slept or eaten in days.

"Yes, come in," Phillip mumbled, without taking his eyes from his father.

"Any change?"

"No. He's still in whatever state that awful witch put him in. The doctor was no help. He built a fire thinking it might thaw him out. Ridiculous."

Daniel waited in the doorway and crossed his arms behind his back. He shuffled his foot along a crack in the stone floor and held his breath.

"Don't linger in doorways. It's rude."

"I'm sorry. I wasn't sure if I should come to see you or whether I should've stayed here. But I couldn't leave without trying to… without saying…"

"You're leaving?" Phillip said, and glanced in Daniel's direction with disappointment in his eyes.

"Well I assumed you would want… I mean I thought I should at least… well, I don't know what I thought I was going to do but I… I feel this is all my fault. If I hadn't crawled into that bed then none of this would've happened."

Phillip shook his head and then looked back at his father. "This isn't your fault. She had it in for me and my father all along. You heard what Peter said about her plans. If anything, you helped reveal her true colors."

"Still, she wouldn't have frozen him if it weren't for me messing up your marriage."

"My marriage. Ha." Phillip scoffed. "It's not you, Daniel. Messing up my supposed marriages was all me. I forgot my role. A king always puts the needs of his kingdom before himself. I was selfish. I should've just married one of those girls and got on with my life. I tried to break the rules. And this," he continued, gesturing toward his father, "is my punishment."

"This is a madwoman's lunacy, Phillip, not punishment. You did nothing wrong. And what rules? You're going to be king and you get to make the rules."

"Not now," Phillip said with a shrug. "Now my future is as frozen as my father."

"Hey," Daniel said as he approached the bed and touched Phillip's shoulder, "we'll fix this. He'll be okay."

Phillip jerked his shoulder away and dropped his father's hand. "We? *You* are leaving."

"Not yet." Daniel sat beside the other prince. "Look, at least she didn't kill him or anyone else."

"There's a little part of me that wishes she had killed me."

"Phillip, don't say that."

"No," Phillip said with a sob, as he dropped his head onto the bed beside his father's still hand. "This just proves I'm not meant to be king. My father is… was… *is* a king. He would know what to do. He would solve this and protect everyone. All I did was make everything worse."

"No. No." Daniel cooed and turned Phillip's upper body until they were face to face. Daniel cupped his hand under Phillip's chin and lifted his face. "Listen to me, this can be fixed. You're his son, so anything that is in him is somewhere in you, too. You've just got to find it. You can solve this. But first you need to eat something."

"Please leave me alone," Phillip begged and jerked his head away. "I just want to keep watch over him until something happens. It's all I know to do."

"Phillip, don't believe all those stories your scribe told you. Magic is not defeated by waiting for someone to come rescue you from it. You have to fight it." Daniel paused and took a breath before reaching out to take Phillip's hand again. "I sat around for two years waiting for someone to come along and fix my problems. No one came, and nothing changed. Then I realized that maybe the person I was waiting for was *me*. So I went out to find my own answers."

"I'm not you. I don't even know where to begin." Phillip sat back on the edge of the bed.

"You begin the way everyone does," Daniel explained, "one foot in front of the other."

"I've barely been out of this castle. I don't know what's out there."

"Well, you're in luck. You know someone who does."

"What? Who?" Phillip cocked his head and stared at Daniel in confusion.

"Me!" Daniel winked and pointed to his chest. "I know what's out there. I've been wandering all over the kingdoms for months now. I've studied the maps and the histories. I know how to fight and how to survive." Daniel stood up. "I'll come with you," he continued. "I'll help you find her, and we'll bring her down together. We *will* fix this."

Daniel could almost see the wheels turn in Phillip's head as he considered Daniel's offer. He looked over at his father, then back down at his feet before glancing up to Daniel with a look of tentative hope. "Why would you do that?"

Daniel pondered the question for a moment, unsure of the answer himself. The pain in Phillip's face touched Daniel's heart and made him want to bring back the mischievous, laughing man he had met just two nights before. This was not his problem, and he had his own concerns to deal with, but looking at Phillip's terrified face, he knew he wanted to help. He knew he had to.

"I'm not being completely selfless. I'm still going to be looking for my own answers. But I can help you look, too." Daniel held his hand out to Phillip. "Come with me. Let's go get you some food and make a plan."

"You're just saying this to get me to eat."

"No. As I said, I feel responsible. If I hadn't gotten in that bed—"

"But you did." Phillip mumbled before turning to look at Daniel with his eyes wide. "And you passed the test. I thought for sure you were the answer—"

"The test? I still don't understand about this test."

"Yes. You were the first to spend the night in the bed and be kept awake by the pea under the mattresses. Okay, maybe some of the others could have passed if I hadn't—"

"Phillip? You think a pea kept me awake?" Daniel stepped back and knitted his brows; he had clearly missed some element of that awful night's events. Though he was glad to see some sign of activity from Phillip, Daniel was thoroughly confused. "Why was there a pea under—"

"Yes. You passed the test. Maybe it is a sign!" Phillip stood and turned to Daniel; excitement spread across his face. "Maybe you *are* here to help me."

"Phillip, I don't think you understand—"

"What's to understand? You told me yourself you hadn't slept a wink."

"Yes, but it wasn't the pea," Daniel explained, his mind racing to figure out what Phillip was talking about "It was—"

"Your Highness?" James's voice called from the doorway, interrupting Daniel.

"Yes?" Daniel and Phillip answered in unison.

"Um, sorry. Just *my* Highness, I mean," James said with a slight bow of his head as he stepped into the room. "I'm not used to two of you. It's so strange having two of you. I mean, I was just telling that man Peter—"

"James, what is it?" Daniel asked, his irritation showing.

"Sorry," James stammered with a blush. "I was just coming to report that the local guards and I have searched the entire castle and the surrounding area. She's not here."

"Well, she has to be somewhere," Daniel said.

"Obviously," Phillip mumbled.

"Phillip, let's go find her," Daniel implored, as he turned back to the prince and reached out his hand. "Let's get some food in you, pack up some provisions and go find her."

"I don't know." Phillip plopped back down on the edge of his father's bed. "Would it be smart or safe for me to go wandering around the kingdoms? What if she comes after me again?"

"Well," James said, as he pushed his shoulders back and grasped the hilt of the sword on his belt, "not to brag or anything, but you would have *the* bravest knight in the kingdoms to guard you."

"And you'll be there, right?" Phillip asked Daniel, with a look of hope. "I mean since the pea kept you awake it must be a sign, right? You're meant to help me."

"A pea?" James said, knitting his brows in confusion. Looking to Daniel he said "He thinks a pea kept you awake? Does he not know about—"

"I was just about to explain that. Phillip," Daniel said, as he took Phillip's hands into his own and stared into his eyes, "I think you misunderstood. I was awake because—"

"Your Highness?" a voice called from the doorway.

"Yes?" Daniel and Phillip answered in unison, both turning to see Peter standing in the doorway.

"Oh, I didn't realize anyone else was—I meant Prince Phillip." Peter stepped into the room and stopped, staring at the two princes holding hands in the middle of the room. He wrinkled his brow and cocked his head. "Am I interrupting something?"

"Peter! Oh, Peter." Phillip dropped Daniel's hands and stepped over to his friend. He grabbed Peter by the shoulders and pulled him to his chest. He leaned back to look into the other man's eyes and said, "I am so glad you came back. I have missed you ever since that woman made you leave, and yet again your stories have saved my life. Thank you so much for coming back, but my father…" He pointed toward his father and wailed, "Look at him. What am I going to do? Sir James and the castle guards have searched everywhere and cannot find that awful woman. He hasn't moved in days, and nothing the doctors do seems to help. Do any of your stories tell what we should do?"

"Prince Phillip, of course I came running back the moment I knew you were in danger. We're fortunate Katerina was smart enough to make me stay and hear Cauchemar's plans." Peter squeezed Phillip's shoulders. "You are my family. You know I would do anything for you. You and your mother are the only reasons I had the life I had; even more, you are why I know how to read and write. But, unfortunately, even my stories don't cover this." Peter looked over at the king's frozen face and frowned. "*This* is too much for words."

"As I feared," Phillip said and sighed. He stepped back toward the king's bed and pulled the heavy, blue blanket up over his father's body. He stared at his father's look of horror before turning back to Peter. "At least you're here to stay with me and help me guard him."

"Well, that is why I came in here." Peter looked imploringly into Phillip's eyes. "I can't stay here with you. I want your permission to go find her."

"You *want* to go find her?" Phillip asked. "And do what? She has powerful magic. You have nothing but words."

"I don't care." Peter brushed away the comment with his hand. "I have something stronger than words. I love Kitty. She took Kitty, and I have to find her. Love is stronger than magic."

"Kitty?" Phillip asked.

"I'm sorry. You know her as Katerina. Kitty is the nickname I gave her."

"*You* gave her? You mean, you are the friend who—"

"Yes. That crazy old woman had her walled away in a tower out in the middle of the forest and I stumbled across her after I was sent away. I was trying to come up with a way to rescue and marry her, but then I overheard Cauchemar's plans to kill you and your father."

"It's a good thing you did!" James said, as he stepped over to the group of men. "Who knows what might have happened if you hadn't."

"It couldn't be worse than this!" Phillip glanced back at his father's frozen form.

"Majesty, please say I can go," Peter implored. "Every minute I spend here is another minute she is getting farther away."

"I don't know, Peter," Phillip mumbled, as he crossed to the roaring fire. "Cauchemar said the kingdoms can be a dangerous place."

"Ever since your stepmother banished me from the castle, I've learned how to survive on my own out there. And why would you believe anything that woman said?"

"Phillip," Daniel interrupted, "why don't we all go together? You won't be alone. You'll have Peter's survival skills, James' sword and both our royal names. We can get all the help we need. All of us. Together."

"But, Sir James," Phillip turned to the knight, "you owe no allegiance to me."

"I will follow Daniel into the mouth of a dragon," James said as he knelt in front of the two princes. "It is my sworn duty. Also, what good is a knight without adventures to his name?"

"And what good are adventures," Peter queried, "without a master storyteller to pass them along? Please, Prince Phillip."

"But my father. My kingdom."

"Your father is guarded," Daniel assured him. "Your people love him. They will protect him and your land until you return."

"If nothing else, sire," Peter said, "we should warn the other kingdoms about what she has done."

"Exactly," Daniel said. He grabbed Phillip by the elbow. "Phillip, you owe it to your kingdom."

"You owe it to Kitty," Peter added.

"You owe it to Clarameer," James said. He stood and pulled his sword from his belt. Turning the hilt away from himself, he handed it to Phillip.

Daniel watched as Phillip chewed his bottom lip while he stared at the golden handle of the sword. He glanced up at Peter and James before shifting his eyes to Daniel with a look that begged for encouragement. Daniel nodded and waved his hand toward the weapon.

Taking the sword and holding it in front of his face, Phillip closed his eyes and took a deep breath. "I owe it to him," Phillip said and glanced down at his father's frozen body.

"Yes!" the other three men answered in unison.

"I owe it to me," Phillip said, as he straightened his back and pushed his shoulders back. Daniel could see the roaring fire reflected in Phillip's eyes as he turned to him. "Okay, let's go. Let's find that cursed witch and bring her down."

# CHAPTER 8

ARLY THE NEXT MORNING, THE FOUR MEN SET OUT INTO the kingdoms in search of Cauchemar. Phillip had secured horses for himself and Peter from the stables and requested provisions be packed for each of the men. Even with packs full of food and clothing loaded on each horse, and his father's glittering sword strapped to his waist, Phillip felt decidedly unequipped for the challenge ahead of him. Yet, Peter would be there with stories to distract him, and James would be there with his sword. Though he couldn't quite put his finger on why, he felt especially relieved Daniel would be riding beside him as well.

After a day of riding north from his castle, they arrived at the dense forest that served as a natural border between Bellemer and the rest of Clarameer. The trees stretched from the center of the continent all the way across the kingdoms until they spread to become what the Sylvanians called the Western Woods, which covered most of Daniel's home kingdom. Phillip had only seen the forest once as a child and had never cared for it. He found the thick, overgrown foliage suffocating when compared to the open expanses of the windy shores of his oceanfront castle. There, the most dangerous creatures dwelt in the waters of the Southern Sea and could not harm a man who stayed safely on shore. But he had heard tales of the bears, dragons and griffins that lurked within the shady recesses of the great woods. As they entered the first line of trees, Phillip slowed his horse to let Sir James and Peter pull to the front, where they could meet any creature first. Daniel slowed his horse as well, to trot along beside the other prince. Trying to keep his mind off the horror in his father's face and the unknown horrors that might wait in the woods, Phillip listened to the two men ahead of him.

"So, Sir Scribbles," James drawled, as he trotted up beside Peter, "you write stories?"

"Yes. I write stories, but my official title was kingdom scribe."

"Scribe?"

"I wrote down all the business of the kingdom. Laws, proclamations, letters to other kingdoms—pretty much anything that needed to be on paper, I wrote. See, my mother was the favorite lady-in-waiting to the former queen, Phillip's mother. She died from the rain plague when I was young, so Queen Marie took me in as a sort of brother for Phillip. She made sure I was taught how to read and write and gave me a career."

Phillip grinned as he listened to Peter talk of their childhood in the castle and remembered the affection his mother had showered on Peter and him. He could still see Peter hunched over a desk with a charcoal pencil and sheaves of parchment, squinting in dim candlelight, with his tongue sticking out of the corner of his mouth, as he practiced drawing letters. Phillip could almost hear his mother's laughter as she sat on a chair between their beds and listened to Peter spin one of his bedtime tales.

James interrupted Phillip's thoughts with, "And they paid you to do that?"

"I was a member of the court, so I didn't really need money. I was fed and clothed and given a room. What more could you need? Phillip and I spent our free time together. He always liked hearing the stories I would make up."

"But you got booted?"

"Banished."

"Whatever." James waved his free hand. "They kicked you out. Did you write something *that* bad?"

"No, I wrote the truth. And some people don't like the truth."

"The truth about what?"

"I was in the room when Prince Phillip's mother died. I wrote down her dying words."

"Okay. And?"

"Well, she had some definite, um, *opinions* on what should happen after she died. I could tell she did *not* want King Henry to have anything to do with that evil witch you met back in the testing chamber. Everyone else thought she was telling King Henry to marry Cauchemar, but I knew she was warning him."

"Why would anyone want to marry that woman?"

Phillip kicked his heels lightly into his horse's flank to speed her up a bit, in order to stay close to Peter. While he had been present for the events at his mother's death, he had never really understood what had happened. He was curious to hear what Peter would say.

"King Henry thought it was what his wife wanted. Her last words *were* a bit vague, at least to everyone else. Also, he knew Phillip would need a mother. King Henry and Prince Phillip were so lost in grief they couldn't see what was happening, but I could. Cauchemar had something to do with the queen dying. She just had to. Before she showed up, Queen Marie was perfectly healthy, and everyone in the kingdom was happy. But in just a few short months, the queen was withering away and dying. Everyone knew that Cauchemar was in Cantera when it fell to the troll king. It just seemed strange to me that every kingdom she showed up in lost its royal family. Then, when she became queen, she started having me write down all these laws that were making the entire kingdom miserable. Work all the time. Music and art were outlawed. It was insane."

"So why didn't you say anything?"

"I tried. But who is going to listen to a peasant boy? Phillip and his father were so lost in grief, I didn't want to add to their troubles. Also, I had no proof. If I accused the new queen of murder, I could've been hanged. So I wrote a story."

"A story?"

"About a rooster that lived in a coop with two hens, one white and one red," Peter said, as he leaned to the left to avoid a low-hanging branch. "The red hen can't lay any eggs so she convinces the white hen to help her. She tells her that the best way to lay lots of eggs is to eat the fur off a fox."

"Oh, I know this one! Lillianne back in our castle read it to me! So the white hen goes looking for a fox to help the red hen. She leaves a trail of her feathers so she can find her way home. She goes up to the fox to ask for fur and gets eaten! Then the red hen sits on the white hen's eggs and claims they're hers."

"But the red hen and the rooster don't realize that the fox follows the trail of white feathers back to the coop."

"And then he eats them both and all the eggs!" James crowed as he slapped his thigh. "Oh, yeah, that's a good one. You wrote that?"

"Yes," Peter said with a smile of pride. "I sent it to the *Kingdom Inquisitor,* hoping someone would figure out it was about King Henry, but the only one who understood it was Cauchemar. She made up some nonsense about me watching her change clothes and had me banished."

"Like anyone would want to see that old bag of bones naked," James said, with a sneer of disgust.

"Precisely. But King Henry was already blind to her lies by then, and I was sent out into the world. That's where I found Katerina in a tower and started telling her my stories. I had no idea Cauchemar was the woman she called auntie until the night before they came to Bellemer. After I heard Cauchemar's plans, I rushed back here, hoping someone would believe me this time. Guess I was a little too late."

"At least you tried."

Phillip pulled his horse's reins. While he had never been pleased with his father's marriage to Cauchemar, he had not known she had a hand in his mother's death. His stomach knotted as he remembered his mother's withering body in the chamber where she died and her final words to his father. Guilt chewed at his mind—she had been trying to warn them of Cauchemar's evil ways, and only Peter had understood. He swallowed the lump in his throat.

"Are you all right?" Daniel asked, as he pulled up beside him. Phillip could see the concern in Daniel's eyes. "Should I make them change the subject?"

"I'm fine," Phillip said, shifting uncomfortably in his saddle. "We should keep moving."

The four men rode on in silence until James finally spoke. "So you wrote *The Rooster with Two Hens?*"

"That was me," Peter said, as he blew on his fingernails and buffed them against his chest.

"I'm just a little surprised, that's all."

"Why?"

"It's just the way you talk," James said, as he pulled his sword out and chopped off a low hanging branch. "I wouldn't think you could write a story that good."

"What do you mean 'the way I talk'?"

"Back in the king's chamber, when you were talking about Katerina, you said 'I don't need magic, I have love.'"

"Yeah? So?"

"Aw, Sir Scribbles, that is awful." James pulled the horse's reins and stopped to shoot Peter a look of disgust. "If your stories sounded like that, no one would want to read them. If you are going to tell the story of my deeds, it has to be a good story. All that love stuff? That's the talk of a silly fool."

"You take that back. I was worried about Katerina."

"It's terrible."

"I was trying to inspire Prince Phillip!

"Just rotten."

"What're you two going on about up here?" Daniel asked, as he and Phillip rode up alongside the two bickering men. "You're squawking so loud you're scaring off the local wildlife!"

"I was just telling Sir Scribbles here that his flowery language is ridiculous. Love is stronger than magic? Oh, please."

"Stop calling me Sir Scribbles!"

"Peter," Daniel said with a chuckle, "you'll have to ignore James. I'm afraid romance is a foreign word to him. He's too busy trying to flirt with every creature with curves to waste time on love."

"Love?" James asked in a huff. "Who needs love when you have battles and glory? Why settle for just one woman when you can woo four?"

"Some of us don't even want one," Phillip sniffed, as he pulled ahead of the group. As he rode off he could hear the other men continuing to argue.

"But love is the food of life!" Peter yelled.

"Ugh. That's just awful," James groaned.

With a roll of his eyes, Phillip clicked his tongue at his horse and trotted farther ahead. Looking around at the massive trees, he began to feel smothered by the thick foliage overhead that blocked out most of the sun. His heart raced as he urged his horse forward toward a small clearing in the path where a bit of sunlight streamed through the branches. Hearing the sound of another horse approaching, he turned to see Daniel ride up to his side.

"Those two will never see eye to eye," Daniel said. "But they are funny to listen to. Are you sure you're okay? You look a little queasy."

"This is the forest where my wedding day hunt would've taken place. This is where I'm supposed to kill a stag for my bride. This is where Cauchemar intended to kill my father and me. And I am just figuring out that she probably killed my mother. I don't have time for stupid arguments about love," Phillip said, as he stared off into the distance. "We need to get out of these woods and find her."

"I know. I'm here to help you with that, remember?"

Phillip stopped his horse in the sunlight and stared up to the small patch of blue sky overhead. Letting the sunlight warm his face, he took a deep breath and then turned back to Daniel. "Why *are* you helping me? Surely your kingdom needs you more than I do."

"Not really," Daniel said with a shrug. "Phillip, I am the *second* son of a king. You know what second sons do, right?"

"Wait for the first son to die? Fight wars? Find a princess from another kingdom to marry?"

"Exactly. But not me."

"I don't follow," Phillip said.

"Phillip, you aren't the only one with no interest in marrying a woman."

"What makes you think that I don't want to—"

"Phillip!" Daniel said with a belly laugh. "You told your parents you were going to marry me! You had to know that I was—"

"Oh yeah," Phillip said with a blush. Urging his horse forward on the path, he mumbled, "Sorry about that. I was just trying to—"

"No. It's fine. I just told you I have no interest in marrying a woman either."

Phillip pulled sharply on the horse's reins and turned back to Daniel. He stared at Daniel, his brows knitting. His face relaxed and then his eyebrows shot up toward his hairline as a thought occurred to him. "Wait? Are you saying what I think you're saying? Are you—"

"Light in the saddle?" Daniel said with a laugh. "Yes. Like you, I prefer the company of men. I thought for sure you realized that after our conversation the first time we met."

Phillip looked at Daniel before turning his face back to the path and riding for a few paces. His eyes widened and he turned back to Daniel. "Oh! Now I get it! You're out in the kingdoms hiding so no one knows your secret! Don't worry, I won't tell. Oh! Does James know?"

"What? No! Of course he knows. I'm not hiding. My whole family knows."

"By Gingerfair's girdle! Did they throw you out? Is that why you're wandering the kingdoms? You've been banished! Are you and James—"

"Phillip, no, no, no. I think it's perfectly clear James likes his ladies." Daniel laughed again at the thought. "No, I wasn't banished. My mother understands my desires. Well, as much as a person not like us can. She knows I'll never marry a princess, so she sent me out to find my own purpose in life. Maybe I'll find love. I don't know. Mainly I just want to find a cure for my curse."

"So you're saying people know and don't care?"

"Believe it or not, some people are happy just to see you be happy."

Phillip let Daniel's words sink in as his horse ambled forward. For the first time since leaving his castle, he felt a sense of relief creep into the corners of his mind. "My mother would've thought that way, I bet," Phillip said. He glanced over to see Daniel nodding in agreement. Phillip sat up higher in his saddle and let the relief spread to his limbs. "Maybe others could, too? Do you think people could ever accept a king with no queen? The rules say I have to marry but maybe I can just… no. A king needs an heir and an heir requires…" Phillip's words trailed off as he looked down at the reins in his hand and frowned. "There I go being stupid again. Now I understand why you said you had a curse. I guess we both do."

"Phillip, *that's* not my curse!" Daniel's chin dropped. "We don't have a curse! I was talking about my birthday fairy curse."

"Your fairy curse? Oh!" Phillip's eyes grew wide with curiosity. "What is yours?"

"I tried to tell you earlier, but we kept getting interrupted. My birthday fairy said that on my eighteenth birthday I would go to sleep and never wake up."

"Daniel, that's awful. Aren't you scared that—hold on. You have to be a least the same age as me."

"Yes, I am twenty."

"Then how did you—"

"The last fairy fixed it, sort of. After the sixth fairy said that, the seventh said that I—"

"Shh!" Phillip interrupted him as he halted his horse. "There is something in the bushes over there."

Phillip pointed to a clump of shrubs to the left of the path. A low growling noise rose from behind the rustling leaves. He watched as Daniel drew his sword and placed his finger to his lips, motioning for Phillip to be quiet.

"Why did you stop?" James asked, as he and Peter trotted up between the two princes.

"Shh," Daniel hissed, as he pointed his sword toward the shaking bushes. "There's something over there."

"Do you think it's a bear?" James squinted and leaned toward the rustling leaves.

"A dragon?" Peter suggested, his voice quivering in fear. "Griffin?"

"Shh."

The bushes shook more violently, and a piercing screech rose as the branches began to part. The birds in the surrounding trees flew away from the commotion, sending leaves fluttering down all around the men. Phillip batted the leaves away from his face and stared toward the bush, holding his breath.

"I'll kill it!" James screamed. He drew his sword and hopped down from his horse.

"Phiiiiii…" the creature in the bush shrieked, as it stumbled out onto the path toward the men.

"Wait!" Phillip yelled at James, as he quickly dismounted. "I think it's saying my name!"

"…liiiiiip!" The creature ended its cry and stood panting before the men. Its wild eyes moved rapidly back and forth between the men as its shoulders heaved with each deep breath.

"It's a girl!" Peter cried, as the four men stared with their mouths agape.

Before them stood a short, thin girl. Her brown hair frayed out wildly around her head with bits of leaves and twigs snagged in its tangles. Dark streaks of mud covered her face and arms, and her yellow dress hung tattered about her petite body. Her angry brown eyes settled on Phillip as she stomped toward him, panting heavily with each step she took.

"Honestly! I should take that sword from his hands and cut your head clean off your body!" the girl screamed as she lunged toward Phillip with her arms outstretched before her. Daniel shoved his sword back into its sheath, jumped down from his horse and stepped between the girl and Phillip. As she crashed into him, the girl growled and swung her arms around his body in an attempt to grab at Phillip. "Out of my way, buddy. I've got a little score to settle with that one!"

"Gwen?" Phillip gasped, as he watched the girl's arms flail at him.

"You know this girl?" Daniel asked. He wrapped his arms around the girl's shoulders and pulled her arms down to her sides. "Easy. Let's just calm down and take a breath."

"This is Princess Gwendolyn of Little Dealonia," Phillip said. Stepping over to the girl, he pulled a twig out of her hair. "At least, I think Gwen is somewhere under all of this mess."

"Honestly?" Gwen choked out, as her eyes flashed in anger. "It's all your fault that I look this way!"

"Phillip," Daniel asked, "what is she talking about?"

"I have no idea. The last time I saw her was in the courtyard of our castle. She was loaded up in a carriage and sent home after failing the princess-test."

"Princess-test?" Gwen yelled as she struggled against Daniel's tight grip. "Your stupid princess-test is why I'm in this mess. I was peacefully sleeping in that ridiculous bed when the next thing I know your stepmother is waking me up and shoving me out the door. She kept saying I failed the test, and I don't even remember taking it!" Gwen's voice grew higher and louder as her frustration grew. "Yes, you loaded me into a carriage to send me away in shame, but we were no more than a few leagues from your castle when my guardians decided that they were wasting their time protecting someone who wasn't a real princess after all. I was riding along in comfort, trying to decide how to explain all of this to my father, and the next thing I knew, the carriage stopped in these woods. The footmen told me I was no more deserving of the carriage than they were and then yanked me out and dumped me on the side of the path! Before I could say anything, they had piled into the carriage and ridden off without me! And they took my trunk with all my dresses!" Gwen began to wail and dropped her head against Daniel's shoulder.

"Hoodlums!" Daniel tut-tutted as he relaxed his grip around the girl's arms. Phillip watched as the anger drained from her face and her body slumped in exhaustion.

"Honestly," Gwen whimpered, as she collapsed at Daniel's feet. "And I've been trying to find my way out of these woods for days now. I've had nothing to eat but rumberries. I fell in a hole and got covered in mud. I got my hair caught in a tree. And my best dress," she said and pulled at the tatters around her crumpled legs. "Well, it's just ruined. And it's all your fault."

"Oh, Gwen," Phillip cooed. He crossed to the girl, sat on the ground beside her and pulled her shaking body to his chest. After picking a few more leaves out of the ratted mass of her hair, he patted her head and said in his most soothing voice, "I'm so sorry. I had no idea those men would do this. Please forgive me. We'll get you out of here. We'll get you home."

"Honestly," Gwen sobbed as she leaned into Phillips arms, "what's the point of taking me home? No one believes I'm a princess anymore. Why should they accept me back into the castle? For all I know, my father won't even want to see me!" Her crying grew more hysterical, and she began to hit Phillip on his chest with her small, muddy fist. "You have ruined me."

Phillip looked up at the other men, imploring them for assistance. They shuffled uncomfortably from foot to foot and looked at the trees around them.

"Okay, listen," Phillip said, as he pushed Gwen away from his chest and looked into her eyes. "I'll just explain to your father that there was a mistake. I'll tell him you're a princess after all."

Gwen sniffled. "But I failed the test! I'm not a princess. And the worst part is, I don't even know what the test was or how I failed!"

Phillip felt a twinge of guilt as he remembered offering Gwen the sleeping tonic. "Actually, I think there may have been a slight problem with the test. I can't really explain it all right now, but trust me. We've got to get going, though. Some bad things happened at the castle after you left, and I need to keep moving." Standing up and brushing the leaves off his backside, Phillip reached out his hand to the girl. "Come on. Up we go."

Gwen grabbed Phillip's hand and pulled herself to her feet. With a hiccup, she wiped the tears from her cheeks. "So you're saying I might still be a princess after all?"

"Yes. Now let's get you home. Then we'll send some of your father's men after those horrid footmen. In just a few days you'll be back in your own bed with all your beloved dresses right there in your room."

"But Phillip, look at me! I'm a mess. A princess can't be seen riding through the kingdoms in a dirty, torn dress!"

"I tell you what, at the next stream we pass, we will get you cleaned up. We'll tame this bird's nest, and then you can put on one of my tunics and breeches. It's not as fancy as your dresses, but at least it will be clean and easier for riding a horse."

"Oh, I don't mind wearing breeches!" Gwen said and her face lit up. "When I played Hugor the Warrior in my play about his life, I wore boy's clothes the whole time! Honestly! Really, your boy clothes are quite comfortable. But is it safe for us to be traveling out here without a carriage?"

"You have nothing to fear with me here, milady," James boomed, as he stepped over and bowed deeply. "Sir James of Sylvania at your service. I will keep you safe, be it from dragon or griffin or angry chipmunk!" Raising his head to look into her eyes, he waggled his eyebrows and beamed at her.

With a giggle, Gwen put her hand out for James to kiss. Seeing the mud caked on her knuckles, she pulled it back and wiped it on the front of her dress. "I guess with a strong man like you beside me, I'll be okay."

"All right, then." Phillip turned to the others and gestured toward the horses. "Shall we be on our way? Peter, let Gwendolyn ride on your horse with you."

"Why me?"

"Shouldn't I ride with Sir James?" Gwen asked, batting her eyes at the knight.

"No. She'll only fit on a horse with Peter. Now let's go."

Peter pulled Gwen up onto his horse. "I still don't see why I have to share."

"It's where she will be the safest, Sir Scribbles," James said and chuckled, as he flipped his reins and trotted down the path. "You can protect her with your love that is stronger than magic."

# CHAPTER 9

"THE TAVERN SHOULD BE AROUND HERE SOMEWHERE," Phillip said, as the group crested a small hill on the edge of the Western Wood. "The old woman in that little cabin said it was the *only* place to stay. I think she said it was called the Lusty Strumpet."

"I'm not sure that is the kind of place we should take a lady," Daniel said, as he stopped beside Phillip. "Sounds like it might be a bit rough."

"Well, it is getting dark, and I don't think we have much of a choice," James added, as he trotted up beside them. "Those clouds look like they are bringing rain for sure. I don't know about you, but I really don't want to spend the night getting soaked to the bone."

"No," Daniel conceded. "None of us will be any good if we get the rain plague."

"We could check it out first," Phillip suggested. "I could stay outside with Gwen while you and James see if it's safe. You both know a lot more about this kind of place than we do."

"Actually, Phillip, we don't spend a lot of time hanging out in gambling halls and taverns."

"Even if some of us have asked nicely," James mumbled.

Daniel rolled his eyes at James and turned back to Phillip. "I guess it's our only option. But if it looks even remotely unsafe we'll just have to keep riding."

Peter rode between them with Gwen holding on tightly behind him. "What's the plan, Highnesses?"

"Well, if this tavern looks safe enough, we are going to spend the night."

"A tavern!" Gwen exclaimed. "How exciting! I've always wanted to go to a tavern. I played a serving wench in one of my plays, but my father wouldn't let me go to the local beer hall to research my part."

"A warm bed and a warm meal sounds good to me," Peter said. "Let's get moving."

"But only if it looks safe," Phillip added.

"I think I see it," Gwen said. She pointed down the road toward a large, well-lit building sitting to one side of a crossroad. "It's awfully bright. Looks popular, too. Let's go!" She reached around Peter, grabbed the reins, kicked the horse's side and they went flying down the road.

"Gwen, wait," Daniel called, as he kicked his own horse and set off down the road behind her.

"That girl is going to get us killed." James sighed to Phillip, then clicked his tongue at his horse and trotted off.

Phillip followed down the road toward the crossroad and the tavern. As he approached, he could see more and more people crowded around the door. Dozens of torches burned around the building's exterior, shedding a flickering light on the faces of the crowd and the sign hanging above the tavern door. The wooden sign had the words "Lusty Strumpet" in bright red lettering above the image of a woman with dark curly hair and a low-cut blouse holding tankards of ale next to her ample bosom. Two velvet-covered ropes lined the path to the door, where a large, muscular man in a dirty black tunic stood with his arms crossed. As people approached, he would occasionally glance at a piece of paper in his hand, nod his head and let a person go into the tavern. On either side of the door, illuminated by lanterns, hung large banners portraying a beautiful, dark-skinned woman in a tight, midnight-blue bodice and long flowing skirts. She held a tiara in one hand and a lute in the other. Above her head was the image of a smiling moon and the words "Appearing tonight: Lady Moon."

"Lady Moon? Who's that?" James asked.

"She appears to be some type of entertainer," Daniel said with a shrug. "Must be good, too. Look at the size of that crowd."

Phillip looked at the poster to the left of the door. *She looks vaguely familiar.* He dismounted and led his horse to the hitching post. "Well, this place looks safe enough. That behemoth by the door doesn't appear to be letting in anyone too unclean. I say we give it a shot."

"Daniel?" Gwen asked, as she slid off Peter's horse. "Why do some of those people by the door have sheaves of paper and charcoal pencils? Are they scribes like Peter?"

"Oh no," Daniel groaned. "Sketcherazzi!"

"What?" Phillip asked.

"Sketcherazzi. They are the lowest life form on earth. No better than worms, really. Just ignore them. No matter what they yell at you or how they ask, just put your head down and keep walking."

Phillip scanned the crowd around the door and noticed that the people standing along the front were in fact scribbling away as each person strolled toward the door. They were clearly poorer peasants, judging by the tattered and dirty beige tunics and dresses they wore. He watched as a young woman in a fancy dress tried to rush past the crowd. They all began shouting at her to look their way, and she turned left and right in confusion. Watching them flock ravenously toward the girl, Phillip was reminded of the seagulls that would chatter and caw around the walls of his castle. He had never cared for those noisy birds and was sure he wouldn't care for these scribbling birds either.

"I don't understand," Gwen said, as she tilted her head. "What do they want from us?"

"My brother, Andrew, loves these people, but I can't stand them. They hang around outside of any place they think lords and ladies and royalty might show up. When you walk by they try to draw a picture of you that they can later sell to someone else. Especially the *Kingdom Inquisitor.*"

"Daniel, that's absurd. Why would someone pay for that?" Phillip asked.

"Phillip, you know people are fascinated by the royal life. They want to see what we're wearing and who we're socializing with. I understand the curiosity, but for these people to profit from it seems wrong. Also, they never get my hair right. Just follow me and don't make eye contact."

"Um… too late," Phillip said as he pointed toward the crowd.

Gwen and James were walking down the path to the tavern door. At the first group of people, Gwen stopped, flashed her biggest smile and posed for the artists. Looping her arm through James's crooked arm, she turned her body slightly toward his and kicked her leg up behind her.

"Come on. We need to go rescue the damsel in distress from herself."

As Phillip and Daniel approached the crowd, they could hear the questions being fired at James and Gwen.

"Princess Gwen! Why are you in a man's tunic? Is that the latest rage with princesses?"

"This old thing?" Gwen replied coyly and flipped the baggy hem of the tunic back and forth.

"Is that hairstyle the latest in the royal world? Who is your date?"

"My date? Why this is Sir James of Sylvania. Only the bravest and most handsome knight in all of Clarameer. Show them your smile, James."

James puffed out his chest and grinned from ear to ear.

"Gwen," Daniel said as he walked up behind her, "I told you to ignore these people and just keep walking."

"Prince Phillip! Prince Daniel! Over here! Look over here and smile!" one of the sketcherazzi yelled, as he furiously scribbled a portrait of the two princes on his pad of paper.

Daniel slowly walked over to the man, grabbed the pad from his hands and ripped off the top sheet. "I'll be taking this. Why can't you leave us be and put your real talents to use? I am sure there is a stable somewhere that needs shoveling." He folded the sketch in two and shoved it into a pocket of his doublet. "Gwen, James, come along."

"Prince Phillip! You have some nerve showing up here on a night Lady Moon is singing!" one of the crowd yelled as Phillip hurried past.

"What did he mean by that, sire?" Peter asked, as he pushed Phillip toward the large man guarding the door.

"I have no idea," Phillip said with a shrug. As he arrived at the door, the large man stuck out his arm and placed his hand on Phillip's chest.

"Are you on the list?"

"List?" Phillip said.

"Yeah, the list," the large man said with a gesture to the piece of paper in his hand. "No one gets in if they ain't on the list."

"Excuse me, sir," James interrupted as he stepped between the man and Phillip. "Phillip, let me handle this. Good man, I am Sir James of Sylvania and I am escorting my friend, Princess

Gwendolyn of Little Dealonia, back to her home. We need a place to stay for the night and we hear this inn is the finest in the area."

"Look, buddy, from what I hear she ain't no princess after all. And if you ain't on the list, you ain't going in. It's a full house tonight for Lady Moon."

"Look buddy, I beg of you," Peter whined as he stepped in front of James. "We just want to have a meal and then turn in for the night. All we need is two rooms."

"List," the guard said as he held the piece of paper out in front of Peter's face.

"Sir," Gwen purred as she stepped forward and batted her eyes at the guard, "I'm awfully tired. Don't you have two little rooms somewhere for me and my friends here?"

"List."

"Maybe a token of our appreciation would help?" Daniel asked as he pulled the bag of gold coins from his pocket and jingled it in the man's face.

"List."

"You know what?" Phillip said with an air of annoyance, as he stepped up to the guard again. "Your little tavern here is in my kingdom, even if I am not on the throne yet. So I suggest you step aside and let your future king through."

"Prince Phillip?" the man said, wide eyed, and then bowed and stammered, "I didn't realize you were you. I mean, I always heard you never left your castle."

"Well, clearly I have. So will you please move aside?"

A look of mischief suddenly crossed the man's face, and he said, "I really didn't expect you to show up on a Lady Moon night. Oh this should be fun to watch!" Stepping to one side, he waved his arm toward the tavern door. "You and your friends go right on in. Go to the bar and ask for the owner, Spud. He'll take care of you."

"Thank you." Phillip swept past the guard and pushed the tavern door open. The loud sounds of laughter and conversation and the smell of spilled ale assaulted Phillip. As he scanned the room, he could not believe the number of people crowded into the main hall. Every seat appeared to be full, and the noise of the crowd made Phillip's ears ring.

Despite the numerous candles and lanterns hanging around the room, it took a moment for his eyes to adjust to the dimness. The tavern itself was rather plain, with only an occasional stuffed animal's head or antlers hanging on the stone and plaster walls. Twenty or so people sat at the long bar that ran the length of the room to the right. Behind the bar, a tall, dark-haired man with an apron tied around his waist scurried back and forth between his patrons and the large oak barrels behind him. He would shove a tankard under the tap on a barrel and wait for the ale to fill the cup, then turn around and send the mug sliding down the bar into the hands of a customer.

A single barmaid rushed among groupings of small tables scattered around the rest of the room, serving full mugs of ale and bowls of assorted foods from the large tray on her shoulder. Each table held at least four people drinking ale and chatting loudly. At the far end of the room was a raised platform where Phillip assumed the evening's entertainment would be performed. A tattered purple curtain hung across the space, and small candles burned along the front edge of the stage.

Phillip had not seen this many people gathered since Cauchemar had stopped the lavish banquets his mother had once served in their grand hall. He had forgotten what the buzz of excitement rumbling around a room was like, and though the excitement made his heart quicken, the noise made him uneasy.

"Shall we find a table?" Gwen asked, pushing past Phillip into the room.

"Looks like a full house," Peter said, as he stood on his tiptoes and peeked over Phillip's shoulder.

"I'll go speak to the owner about some rooms for the night," Daniel said and made his way toward the bar, winding through the maze of tables and patrons. "James, you take the others down front. I think I see an empty table there."

"Okay." James wrapped his hands around Gwen's waist and steered her toward the table at the foot of the stage. "Bring some ale, too. All that riding has me thirsty. Oh! And some dragon wings if they have them."

Phillip followed to the lone empty table. A hush fell over each table as the entourage passed it. Phillip could feel the eyes of the silent patrons following him until he had walked by, when the murmurs began. He was sure he could hear whispers of, "is that…" and, "I can't believe he would…" When he finally reached the empty table, he grabbed a chair, slid it back and gestured for Gwen to take a seat. She looked over her shoulder and said, "Thank you. Aren't you excited about the show?"

"I guess," Phillip said with a shrug, hoping to disguise the discomfort the crowd and its chattering were causing. Sitting down beside Gwen, his stomach churned. The people around him seemed to be practically sitting at the table with him. The room felt increasingly hot. "I've just never been big on crowds. Especially when they seem intent on staring a hole in me."

Phillip glanced at the bar to find Daniel among the crowd. He could see Daniel pointing in their direction and holding up two fingers. The tavern owner glanced over Daniel's shoulder and nodded a greeting. Daniel pulled a sack from his belt, removed several coins and handed them to the barkeep. As he leaned over the bar to speak into the bartender's ear, Daniel's doublet rode up in the back to reveal his muscular thighs. The fabric pulled tight across his shoulders, accentuating his strong back and arms. Phillip had not noticed the strength and grace of Daniel's movements. He stared as the other prince haggled with the barkeep. Daniel dropped back onto his heels, looked back over at Phillip and winked. Phillip felt the blood rush to his cheeks. Hoping no one noticed his ogling, he moved his gaze to a painted sign on the edge of the stage. The woman pictured on the banners smiled out from the painting. Phillip leaned over the table to get a closer look.

"She's beautiful, don't you think?" Gwen asked, as she wrapped her arm around Phillip's and leaned into his side. "That olive skin shows she's from Osterling. My father says everything in Osterling is exotic. Oh, how I would love to go there! Can you believe the best wines, the most lavish clothes and the wildest dances all come from just over Clarameer's eastern border? I know Lady Moon is probably a made-up name, but she does look like a princess."

"Yes," Phillip mumbled as he studied the painting. "She seems very familiar. She reminds me of… oh, no."

"Well, the barkeep was more than happy to provide two rooms for his future king and a few royals," Daniel said and dropped into the chair on the other side of Phillip. "All it cost was a few too many gold pieces and a promise that we would each pose with him for sketches to hang behind his bar."

"Daniel, we need to leave," Phillip whispered into the other man's ear.

"No." Daniel shook his head and laughed, "we just got here, and I just overpaid for rooms and food."

"We aren't leaving, are we?" Gwen gasped and opened her eyes wide. "I really want to see this singer!"

"Please," Phillip begged, "I need us to leave right now."

"Leaving?" Peter said. "I'm not going anywhere until I get some food and ale. I'm in no hurry to get back on that horse with her highness, here." He pointed his finger at Gwen, who stuck her tongue out at him.

"Relax," Daniel said, as he clapped Phillip on the shoulder. "I know you're in a hurry to help your father, but we need our rest. We can't fight a battle when we're tired and hungry."

"No. It's not that. It's the singer. She—"

Phillip was interrupted by a roar from the crowd. He looked up to see a short man in pink and green jester's motley step through the curtain.

"Ladies and gentlemen!" the man yelled, as he danced from one foot to the other. The bells on his hat jingled with each bounce, and he grinned broadly at the crowd. "And from what I see, that term applies to some of you more than others!" The crowd cheered and laughed, as Phillip sank farther down into his chair. "It appears some of you paid a *princely* sum to be here tonight!"

"Please. Let's go."

"Shh," Gwen chastised him. "The show is starting. It would be rude to leave."

"But enough about the crowd! Let's bring on that lovely Osterling maiden you all came to see!"

The crowd cheered again and several of the men whistled and stamped their feet.

"I give you… the fallen princess!"

"Oh, by Godrick the Golden…" Phillip mumbled and dropped his head into his hands.

"The Queen of the Night! Lady Moon!"

Grabbing the edge of the curtain, the little man ran to one side of the stage, pulling the curtain open behind him. Phillip raised his head and spread his fingers slightly to peek between them. The stage was bare except for a scarecrow standing in the center wearing a light blue tunic with Phillip's family sigil, the seahorse, painted on its breast. Its head was a burlap sack daubed with blue eyes and a large frown, and on top sat a wooden crown colored a faint yellow.

"Is that supposed to be you?" James turned to Phillip. "Do you know this woman?"

A flourish of horns played from behind the stage and the crowd began to cheer even louder.

"Unfortunately, yes."

As the music began a jaunty bounce, Lady Moon stepped out onto the stage in a deep blue velvet dress that was cut low on her chest and flowed full around her hips. As she approached the scarecrow, her dark black hair glistened under the flickering light of the candles along the front of the stage and bobbed around her shoulders as she danced to the music's rhythm. As the music swelled to a high note, she stopped in front of the scarecrow prince and gathered her flowing skirts in her hands. With a flourish, she dropped into a deep curtsy, glanced at the crowd and gave a long wink. Rising from the floor, she rested one of her hands on the scarecrow's chest and batted her eyes. "Ha!" she spat out and pushed the scarecrow over onto the floor. Putting her hands on her hips, she began to sing:

*When I came on the scene, they said I'd be queen*
*But have you heard what's happened since?*
*I failed his little test, and, well, you know the rest*
*All because of that darn little prince!*
*Now I'm blue! Royal blue.*
*Up all night. Won't sleep anytime soon.*
*So blue! Royal blue.*
*Up all night. I'm now Lady Moon.*
*So, Princess Monique, you've lost your mystique.*
*No more of life high on the hog.*
*He's a seahorse? Well I know, of course,*
*He's really a stable yard dog!*
*I'm just blue. Royal blue.*
*Can any princess ever pass?*

*So blue. Royal blue.*

*Little prince you can just kiss my...*

"Enough!" Phillip yelled. He stood and turned away from the stage. As he began to run toward the door, he tripped over the feet of a man at the table behind him and fell on his hands and knees on the dirt floor. The music stopped, and a gasp spread through the room.

"Phillip!" Daniel cried out and leaped up to help the fallen prince. "Are you hurt?"

Shoving Daniel's hand aside, Phillip stood and brushed the dirt from the front of his tunic. With tears stinging his eyes, he looked into Daniel's face and sighed. "Not from the fall. I told you we needed to leave." Turning again to the door, he stormed past the silent crowd and into the cool night air.

"Prince Phillip! Over here!" a little man with wiry hair and a large nose screamed from the crowd outside, as Phillip rushed by him. "How was the show? Come on! One little sketch so I can feed my family!"

"Leave me alone or I will take that parchment and shove it up your—" Phillip was interrupted by a hand landing on his shoulder and turning him around.

"Now, now, young man," Monique said with cluck of her tongue. "I'm the only one around here who gets to use that word." She smiled at Phillip and slid her hand down his arm from his shoulder to his hand. "Come back inside. You and I need to have a little chat."

"Monique. I'm sorry. I just—"

"Not here," she said quietly while pulling Phillip toward the tavern door. "There are too many little vermin with ears to hear." Turning to the sketcherazzi, who were scribbling away beside them, she raised her voice and said, "Shoo! Go back under whatever rock you crawled out from."

Monique yanked Phillip through a small door to the right of the entrance. He stepped into a room that was not much bigger than a storage closet. A small table was covered with pots of face paint and hairbrushes, and a large, gilded mirror sat in the corner next to a rack stuffed with a rainbow of ruffled and embroidered gowns. Several wigs in various hues hung on hooks alongside the mirror, and a small stool was knocked over in front of the table. Monique shoved Phillip onto an overstuffed chaise on the other side of the room.

"My dressing room." She waved her hands. "It's no palace, but at least it's private."

"Monique, I really don't know what to say." Phillip tugged at the hem of his doublet and avoided making eye contact with the singer. "Please, just let me get my friends and leave."

"Little man, I just walked off the stage in the middle of a song for you. Lady Moon does not stop in the middle of a song." She put her hands on her hips and glared at Phillip. "If you walk into that room, you're going to face a *very* angry crowd of people who either want me to sing or want their money back. And I am not singing until you listen to what I have to say."

"I know," Phillip mumbled and his shoulders dropped. "I ruined your reputation. You can't go home and now you've been reduced to singing in a tavern."

"Reduced?" Monique gasped. "Sweetheart, I am a *star*.

"Yes. But you were a princess. You could've been a queen. You must hate me."

"Phillip, I don't hate you."

"But—"

"Sugar, I'm doing just what *I* want to do." Monique poked herself in the chest with her finger. "No rules. No expectations. I'm free."

"Yes, but you could've had anything you wanted."

"And maybe singing in this tavern is it! Honey, don't let those storytellers fool you. The princess life isn't all it's hyped up to be." Monique righted the stool and sat down on it. She turned to the mirror and inspected her reflection before grabbing a brush from one of the pots and applying red color to her lips. Glancing at Phillip in the mirror, she explained, "Sure, your parents are royalty and your bankroll is endless. But, by Gingerfair's garters, your only friends are forest animals or dwarves, neither of which are any good at conversation. Your stepsisters are wicked and, oooh, all those witches. Every time you turn around, some jealous hag is putting a curse on you or giving you toxic fruit. Glass coffins and glass slippers? No, thank you." She punctuated the sentence by stabbing at the air with the paintbrush.

"But if it weren't for me you could have found—"

"What? Another prince?" Monique spun on the stool and smiled at Phillip. "Oh, please. Who wants to sit around waiting for a man who may never come? And so what if he does show up? Shining armor rusts, and white horses are just albino black ones. I'm doing perfectly fine with that man behind the bar."

"But what about happily—"

"Sugar, I found it. And I didn't need some silly crown."

"But what about that song you were singing?"

"Sweetums," she cooed, "that is just part of the act. What I really want to say to you is 'thank you.'"

"Thank *me*?"

"Yes. For the first time in my life, people love me for what I do and not who my parents are."

"Honest?"

"Honest." She turned and checked her reflection one last time, "Now, let's get back out there before that crowd starts a riot. When you talked to me in that ridiculous bed, didn't you tell me your mother taught you to sing?"

"Yes. She adored music. She would've liked you a lot."

"Then come up on stage with me. Do you know "True Love Someday Will Be"?"

"Of course, but is it appropriate for the future king to be singing in a tavern?"

"Who cares? When you're king you can turn your whole castle into a tavern if you wish. I'll come sing for you any time you want." Monique walked to the door before turning around and offering her hand to Phillip. "Now, come show that crowd who you really are, and sing with me."

"Ok. Fine." Phillip shrugged as he rose and took her hand. "But you have to do the harmony."

"Whatever you say," Monique drawled, "Your Highness."

# CHAPTER *10*

"**E**ASY, GIRL," DANIEL MURMURED TO HIS HORSE AND clicked his tongue. He looked out at the vast golden fields swaying in the afternoon breeze on both sides of the road ahead. Since he had grown up in the thick overgrowth of the Sylvanian woods, the sheer openness of Grand Dealonia made Daniel's stomach uneasy as he searched the horizon for a single tree. All he could see was dancing leaves of corn and stalks of wheat that flowed all the way up to the walls of a glimmering white castle at the end of the road. He knew Dealonians provided the produce and grains for all of Clarameer, but he had never imagined this much of anything growing for as far as the eye could see. *Oh, Ems, how do you stand all this emptiness? Where on earth do you hide here?* He mused until his thoughts were interrupted by the noisy, off-key singing of his companions.

"Second verse!" Peter hooted into the clear blue skies. He swung his arms about in front of Gwen's shoulders as he directed an imaginary orchestra. "This time even louder! These fields are full of corn, so there are thousands of ears that need to hear us!"

"Must we?" Daniel begged as he turned to look over his shoulder at James and Phillip ambling along. "I appreciate a good traveling tune as much as the next guy, but can't you think of something else to sing?"

"Sorry, Highness," James said, as he trotted past Daniel to pull up alongside Peter and Gwen, "it's just a wickedly catchy little tune."

"*Royal blue!*" Peter sang at the top of his lungs and he threw his head back. "*I'm royal blue.*"

"Ow! Peter," Gwen laughed as she put her hands over her ears and scrunched up her shoulders. "At least try to get the tune right! It's '*Blue!*'" she sang. "Up here. Not down low like that. Try again."

"*I'm blue!*" Peter bellowed, as James joined in. The three of them laughed again as they moved farther up the road toward the castle looming ahead.

Daniel rolled his eyes and waited until Phillip's horse drew up. He was surprised to see Phillip smiling at the singers. "I tried to get them to stop."

"It's fine," Phillip shrugged. "I'm dragging them all over the kingdoms on what may be a fool's errand. Let them have their fun. It *is* a catchy tune. '*Royal Blue!*'" Phillip sang softly, then turned to Daniel and grinned broadly.

"Well, there he is," Daniel grinned back.

"Who?" Phillip asked, knitting his brow.

"The handsome, smiling man I saw when I opened my eyes in that ridiculous bed. I was a little worried he'd gone away forever."

Phillip blushed and abruptly shifted his gaze back to the road ahead. The smile quickly disappeared, and Phillip dropped his chin to stare at the reins in his hands. Daniel looked away and grimaced, regretting instantly that he had reminded Phillip of the events in the testing room. He wasn't sure what had transpired the previous night in Lady Moon's dressing room, but Phillip had been much calmer since then. Phillip had even climbed on stage to lead the tavern in a rousing song. Daniel hoped he could keep Phillip's mind off his troubles, but he was failing.

"I'm sorry, Phillip. I shouldn't have brought up the bed. I know it reminds you of…"

"My father? No. I never stop thinking of my father. How could I?" Phillip flipped the reins and started the horse down the road again. "No. It's the bed. We're about to see King Robert of Grand Dealonia. He may be… um… less than happy to see me."

"Because Gwen is his cousin? At least you've rescued her and brought her back to the kingdom."

"Well, not just Gwen. Robert's little sister, Dinah, was sent to marry me, too. She was in the bed and…"

"Let me guess. Didn't pass?"

"Slept like a log." Phillip shook his head and frowned. "I thought we'd never wake her up. When we finally got her awake, and my stepmother told her she had failed the test, she was livid. She screamed and yelled and threw a shoe at me. A shoe!"

Daniel laughed and then quickly stifled it with his hand. "Sorry, but I'm just imagining you ducking the flying footwear!"

"It's not funny. I thought she might try to kill me! Oh no! What if she is at the castle?"

"We'll just insist she meet you barefoot," Daniel laughed louder. "Come on, Phillip, it's kind of funny." Daniel watched as a smile began to creep across Phillip's face. "But I do have one question. We've got Monique, Gwen and now Dinah, right? Exactly how many murderous princesses are we in danger of running into on this trek?"

"Um… Seven? No, Six?" Phillip shifted his eyes up in thought and began counting silently on his fingers. "Six if you count Katerina, but I guess she never got the chance to take the test. I kind of lost count. Nobody ever made it all night without sleeping. Until you. You're lucky number seven! It's a good thing your sister married King Robert before I had the chance to ruin her reputation too."

"You'd have been lucky to marry Emmaline. She's my favorite woman in all of Clarameer." Daniel grinned at Phillip while he thought of his sister. "Between James and Emmaline, I was never lonely. When we played hide-and-seek in the castle, I could never find her. She was always the best at hiding. She would run out of a hiding spot and grab me in a big hug and swing me around until I almost died from laughing."

"Sounds wonderful." Phillip stared wistfully at the few small houses and the large castle on the horizon. "I always wished I had a brother or a sister. Peter was as close as I got, but then he was banished. It was always kind of lonely."

Daniel could see the loneliness that Phillip had endured in the sudden weary droop of his shoulders. Hoping to move Phillip's thoughts back to happier things, Daniel continued. "Sometimes, I think she is the only reason Andrew and I made it to being adults without killing each other. When we were little and Andy was being especially mean to James and me, she would punch him in the nose! Mother had forbidden us boys to hurt Emmaline, so there was nothing Andrew could do! Then she would use her little lace handkerchief to dry my tears and sneak me into the kitchen for a treat. She's also beautiful, if I say so myself."

"Long, curly black hair?" Phillip asked. "Looks a bit like you, only shorter?"

"Yes. How did you know that?" Daniel followed Phillip's pointing finger down the road until he saw his sister standing at the end of the castle's drawbridge waving a bright yellow scarf over her head.

"Emmaline!" Daniel shouted. He kicked his horse and raced past the other travelers. As he drew close to his sister, Daniel jumped down and ran into her open arms. Wrapping his arms tight around her chest, he picked her up and spun her around. "Oh, Ems! It's so good to see you!"

"Daniel, put me down. A woman in my condition shouldn't be spun around like that!"

"Your condition? Oh, Ems! Are you?"

Emmaline nodded her head in assent and placed her hands lovingly on her stomach. "But don't tell anyone! We're trying to keep it out of the *Kingdom Inquisitor* as long as we can, so that I can have some peace. Speaking of which, you and James have been making a little front page news lately."

"Me?"

"Yes, you. Well, you and that man." Emmaline scowled as she pointed toward the approaching group. "It seems the two of you were seen larking about in taverns all over Bellemer. Really, Daniel? After the way he ruined the reputations of Robert's sister and cousin? This is the kind of man you choose to take up with? And you let Gwendolyn traipse about in men's clothes on James's arm! I had to hide it from Robert so he wouldn't hunt you both down!"

"Ems, I've been wandering the kingdoms for months now and I rarely read that garbage. I had no idea what had happened with Robert's sister. Also, you should know better than to believe the stories in that rag. It was one tavern for one night. I can explain everything. Prince Phillip is—"

"Prince Phillip is standing right behind you," Phillip said, as he stepped around Daniel and reached out for Emmaline's hand. "Queen Emmaline. Prince Phillip of Bellemer. I have come to seek the forgiveness and aid of your kind husband." He raised her hand to his lips and kissed it.

Emmaline pulled her hand back sharply and said, "That will all be his decision. Gwendolyn! Come here! Let's get you into the castle and back into clothes more appropriate than this man's tunic. I will take all of you to speak with Robert." The young queen commanded, "Daniel, walk with me. We've a few things to talk about."

Daniel shuffled forward like a reluctant child and took his sister's outstretched hand. She turned and headed across the drawbridge, pulling Daniel along behind her. Gwendolyn looked at Phillip and shrugged before turning to follow the pair into the castle. Daniel turned to see Phillip standing with a blank stare.

"Well, that was chilly." Peter pulled his horse toward the open gate. "Why don't James and I take the horses to the stables while you handle this?"

"Phillip, come on!" Daniel called back to the other prince and watched as Phillip hurried across the drawbridge to join the group. Daniel nodded at the guards standing on either side of the castle's main gates as they strolled into the bustling courtyard.

At first, Daniel assumed it must be market day, until he remembered that Dealonians were known for having voracious appetites, sumptuous daily feasts and continuous markets. All around the edges of the large cobblestone-paved enclosure, farmers sat at small, multicolored tents with table after table of fresh produce spilled out for purchase. A few hens and roosters fluttered about, chased by three yapping dogs. Women in aprons ambled among the tables, inspecting fruit and vegetables and gossiping about the day's events. Children ran around the edges of a stone fountain that gurgled in the center of the courtyard, as they chased the small paper boats they sailed in the basin. In the solitude of his wanderings, Daniel had forgotten how exciting the flurry of castle life could be. He was glad Emmaline's marriage had brought her to such a busy place.

He turned to his sister and asked, "So, have you forgiven me for missing your wedding yet?"

"No. I know you were seeking a cure for your birthday curse, but it's a shame you didn't come home for the wedding. You know, the fairies all showed up to bestow their blessings. You could have just asked them then."

"Wait? What?" Daniel asked as he stopped, dropped his sister's hand and stared at her in disbelief. "The birthday fairies came to the wedding?"

Phillip gasped for breath as he trotted up beside Daniel. "Everyone knows that, Daniel. Weddings, engagements, births. They always show up for the big events." Phillip placed his hand on Daniel's shoulder while leaning over to catch his breath and holding his side with his other hand. Daniel reached up and patted Phillip's hand.

Emmaline shifted her gaze between Phillip's hand lying casually on her brother's shoulder and the gentle smile Daniel cast toward the gasping prince. Arching her eyebrow, she smirked before taking her brother's free hand and turning to continue down the hallway. At the end of the hall she stopped in front of a pair of wide doors, which were painted with motifs of wheat and corn in the gold and burgundy colors of the Dealonian royal family. Emmaline turned her back to the doors and bumped them open with her backside. "This way."

Daniel and Phillip gasped as they entered the enormous room. Daniel was awestruck by the ceiling paintings of farmers working in fields. At the far end of the hall were two thrones beneath a long burgundy banner with the words "Sow the seed. End the need." embroidered in golden lettering. Beneath the banner hung a large wooden shield with the family sigil of a sheaf of wheat.

"Welcome to my little chateau!" Emmaline said with a sweep of her hands, as she crossed toward the thrones. "What were we talking about? Oh, the wedding. All seven fairies were there. For less important events, it's just one at a time, and they don't let you know they're there. But at engagements, weddings and births they show their faces. Dima, my fairy, gave me a fertility blessing, which has clearly worked. Instead of wandering all over the kingdoms, you should just get yourself engaged." Daniel felt his face flush as Emmaline shifted her eyes to Phillip. "Phillip, how did my silly brother talk you into wandering around the kingdoms with him looking for a good night's sleep?"

"What?" Phillip asked, as he and Gwendolyn followed the pair into the hall. "What are you talking about? We aren't just wandering. We have a mission, and Daniel is helping me with my problem. We're not just looking for a good night's sleep. Daniel, what is she talking about?"

"Phillip, let me explain—"

"Here we are!" Emmaline interrupted, dropping her brother's hand. Gathering her skirts, she carefully stepped up the three steps of the dais that held the thrones. A young man with sandy blond hair and a thick beard slumped in the larger throne with his head resting on his fist. His shoulders rose and fell slowly in the quiet breath of sleep. "Robert! Wake up!" Emmaline shouted and punched the dozing man on the arm. "We've got guests!"

King Robert's crown slid off his head onto his lap as he jolted awake. He fumbled with the crown as it rolled across his thighs, barely catching it before it tumbled to the floor. After shoving the crown back on his head, he yawned, stretched and scratched his ribs. Shooting an irritated look at his wife, Robert said "Ouch! What did you go and do that for? I was just getting to a good part. The chefs were serving an enormous cake covered with chocolate and… Daniel? Is that Daniel? Come here, lad, and give your new brother a big hug!"

Robert leapt from the throne and stretched his arms out. Daniel stepped onto the dais and wrapped his arms around the king. Robert pulled Daniel close and clapped his hands on his back several times, then leaned back to inspect the prince's face. "Yes. You are definitely from the Sylvanian house. Emmaline, why didn't you tell me how much your brother looks like you?"

"Guilty," Daniel said with a grin.

"Yes. You *are* guilty," Robert boomed and released Daniel from his grasp. "Guilty of missing the fanciest wedding the kingdoms have ever seen! No one warned me your sister would try to empty my coffers with one little party. By Godrick's curls, there were flowers and foods I'd never even heard of! Some of those desserts haunt my dreams to this day! And I'm not forgiving you for missing a second of it, baby boy, no matter what your excuse. Wandering the kingdoms like some peddler. If this little lady hadn't swept me off my feet with those big green eyes, I might have questioned marrying into a family that lets the youngest boy go traipsing about!"

"I'm truly sorry to have missed it," Daniel said with a laugh. "But you didn't give us much warning. You met, proposed and married in the span of a week!"

"Well," Robert said as he plopped back down on the throne, "I couldn't run the risk of some other prince snapping up this little gem, now could I?"

"Oh, Robert," Emmaline said with a chuckle, as she batted him softly on the shoulder, "it's not like you had much competition. There was only one other eligible prince in the kingdoms that I wasn't related to."

"Oh! Him," Robert said with a huff. "He was no competition. Why, that fish-brained prince—"

"Is here," Emmaline said and pointed at Phillip.

"What?" Robert bellowed. He abruptly stood up, almost knocking Daniel over in the process. He leaned to look around Daniel's shoulders at the two figures standing below. "Emmaline! Fetch me my sword! I am going to skewer that little fish and roast him on a fire!"

Daniel turned to watch Phillip back away from the thrones. He could see the fear in the other prince's eyes as he fidgeted with the hem of his doublet. "Now, Robert, calm down. I've brought Phillip here to seek your forgiveness and aid. You simply can't—"

"I can," Robert raised his voice even louder. Leaning close to Daniel's face, he spat, "Do you realize this shrimp has ruined the reputation of my dear sister, Dinah, and my beloved cousin, Gwendolyn. The whole kingdom is laughing at me and claiming that we all might be frauds! I think a sword through the belly is better than he deserves!"

"Cousin Robert," Gwendolyn said, as she took a step toward the thrones.

"Dinah was so embarrassed by the whole tawdry affair that she has run off to who knows where!" Robert continued his rant as he clomped down the steps. "And no one has seen my beloved cousin since she was unceremoniously dumped out of your little seaside castle."

"I can explain," Phillip whimpered, as he cowered away from the king's advancing form.

"Cousin Robert!" Gwendolyn stepped between Robert and Phillip. "I'm right here. You'd think if I'm so beloved you'd notice me in the room! Honestly."

"Gwendolyn?" Robert gasped, then turned and swept the girl into his arms. "Oh, Gwen. You've come home! Your father will be so pleased!"

"Yes. I'm fine, and Phillip is the one who brought me home." Gwen said huffily, as Robert dropped her back to her feet. "If anything, you should be thanking him. I mean, honestly. Those ruffians you and Daddy hired to escort me dumped me outside the castle. Not Phillip."

"Why, those no good—I ought to round them up and have them baked into a—darling, I'm sorry. But he still ruined your reputation! Thanks to those blubbering idiots at the *Kingdom Inquisitor*, everyone in Clarameer thinks you and Dinah are frauds!"

"It was never my intention to—" Phillip tried to enter the conversation.

"Hush, boy. I'll deal with you in a minute," Robert said and put his hand up in front of Phillip's face.

"Cousin," Gwen said, as she grabbed Robert's outstretched arm, "if you will calm down and think about it, Phillip has done you a favor."

"A favor?" Robert asked, his chin falling.

"Yes. Think about it. When Granddaddy split Dealonia between your daddy and mine, nobody intended it to stay that way."

"Yes. The first of their children to marry and produce an heir would reunite the two halves."

"Right. So, if anything, Phillip made it easier for you to have a child first. When my father is gone, you will rule both kingdoms. Without a true princess to produce a child, you've got no competition."

"It's true, Robert," Emmaline cooed. She stepped forward and grabbed her husband by the hand. Leading him back up to the thrones, she gently nudged him to his seat. "And if Gwen had married Phillip, you'd have her father to your north and her husband to your south. They could've made an alliance and tried to run you off the throne!"

"You're not helping," Daniel hissed at his sister.

"This minnow? Wage war on me? I'd like to see him try."

"King Robert," Phillip said and stepped up to the throne again, "that was never my intention. I just want to rule my own kingdom in peace. Which is why I have come to ask your help with—"

"I'd have been happy to leave you in peace, son. If you'd married Dinah, I'd have an ally to the south and the use of your ports. But you had to go and—"

"Again, my intentions were—"

"Intentions. Ha! Your intentions have made my little sister just disappear! First she spent all her days locked up in her bedroom reading books on magic. Then one day she came storming in here in a downright fit. Dinah's always been an ornery sort, but that day she was so mad I thought she would spit fire. Said there was no way she could've failed his test. Claimed there was some hokum pokum going on in that castle and, by Gingerfair's crook, she was going to go and prove it. Stormed out of here like a Dealonian cyclone, and no one has seen her since. That is all your fault!"

"Robert," Daniel said calmly, as he stepped beside Phillip and rested his hand on the other man's shoulder, "you make Phillip sound so heartless. How could he know Dinah would fail the test? How could he know she would storm out of her own home? Phillip is not an evil man. I've seen evil. His stepmother attempted to kill us all and has cast a spell on King Henry. That is why we've come here, to seek your help in finding and capturing her."

"A spell, you say?" Robert said with a frown. "Almost killed you all?"

Phillip nodded as tears began to form in his eyes. "My stepmother, she did something to him and now he's... I don't know... but I have to help him. I have no interest in conquering or ruining anyone."

Daniel stroked his hand across Phillip's shoulder. "I've watched him go through sheer torture in the last few days, and yet he's been nothing but kind and caring to Gwendolyn. All he is asking is that you search your kingdom for Cauchemar. Help him bring her to justice and save his father's life."

"It's true. He's rescued me, clothed me and brought me to you. I mean, honestly."

"Despite fearing for his kingdom and his father, he even agreed to help me on my quest. Phillip wishes no ill on you or your house."

Daniel looked at Phillip and smiled before turning back to the king. "True, Phillip's not a warrior. But some men can conquer with kindness. Won't you follow his example?"

Leaning down to bring her lips close to her husband's ear, Emmaline whispered, "Leave them be, darling. I think you might be gaining a family ally in the south, after all."

Turning his head to look his wife in the eye, Robert raised an eyebrow and whispered, "You mean—"

"I'm a wise woman, you old goat. I know my little brother. Just help them."

"Well," Robert said quietly, as he turned back to face the princes, "King Henry is a good man. A fine man. Yes. I will gladly send my men to search every corner of Grand Dealonia. However, I have to ask two favors in return."

"Anything," Phillip said as he grabbed Daniel's hand.

"Take Gwendolyn back to her father. If some lunatic woman is roaming the kingdoms trying to kill royals, I can't have my cousin wandering about like a wild filly."

"Of course," Phillip replied.

"Secondly, find my little sister. Bring her home to me, and I'll forget what you've done to our family."

"Consider her halfway home," Phillip replied, as he loosened his grip on Daniel's hand and stepped up to Robert's throne. He reached out his hands to the king. "Your trust is not misplaced, and your forgiveness will not be forgotten."

Taking Phillip's hand in his own, Robert looked Phillip in the eye and said, "Bring her home." Turning to his wife, he rubbed his belly and yelled, "Emmaline, I do believe all this hollering has grown me a fierce hankering for some sweets. What do you say we all head down to the kitchens for a little treat? My dumpling here has found one of the best pastry chefs in all the realms. Makes an éclair I'd slap my pappy for."

"Sounds delicious," Phillip grinned and followed the king toward the doors of the hall.

"Daniel," Emmaline called to her brother as he followed Phillip, then dropped her voice as he slowed beside her. "While I'm glad you have found a companion for your travels and are helping Phillip with his task, please tell me you're still working on your own little problem."

"Yes," Daniel sighed as he crooked his arm around his sister's waist. "I'm looking still. James has been very... um... helpful, but so far, no luck. If only I'd been here to meet the fairies."

"I should've asked them myself, but I was a little busy with the wedding and all."

"That's okay, Ems. But don't you worry, I will find a cure for this insomnia and I will sleep again." As they passed into the hallway, Daniel looked up to see Phillip standing before him with a look of utter confusion.

"Insomnia? What do you mean insomnia, Daniel?"

# CHAPTER 11

"**I** CAN'T SLEEP. TELL ME A STORY." THE GIRL IN THE CELL next to Katerina groaned, as she slid off her bed to the floor. Katerina startled awake at the girl's voice. In her exhaustion, she had almost forgotten the girl was there, and the girl had barely spoken to her until now. Katerina turned her head to look at her. The girl's sandy blonde hair hung in loose clumps about her shoulders and fell onto the stained embroidery of wheat sheaves on the breast of her tattered burgundy gown. The flickering torches on the walls of their cells barely illuminated the girl's face, but Katerina could tell that under the dirt and tear stains the girl was pretty. Katerina watched her out of the corner of her eye as the girl struggled to shuffle closer to the bars that separated them. "You keep moaning about somebody named Peter. Tell me about him."

"I don't want to talk about that," Katerina mumbled, as she looked around the cell for a way to move away from the other girl's complaining. The back wall was solid stone with a large slab embedded in it to serve as a bed. Foul-smelling water trickled down the wall and kept the bed far too damp for Katerina to sleep on it. The cobblestone floor had not been much better, but the moss that covered it made for a slightly softer bed. Thick iron bars stood between her and the cells on either side of her. The bars extended across the front of the room as well. With only one torch burning in the hall outside, Katerina could barely see another row of cells across the hall. Her teeth chattered as she shivered in the cold air of the dungeon; the thin, frilly gown she was wearing provided no warmth.

"That's not very neighborly," the other girl groused and glared at Katerina through the bars. "And you're wearing that dress wrong. The ruffles are supposed to be down on your arms, not up on your shoulders."

"Well, it's so cold in here, it's hard to think, much less tell a story." Katerina wrapped her arms across her chest and tried to rub some warmth back into her limbs. "And I like the lacy parts better up here," she mumbled as she pulled the frills higher onto her shoulders. "Why is everyone determined to make me feel half-naked?"

"If my hands were unbound, I could use my magic to make a fire," the girl in the other cell said, as she lifted her hands to show Katerina the leather straps that bound her hands. "But I can't do anything with these straps tying my hands together." She lifted her chin to stare at the ceiling above and yelled, "Big bad troll king has to tie me up! If he'd show his face down here, I'd—"

"You can do magic? You can get us out of here! Come over here, and I will untie you!" Katerina cried out, She scrambled up and reached her arms through the bars into the next cell.

"Won't work," a man's voice called out from across the dimly lit passageway.

Katerina jumped. She had forgotten the man was there. He had barely said ten words to her since the guards had dragged her down into the dungeons and thrown her into this room a few days earlier. She didn't even know his name. She hurried to the door, hoping she could see his face.

"Those are magic bonds," the man continued. "For every knot you untie, three more will appear. Eventually they will grow so tight her hands will fall off. Also, a fire would just choke us all on smoke. While I expect full well to die in here, I see no need to rush it. Now, could you both hush so I can try to get some sleep?"

"Oh," Katerina cried, as she dropped back to the cold stone floor. Grabbing the ratty blanket, she pulled it around her shoulders and curled up into a tight ball. She sat shivering before turning to the girl and whispering through the bars, "Did they put you in here because of your magic?"

"To be honest, I don't know much magic," the girl said, as she shuffled on her haunches across the floor toward the bars. "I was just starting to learn, really. See, until recently I just assumed I'd marry a prince and do the same thing my mother and every woman in my family has done for generations. There aren't a lot of options for us royal girls."

"Oh! You're a princess, too?"

"Yeah. My name is Dinah, Princess of Grand Dealonia. Are you a princess?" Dinah stopped her shuffling and leaned her face against the bars.

"That's sort of hard to answer," Katerina said with a grimace. "My name is Kitty. I think I may be a princess."

"That isn't a hard question. You either are a princess or not!" Dinah leaned back and rolled her eyes. "Everyone knows I'm a princess. At least, they did, until I failed Prince Phillip's test."

"Oh, I know Phillip!" Katerina said. She leaned closer to the bars and whispered to Dinah, "I was supposed to take his test, but some bad things happened before I could."

"Well, be glad you didn't. There was some funny business going on in that castle, let me tell you." Dinah puffed a few breaths at her hair to move it out of her face, before lifting her bound hands and shoving it away. "No matter what Phillip's stepmother says, I know I'm a princess, and there is no way I failed that test without someone making me fail."

Katerina's stomach flipped at the mention of her aunt. She decided that her relationship to Philip's stepmother might not be the best information to share at the moment. "You know what the test is?" Katerina gasped. "I thought that was a very guarded secret."

"Well, it took me a little while to figure it out, but eventually I got it. I'm smart that way." Dinah shoved back her shoulders in pride. "Well, it seemed strange that they put me in that humongous bed. I mean, who has furniture like that? And then that prince kept asking me over and over if I was sleepy. He was obsessed with my energy level. He even offered me a sleeping tonic."

"That is strange," Katerina mumbled.

"Then I woke up and was told I failed a test I don't even remember taking. I don't fail tests! Like I said, I'm smart that way. So I thought about it all the way home and I just couldn't stop thinking about that big bed."

"I saw it. It *was* very big."

"So the minute I got home, I ran to our library and did some research." Dinah lifted her bound hands and pretended to rifle through the pages of a book. "I found out that hundreds of years ago they used to test a girl's royalty by putting a pea under a big stack of mattresses."

"That seems silly," Katerina said, hoping to change the subject.

"I know!" Dinah said. "But the crazy thing is that it's true! I tried it. I put the tiniest pea I could find under a bunch of mattresses, and it felt like a boulder! That was when it occurred to me that someone must've used magic to make me fail, and I decided to prove it."

"Prove it how?"

"Well, I tried to tell my brother, but he told me to be a good girl and keep quiet. After I hit him with my shoe, I started reading everything I could about magic to figure out how Phillip did it. I thought I could expose him for a fraud, ruin his reputation, and get my rightful title back. If nothing else, I could at least learn how to turn the twit into a toad. I was a woman on a mission!"

"Did you figure something out?" Katerina said meekly. She dreaded having to tell the girl that her aunt had been the one to make her fail.

"No," Dinah said, as she leaned against the bars. "But something strange did happen. I started to learn things no one had ever bothered to tell me. Useful things! Not just dancing and conversation and how to wear your hair. Did you know rumberries can cure rain plague? A dragon scale can cure hiccups! It's fascinating!" Dinah's face lit up with excitement as she thought about what she had learned. "I read everything I could in Dealonia's libraries and I just needed to know more. So, I ran away in the middle of the night and sought out every person and book I could find to teach me more. I began to be able to do a few spells, and it was so amazing. I had power!" Dinah lifted her hands and wiggled her fingers, making a few purple sparks glitter out of her fingertips.

"How exciting!" Katerina said, her eyes widening.

"Eventually I ran out of things to read. And the really powerful people won't tell you their best secrets. So, I came here, thinking I could learn something from the troll king. I mean, anyone who can build a magical wall around an entire kingdom must be powerful."

"But how did you get over the wall?"

"Not by choice. I was walking along the base of the wall looking for any way in, and some men grabbed me. They pulled me right through the wall, somehow, and then I woke up in here." Dinah shrugged and kicked at the bars. "I tried to throw a few spells at them, but all I managed to do was shower them with rose petals. They bound my hands anyway," she yelled at the ceiling again, "because the troll king is a spineless goat!"

"Dinah, please!" the man across the hall groaned. "Enough with the yelling. Can you both be quiet so I can think of a way to get us out of here?"

"That's my uncle, King Edward. He's an old grump. They captured him outside the wall too. How did you get in here?"

"My aunt brought me here to marry the troll king," Katerina said. "I refused. I told her I already loved someone else and wouldn't accept a life of misery married to some old troll." Katerina stared up at the torch on the wall across the cell and tried to stop the tears she could feel burning in the corners of her eyes. "She had the troll king's guards toss me in here and said I'd see what true misery is, so I'd appreciate my life as his queen."

"Well," Dinah said, as she shuffled back into the darkness of her cell, "this place is awful, but I'd take it any day over marriage to a troll."

"Yes. It's awful. I wish I were back in my tower," Katerina said with a whimper, as the tears began to roll down her cheeks. "Everything was better in my tower. I was safe. I had Peter's stories." Her breath caught, as she sobbed and closed her eyes. "Things moved so much slower when I measured the days by sunsets. This is all moving so fast now. I just want things to slow down. Slow down. Just slow down."

"PHILLIP, PLEASE SLOW DOWN," DANIEL PLEADED, AS HE RACED his horse up to Phillip's side. "Your horse can't take this pace and, frankly, neither can I."

"She's fine," Phillip muttered, with a glare in Daniel's direction. "We're all fine."

"Please, just let me explain. Slow down and let me explain!"

"There's nothing to explain," Phillip said with a glare, his anger making his voice tremble. "You lied to me. All clear. Now, can we please just get Gwen back to her castle so I can go home and tend to my father?" Though he knew it wasn't true, Phillip added another twist of his verbal knife. "I only came along because I thought you might have passed the test. But that was just a lie."

"I never lied to you! I tried to tell you several times, but we kept getting interrupted. It's like someone wants me to always get—"

"Oh! Look!" Gwendolyn squealed as she trotted up between the two princes with her arm gesturing to the horizon.

"—interrupted." Daniel sighed and rolled his eyes.

"What am I looking at?" Phillip said. He turned away from Daniel to look where Gwendolyn was pointing. They had agreed it was safer to stay off the main roads, and the dirt road they were following wound its way back and forth in front of them across golden wheat fields. It met the main road at the gates of a small castle. The fields were in full fruit, but not a soul could be seen working in them. Phillip was surprised at how tiny the castle seemed, compared to his own. He was also surprised to see no banners flying from the towers, and the gates sitting half-opened.

"It's my home!" Gwen shouted, as she popped her horse's reins and sped off toward the small castle with the golden gown Emma-line had forced her to change into fluttering in the breeze behind her. "Look at our pretty little castle! Daddy, I'm home!"

"Gwen!" James yelled, as he and Peter rode up to the two princes. "Wait! You need one of us with you. That crazy woman could be in there!" Kicking his spurs into his horse's side, he sped after Gwen. With a glance back over his shoulder, he called to the others, "A little help here! Before she gets herself killed."

"Some of us won't particularly miss her." Peter sighed, as he trotted after James.

"Come on," Phillip said icily to Daniel. "Let's make sure she's okay. Something doesn't look right about that castle."

"Fine, but we're not finished with this conversation."

Phillip rolled his eyes before clicking his tongue at his horse and setting off toward the castle. As he approached, the hair on the back of his neck bristled. The windows along the front of the castle seemed like empty eye sockets staring back at him. The gate hung half-open like the mouth of a fish pulled from the water. Glancing at the empty sentry box by the gates, Phillip asked, "Where are the guards?"

"Where is *anyone*?" Daniel whispered, as he slowed his horse and dismounted. "Something is definitely wrong here."

"Whoa, girl," Phillip murmured to his horse and patted her neck. He dismounted and grabbed the loose reins to lead the horse to the gates. The horse whinnied and chuffed as Phillip led her into the courtyard of the castle. With a pat on her hind leg, he sent the horse to stand with the rest of the traveling party's horses in a corner of the courtyard, where they shifted from hoof to hoof.

Phillip glanced around to see all of the doors and windows hanging wide open. A few carts lay toppled over on the cobblestone floor of the courtyard with the last bits of a straw spilling out of them onto the ground. Phillip stepped carefully over a few toppled chairs and an empty barrel, and walked on toward the carts. As Phillip reached down to grab a handful of the straw, a screech from the opposite corner made him jump. He jerked his head in the direction of the sound to see a single rooster flapping its wings and crowing on top of a carelessly dropped basket of clothes. "Hush, you stupid bird," he scolded.

Phillip took a few steps toward the main hallway of the castle and strained to see inside. "Gwen? James?" he called into the darkness, his words echoing slightly off the empty walls around him.

A touch on his arm made him jump again, and he swung out at the person grabbing him.

"Careful!" Daniel exclaimed, as he ducked under Phillip's swinging arm. "It's just me!"

"You scared me," Phillip hissed. "This place is making me jumpier than a Glorianna hare. Something bad has happened here."

"Sorry, I didn't mean to scare you," Daniel whispered. "Where did they go?"

As Phillip opened his mouth to answer, a wail came echoing down the empty hallway. Phillip and Daniel jerked their heads in the direction of the sound and then looked back at each other. "That was Gwen! Come on," Phillip said. He turned and began running down the dark hallway toward the sound.

"Phillip, wait," Daniel called, as he pulled his sword from its scabbard and followed. At the end of the hall, large double doors sat wide open, and the hallway opened into the castle's spacious throne room.

As Phillip rushed into the room, he saw Gwen sitting on the floor with her head and arms draped across an empty throne. She held a jeweled dagger in one hand and a crumpled piece of parchment in the other. Her shoulders shook with sobs, and her cries echoed around the empty room. James knelt behind her and rubbed her back. Peter stood off to the side, staring at his feet. As Daniel clattered into the room behind Phillip, Peter looked up and shook his head.

"Peter," Phillip asked as he approached the boy, "what is going on here?"

"I'll tell you what is going on here! He left!" Gwen screamed as she swept up from the floor and charged toward Phillip. "Your stupid test made him leave!"

"Who?"

"My father!" Gwen sobbed. Shaking the crumpled paper in his face, she said between gasps, "I found this note stuck into the back of his throne with this dagger. Oh! He's gone. Honestly." The girl dropped the paper at Phillip's feet and raced back across the room toward the empty throne. In her frustration, she threw the dagger toward the throne, spinning it end over end until it stuck into the back of the throne with a loud "thunk."

"James! He's gone!" she wailed as she draped her body across the knight's chest.

James wrapped his arms around her shoulders and ran his hand gently down the back of her head while he looked at the dagger sticking into the back of the throne. "How did you do that?"

Daniel reached down to retrieve the paper and quickly scanned it. "It says he abandoned Little Dealonia and surrendered it to King Robert. He told his people that since the princess is gone, he has no claim to the throne. He sent them all to swear allegiance to King Robert and reunite the two Dealonias. He is heading into the kingdoms to hide. This must have happened while we were coming here! "

"If we had stuck to the main roads like I suggested," Peter said with a sniff, "we probably would've seen them all leaving."

"This makes no sense!" Phillip said, as he pulled the paper from Daniel's hands and read it quickly. His stomach churned with guilt and he feared he would vomit. Though Dr. Hickenkopf's Miracle Tonic was supposed to cure what ails you, it was causing Phillip nothing but more and more trouble. "It was a silly test. Why would he abandon his whole kingdom over that? His princess isn't gone!" Phillip read more of the letter and gasped. "Gwen, did you read all of this? He thinks you're dead!"

"Dead? Why?" Gwen asked with a sob, as she raised her face from James's chest.

"Those men that were bringing you home must've told him they were attacked and you were killed."

"But Emmaline said we're all over the front of the *Kingdom Inquisitor*," Daniel said. "Surely he saw that and knows you are alive!"

"Oh, Daddy, honestly," Gwen said with a deep sigh. "After my mother died, he never allowed the *Inq* in our castle because it reminded him of her. Mama read it every morning at breakfast. She's the one who called it the *Inq*. Daddy said it was a good name because it wasn't real news, just ink. He told me to spend my days learning my princesscraft, not reading that. I had one of my maids sneak it in for me so I could read the reviews of my plays, but I had to hide it from him. Honestly, Daddy, it's just a newspaper."

"He says he hopes the news is wrong, and Gwen will find this— and him."

"Gwen," James said and reached out to take her hands. "You know what this means?"

"Uh-uh," Gwen said with a sniffle.

"We have to find him and let him know you're alive," James said as he swung her hands excitedly back and forth. "You can come with us!"

"Yes!" Phillip said with a broad smile as he stepped over to put his hands on her shoulders. "This can be fixed. We can find him. We're already looking for half the royals in the kingdoms. Why not one more?"

"I don't know," Gwen said as she dropped James's hands and wiped the back of her hand across her nose. "I don't know anything about surviving in the wild. I was raised to be a princess, not a vagabond. I'd be scared."

"Oh, really?" Peter said with a laugh. "So far, all I've seen you do is run into every situation without a care in the world. I don't think you can even spell the word scared."

"Peter," Gwen sniffled again, "don't be mean. I'll just be in the way. All I know how to do is act and sing and other silly things."

"Like dagger throwing?" James asked.

"As much as it pains me to say this," Peter mumbled, "I actually like your singing. You and Phillip are the only ones of this bunch who can harmonize, and he's too busy with… well… if nothing else, *The Vagabond Princess* might be a good story for me someday."

"But a princess doesn't go wandering around with a bunch of men unchaperoned."

"Says who?" James asked.

"I don't know. The rules?"

"The rules say an orphan shouldn't be the bravest knight in all the kingdoms, and, well, just look at me now," James bragged, putting his hands on his hips and striking his most heroic pose.

"Well, it's not like I have anything else to do," Gwen said. "Not a lot of opportunities for ex-princesses. What am I supposed to do? Sit in this empty castle and rule over nobody?"

Phillip watched as Gwen twisted the rings on her fingers. He was reminded of the nervous energy that had made her so talkative in the testing bed. Remembering the excitement in her voice that night as she dreamed of possibilities and encouraged him to do the same, Phillip felt the need to return the favor.

"Gwen," Phillip said "remember when we were talking in the testing chamber? You told me that if we got married we would find adventure together. Okay, we didn't get married, but we can still find adventure, right? Come with us. Let me help you find your father to make up for all the mess my stepmother's stupid test has caused."

"You know," Gwen said, as she set her shoulders back and stuck out her chin, "that princess life is behind me now, so I think I'll leave all those princess rules right here with it." She crossed the room to the empty throne and propped her foot on the seat. She grabbed the dagger by the handle and yanked it out of the wood. "But I'm taking this with me."

"Why don't we see if there are any supplies we can use?" Daniel suggested, as he walked to the side of the room and pulled an overturned bench upright. Sitting down on the bench, he pulled off his boot and turned it upside down to shake out a pebble.

"Well, I am definitely getting some better traveling clothes than this ridiculous gown Emmaline put me in." Gwen laughed and spread the skirts of her golden taffeta gown out around her legs. "James, why don't you and Peter come help me pack."

"Okay, I said you could come," Peter groused, "not that I'd be your valet."

Phillip walked over to the bench and sat beside Daniel. He laughed as he watched the others leave the room arguing, and then looked at Daniel. The prince sat staring at him with a smirk. "What?" he asked gruffly.

"So you aren't going back home?"

"Well, I have to fix all these messes I've caused," Phillip pouted and crossed his arms. "This in no way means I've forgiven you for lying to me."

"Phillip," Daniel said as he reached over to uncross Phillip's arms and take his hands, "I never lied to you. I tried to tell you about the insomnia curse but I never got a chance. It's not my fault that you assumed—"

"Assumed?" Phillip jerked his hands from Daniel's. "*I* assumed? Well I… guess… I did assume. But that's beside the point. The only reason I agreed to come out here was I thought you had actually passed that stupid test. That nonsensical, pain-in-my-backside test. I thought it was a sign that you were here to help me." Phillip stared down at the stone floor as he thought about what he had just said. "Which, in hindsight, is maybe not the best basis for making a plan. Look at Gwen's father. He should have waited until he had the full story. Was I really letting a stupid little pea under a mattress control my life?"

"You really thought I was kept awake by a pea under the mattress? Phillip, that makes absolutely no sense. A pea under all those mattresses? Why would you use that as a test?"

"I know. I know. But it was my birthday fairy. Her curse stated that marriage to the wrong person would lead to me losing my throne. So we knew we would have to be very careful with my marriage. As I grew older, I decided that was a good thing because I knew I didn't want to marry a woman and I couldn't marry a man. No marriage, no curse. You know? But a king has to marry, so—"

"But that was your birthday fairy. What about the last fairy who sort of fixes it?"

"Well, that fairy said I would be happy if I waited for 'the one who keeps a vigilant watch in the night.'"

"So someone decided—"

Phillip nodded. "Cauchemar decided that we would test any princess to make sure she was the right one. Princess-testing used to be a pretty common practice in the old days when the seven kingdoms were just one land. Anyway, she interpreted the last part to mean my bride needed to be a girl who could be sensitive enough to know my needs even in the middle of the night. Sensitive enough to feel—"

"A pea under a mattress. That is the craziest thing I've ever heard, and I was cursed with insomnia. Who could pass that test? No wonder all the girls failed."

"Um. Maybe."

"Maybe?"

"Well, a couple of them had a little help falling asleep."

"I don't follow you."

"Okay. Before I tell you this I want you to know that I'm not proud of it at all." Phillip turned his face away. "Also, I realize that

I accused you of lying and I haven't been honest with a bunch of people."

"Phillip," Daniel said, cocking his head, "did you do something to make the girls sleep?"

"I kind of gave them a sleeping tonic."

Daniel stared at Phillip. Phillip watched his eyes move back and forth across Phillip's face as if looking for a sign he was lying. Phillip held his breath as he waited for the blast of anger he knew would arrive. Daniel suddenly threw his head back and erupted in a belly laugh.

"Why you devious little scamp! That is absolutely brilliant. You found a way to play around the rules!"

Phillip released the breath he had been holding. "You don't think I'm a terrible person?"

"Okay. I will admit it was really unfair to do that to all those poor girls, but it *is* hysterical. They get the best night's sleep of their lives, and you get out of a marriage!"

"That's why I said I have to fix the messes I made. Not my stepmother's messes. Mine. They really are princesses, and I'm the reason no one believes they are." Phillip swallowed and shook his head. "If I had just followed the rules, left things alone and married one of the princesses, then none of this would be happening."

Daniel stared at Phillip for a second before making a tut-tutting sound and shaking his head slowly. "And the birthday fairy's curse would have come true!"

"What?" Phillip said in confusion. "No. I would have married—"

"Phillip, you were right about needing to be honest with people, and that includes yourself." Daniel took Phillip's hands in his again and squeezed them. "If you had married one of those girls, you would both be miserable, and you probably would have lost your kingdom. A miserable king makes a miserable kingdom."

"I hadn't thought of it that way." Phillip let the tension slide out of his shoulders as he thought about what Daniel was saying. "So you don't think I'm a terrible person?"

"You are out here trying to make everything right, aren't you? To me you are just proving what I said to King Robert. You are one of the kindest men I have ever known."

"Thank you. And I promise, no more lies."

Daniel suddenly laughed again.

"What's funny now?"

"I was just thinking about that 'vigilant watch in the night' business," Daniel chuckled. "That could almost be me. I mean, who's more vigilant in the night than a man who never sleeps?"

"That is funny," Phillip said, as he joined in Daniel's laughter, "but ridiculous. I mean, two princes can't marry each other."

The two princes laughed loudly together until their laughter died down to silence. Turning to face Daniel, Phillip stared into his eyes. He watched Daniel's eyes crinkle at the edges as he smiled back and tilted his head slightly to one side as if in thought. Phillip's heart beat in his ears and he felt the same urge he had felt in the testing chamber: to lean over and place his lips on the other man's. He lifted his hand to touch the other man's face, but Daniel suddenly stood and walked toward the hallway doors. Phillip felt a rush of heat to his face as he blushed and looked at the floor.

"Well," Daniel broke the silence, "let's go find the others and get on our way. Not going to solve these problems sitting here giggling."

Phillip rushed past Daniel into the hallway, not noticing the other prince lean his head against the doorframe. "Yes," Phillip mumbled, "I should go find Gwen." He raced down the hallway, unsure if the loud thuds in his ears were his footsteps on the cobblestones or the heart pounding in his chest.

# CHAPTER 12

"NINETY-ONE," DANIEL COUNTED, AS HIS HORSE STEPPED off the wide wooden bridge onto the rocky soil on the other side of the wide, rushing river. *When did I start counting again? I don't remember counting anything since I first met Phillip in that ridiculous bed. Of course, it was the cobblestones.* The previous day in the abandoned throne room of Gwen's castle, he had been overtaken by a sudden desire to kiss Phillip. Hoping to suppress the feeling, he had walked away from Phillip to lean his head against a doorframe. He heaved a deep sigh. *No. Two princes can't marry. Two princes. Two. Two, Three, Four...* Suddenly he was counting the cobblestones and trying to steady his breathing. Now he had just counted each step his horse had taken on the bridge across the river.

"Ninety-one whats?" Gwen asked as her horse stepped off the bridge beside him. Her question pulled Daniel out of his thoughts.

"Did I say that out loud?" Daniel asked, with a bit of red coming into his cheeks.

"Yes. Ninety-one whats?"

"Steps. Across the bridge. I count steps. Long story." Daniel turned to watch the rest of the traveling party cross the bridge. "Are we in Upper Lipponia now?"

"Yes," Gwendolyn said. "That was the Rupert River we just crossed and it is the border between Dealonia and Upper Lipponia. Look how rocky it is here. Upper Lipponia is nothing but rocks and dirt. Daddy always said the people here are as harsh as their landscape and have as many rocks in their head as they do on the ground. Lower Lipponia is the prettier half with happier people. It has grassy hills and sheep, and the people live an easy life. Also, those are the Pearl Mountains in the distance. They separate the two halves of Lipponia."

"Why would they call them that?" Phillip asked as he led his horse to the river to drink. "Pearls aren't in mountains. They're in the sea."

"Well, it's getting too dark to see them right now, but when the sun hits them they are the milky color of a pearl. They are really quite beautiful. The locals call them The Teeth."

"I get it," Peter said. "Teeth are like pearls?"

"Well, I guess, but it has more to do with the fact that they run right down the middle of Lipponia."

"I don't get it," James said, as he scratched his blond head.

"The locals call the two kingdoms Upper and Lower Lip. So, The Teeth are between them. There is a passage through the mountains that they call The Tongue."

"That's actually clever," Peter said and laughed. "How do you know all this?"

"I'm a princess of Dealonia," Gwen said with a shrug. "Well, I was. I had to learn all about my neighbors in case I beat Robert to the throne. Plus, I studied all kinds of history and geography when I thought that might be what Phillip's princess-test would be."

"Look, Gwen, I've already apologized for that. It was Cauche-mar's decision, not mine, to do that pea test. Can we stop for a bit? My backside is killing me from all this riding, and I think the horses could use a break."

"I could use a leg stretch too," Daniel said and swung off his horse. "James, can you make a fire? It's going to be dark soon, so we might as well make camp for the night."

"Sure. Gwen, you want to help me find some firewood?"

"How exciting! Can we tell stories? My maids always said the best part of sitting around the fire was telling stories."

As James and Gwendolyn set off into the surrounding scrub looking for firewood, Daniel could hear James saying, "No need to fear mountain lions, my dear. I will protect you."

"If she meets a mountain lion," Peter said, unpacking blankets from his saddlebags, "I feel sorry for the creature. She'll talk his ears off."

After the fire had been built and a meal cooked, the group sat in a circle and listened to Gwen's performance of "The Tragic Tale of the Lips." Daniel glanced out of the corner of his eye to admire Philip's body as he stretched his arms above his head and yawned. Stretching tightened the doublet against his firm chest and pulled the sleeves snug on his toned arms. As Daniel watched the heat of the fire and the weight of the day's travels push down Phillip's eyelids, he saw Phillip shift to lie on his side and rest his head on Daniel's thigh. "Is it okay if I do this?"

"You're not mad at me anymore?" Daniel teased.

"Uh-uh," Phillip muttered. "You mad at me?"

"No, Prince Sleepy," Daniel said as he reached down and brushed a stray lock of hair from Phillip's brow. "It's fine. I won't be sleeping, remember? I'll keep watch."

Phillip smiled at the prince and shifted his attention back to Gwen across the fire. Daniel sighed as he looked at Phillip's features in the flickering firelight. The boy's blue eyes sparkled with laughter as he watched Gwen's performance. Daniel looked at Gwen and played with a lock of Phillip's hair. He laughed as Gwen strutted back and forth with her chest puffed out.

"And King Rupert the Fourth was very proud that his wife would be giving him not one child, but two. The queen complained daily that it felt as if the two babies were waging war on one another in her belly." Gwen grabbed at her abdomen and howled as if in pain, making the boys laugh. "When the day of the blessed event occurred, Rupert called the very old woman who had been his own nanny to help with the delivery of the children." Gwen changed her posture into the stooped frame of an old woman and hobbled back and forth.

"But the old woman had grown nearly blind. The birthday fairies felt particularly devious that year, for they had the boys come out one right after the other." The girl squatted, put her hands on her knees and began panting and screaming in a pantomime of childbirth. As the boys clapped and hooted, she shifted back into the posture of the old woman. "Nanny grabbed each boy as he was born and set him on a table behind her before turning back to check on the good queen. When she turned back around, the two babies were wrestling each other all over the table top. The old woman could not tell which boy had been the one to come out first!"

"That can't be true!" Daniel laughed as he rested his hand casually on Phillip's upper arm.

"Even I couldn't come up with a story this strange," Peter said with a laugh. "What happened next?"

"So, no one knew for sure which boy was supposed to be next in line. Old Rupert thought he would just wait and see if he would receive a sign."

"And?"

"Nope, no sign. The two boys continued to fight each other daily all through their childhood." Gwendolyn bounced and punched the air in front of her face. "When Rupert the Fifth and Frederick the Third turned eighteen, they began to fight for the throne. Eventually, their father threw up his hands and divided the kingdom, east to west, right across the middle. So now we have Upper Lipponia and Lower Lipponia."

"Upper Lip and Lower Lip!" James cried out as the group applauded. "I get it now!"

"Anyway," Gwen said as she dropped onto her blanket between James and Peter, "Old Rupert was worried that the two boys would wage war with each other to gain control of both halves, so he declared that the first to have a male heir would reunite the kingdoms."

"Let me guess…" Daniel said, as he rubbed his fingers up and down Phillip's upper arm.

"Yes, both men had daughters. Marina and Bianca."

"Okay, aren't all these rules kind of stupid?" Peter said. "I guess in a story maybe, but in real life?"

"Well, Old Rupert finally said that the first girl to marry a prince and bring him back to the kingdoms would reunite them."

"I've met them both," Phillip said and shifted his head slightly on Daniel's thigh, his hair tickling Daniel's skin through his tights. "They both tried to marry me."

"And we all know how that turned out," Gwen said with a roll of her eyes. "Now stop interrupting me."

"I think I heard something behind those rocks," Peter said as he slowly lifted up on his elbows.

"Peter, hush. I know you want to be the storyteller, but let me finish."

"Highnesses—"

"Since neither girl passed Phillip's test, no one knows for sure who should rule the kingdoms?" James asked.

"Why not just let them both have their kingdoms?" Phillip mumbled as his eyes drooped. "Why do they have to marry some man to do that? Why do any of us have to get married?"

"Phillip, don't you want to marry?" Gwen sighed as she lay down on her blanket. "Don't you want someone to love you?"

Daniel felt the pleasant weight of Phillip's head leave his thigh as the other prince sat up. "I think I heard something too, Peter."

"Now you're just changing the subject. Don't—" Suddenly a pair of leather-gloved hands grabbed Gwen from behind and dragged her away from the fire. As Daniel jumped up, another pair of hands grabbed him from behind and wrestled him back to the ground. Daniel looked over to see Phillip being lifted by a burly man in a knight's garments. A large ram's head was emblazoned on the man's chest. "Unhand us!" Daniel yelled, as he struggled against the heavy weight of the man pressing on his back. "Do you have any idea who we are? We are royalty!"

"Oh, pardon me," the man on his back growled sarcastically. "Boys! Be sure you curtsy before you tie them up." The man pulled Daniel's arms behind his back. "King Rupert kindly requests your presence in his dungeons. I'll let you respond in person."

"Ooof," Daniel grunted as he landed on the cold stone floor of the tower where the guard had tossed him. As the guards shoved his companions through the door, Daniel had to quickly roll to the side to keep from being crushed. "Careful!" he yelled at the men, as his friends landed in a jumbled pile beside him.

Phillip crossed the cell just as the guard slammed the iron-barred door shut in his face. He shoved his face between the bars and yelled into the hallway beyond, "Where is King Rupert? I demand to speak to King Rupert!"

"No need to shout, boy. It's rude," a tall man with thick gray hair said, as he stepped out of the darkness of the hallway. The man wore a long black tunic with a deep purple overcoat and a large silver crown that looked like a pair of ram's horns curling down around his ears. "I'm right here."

"Do you have any idea who I am?" Phillip demanded, as he shook the bars of the door. "You have no right to imprison me like this!"

"I know perfectly well who you are. You're the boy who ruined my daughter's reputation and all my plans. Your presence in my kingdom can only be seen as an invasion of my lands, since you are most assuredly here without an invitation. I'm within every right I have as king to imprison a man who is clearly here to take over my lands and commit unspeakable acts against my people."

"Unspeakable acts? That's ridiculous. I'm merely here to seek your aid and warn you of a great danger. There may be a woman hiding somewhere within your borders who has made it clear her goals are to conquer every kingdom in Clarameer and rule the realm as her own. My stepmother, Cauchemar, has disappeared, and I can only assume she is hiding and plotting against us all. She had plans to murder my father and me both in cold blood."

King Rupert shook his head and made a tut-tutting sound with his tongue. "Pity."

"Yes. It's true," Daniel added, as he stepped behind Phillip at the door. "I'm Prince Daniel of Sylvania and I can vouch for the truth of Phillip's words. I was there when Cauchemar made an attempt on Phillip's life."

"I'm aware of who you are and that little girl with you too. I see the *Inquisitor* and I know what you've been up to, larking about the kingdoms while Marina and I suffer here. I'm afraid you misunderstood me," King Rupert said with a snide grin. "I meant it is a pity she failed. She could have saved me the bother of having to kill you myself."

"Kill me?" Phillip yelled. He took a step back and bumped into Daniel's chest. "Because I didn't marry your daughter? This is crazy!"

"It's not just that you didn't marry Marina." Rupert spat his words at the prince as he leaned his face between the bars. "You ruined all my plans. You see, my imbecile brother refuses to cede his half of the kingdom to me, even though I know I am firstborn and the rightful ruler of these kingdoms. His stubborn insistence on remaining on the throne has made it necessary for me to come up with some, shall we say, *alternative* methods of removing him from that throne. I need an army to march down The Tongue and take what is rightfully mine."

"Bellemer is a peaceful land. I have no army to give you."

"True," Rupert said, as he moved back from the cell door, "but you have riches. And riches can buy many a soldier's allegiance. I had hoped Marina's marriage to you would bring me the funds that Upper Lipponia lacks. However, you weren't content just to not marry her. No! You had to convince all of the kingdoms that she is not a real princess. Now no king will marry her, and my opportunities for funds have died. I'm afraid you will have to die now, too."

Daniel stepped beside Phillip and shoved his hands through the bars at the king. Pointing his finger at the king's face he yelled, "Killing us will seal your fate. You will have the wrath of Bellemer, Dealonia and Sylvania raining down on your house!"

Rupert grabbed Daniel's finger and pushed it away from his face. "Don't point, boy. It's rude. And don't insult my intelligence. Your bodies won't be found in *my* kingdom. No. My dear brother will be in for quite the surprise when your headless bodies are found in Lower Lipponia, and he is the one accused of your murders."

"Sir," Gwendolyn pleaded as she stepped up to the door, "please have a heart. I had nothing to do with any of this. Isn't there something we can do to change your mind?"

"Why, aren't you a pretty one." Rupert reached between the bars and patted Gwen's cheek. "Those sketcherazzi did you no justice.

If I thought you had a penny to your name, marriage to you might have been a pleasurable alternative. But, alas, no. However, don't you frown, my dear, I'm not a heartless man. Look behind you."

Daniel and Gwen turned to look at the room behind them. In the center of the room, an enormous woven straw basket with hundreds of skeins of multicolored yarn spilling out of the top took up most of the floor space. Next to the basket sat a simple wooden spinning wheel and several piles of thatch and hay, along with bales of raw wool. In the dim light of the torches flickering on the tower walls, Daniel could see the floor was covered with feathers and bird droppings. Looking up, he saw that the tower was slowly crumbling, and half of the thatched roof was missing. The wooden rafters were filled with hundreds of birds that ruffled and cooed. Turning back to the king, Daniel mumbled, "I don't understand."

"This was my late wife's spinning and sewing tower. She and I weren't what you would call close, and she spent most of her days in here working on dresses for our little girl. She never cared for the austere lifestyle of Upper Lipponia. She had her ladies weave that absurdly large basket to hold all of her fabric and thread. I'm afraid, after she died, I let the roof fall into a state of disrepair. Then I remembered the old tale that a true princess could spin straw into gold, so I put Marina in here and set her to work. I thought she could kill two birds with one spin, so to speak. She would prove she is a true princess again by spinning the gold and, conveniently, provide me with the gold I needed to raise my army. It appears, Phillip, your test was correct, though. The idiot girl could spin nothing but yard upon yard of yarn."

"Straw into gold?" Phillip said with a look of disgust. "That's absurd."

"Absurd or not, I suggest you and your little friends here get busy. I see from the *Kingdom Inquisitor* that you proved this girl is not a princess either, so I guess she'll be no help. Since you two appear to still be royals, you may be able to pull it off. If you succeed, I will keep you alive until I have the gold I need. Otherwise, when you see the sunrise through that missing roof tomorrow morning, it will be your last." King Rupert spun on his heel, letting the long tails of his overcoat flare out behind him. He grabbed the large oak door of the chamber and slammed it closed over the iron bars.

Daniel began beating on the wooden door and screaming at the top of his lungs, "Come back here! You cannot do this! Ow!" Daniel jerked his hand back and cradled it in the crook of his arm.

"Daniel! Let me see your hand," Phillip said and took Daniel's hand into his own. "Please, stop. You'll hurt yourself. I need you able to fight if it comes down to that. James, do you think we can overpower them if they come back?"

"Sirs," James said and dropped his head, "I've let you both down. I should've been more aware. I should've fought harder. I should've—"

"James," Daniel interrupted, "can we overcome them?"

"Four of us? With no weapons?" James asked, shaking his head.

"Five of us and one weapon," Gwen said as she pulled the jeweled dagger from a sheath under her skirts. "They didn't find this!"

"A dagger? Against swords? No."

"Phillip?" Peter called out, as he walked over and spun the spinning wheel with his finger. "Did he say Marina tried? The spinning, I mean."

"Yes," Phillip replied and glanced up from Daniel's hand. "Why?"

"Um, where is she now?"

"Oh no. Do you think he—" Daniel gasped as he pulled his hand away from Phillip.

"I'm right here," a voice lilted out from the shadows in the corner of the tower.

Daniel jerked his head in the direction of the voice and breathed a sigh of relief as Marina stepped out into the flickering torchlight. Her red curls frizzed out around her head, and her snug-fitting dress was covered with bits of straw and feathers. Around her neck, she wore a knitted scarf that stretched down to the floor and trailed several feet behind her. She held a ball of yarn in one hand and knitting needles in the other. She kept her head bowed demurely as she stepped over to stand beside the spinning wheel. "You'll have to forgive me. I'm sure I look a sight. My father won't let me have a mirror, so I have no idea what I look like. I miss my mirrors. Do I look bad? How is my hair?"

Daniel watched as Phillip ran over and scooped the girl up into his arms and spun her around. "Marina, you're a beautiful sight in my eyes. I was worried your father had—I don't even want to think about that! Why didn't you let me know you were in here?"

"I was scared for you to see me."

"You were scared? Marina! I'm the reason you're in here! If anyone should've been scared, it's me. This is all my fault. I'm surprised you didn't come after me the minute I was thrown in here and try to stab me with those needles!"

"My dress doesn't fit right," Marina said with a blush, ignoring Phillip's words and fidgeting with the collar of her dress. "I didn't want you to see it."

"What?" Phillip leaned back and eyed the girl up and down. Her dress was a bit tight around her waist and arms. "Why would I care about that?"

"Phillip," Marina said as her bottom lip trembled, "it's been awful in here." As a tear rolled down her cheek, she stared up at the birds in the rafters. "I tried spinning the straw into gold but that didn't work, and there was nothing else to do. So I knitted. A lot." She lifted the yarn and needles in her hand and Phillip could see the yarn was still connected to the end of the scarf around her neck. "But I'm not very good and that made me sad. Plus, looking at all my mother's sewing supplies made me miss her. And that made me sad. I miss my lovely dresses and my hair brushes and my pretty little mirror. And that made me sad. So I ate. A lot. And now my dress doesn't fit right. And that makes me sad. And that makes me want to eat!" The girl flopped onto the pile of straw beside the spinning wheel and bawled.

Phillip looked over to Daniel and Gwen, and Daniel could see the panic dancing in his eyes. Daniel just shrugged, and Gwen rolled her eyes.

"Sweetheart," Phillip cooed, as he knelt down beside the girl and stroked her hair, "that's not important to me. Actually, if you hadn't mentioned it, I never would've noticed. Okay? We can get you out of here and back to your pretty dresses, okay? But I need you to stop crying and help me first, okay?"

Marina sniffled and dropped her head onto Phillip's chest. Rubbing her face across his shoulder, she wiped her running nose on his sleeve. "How can I help you? I was raised to be pretty, not helpful. I don't know what to do."

"Think," Phillip encouraged the girl. "Is there maybe another way out of this tower besides that door?"

"No. Father made the room with only one door, which could be guarded when my mother was in here sewing. That way my uncle in the south couldn't send someone to hurt her. Oh, if only I were really a princess, I'd spin this straw into gold and maybe he'd let us all go. Gwen, do you think you can try?"

"Don't look at me," Gwen said. "I'm no more princess than you are. I failed his test, too. If I were a princess, I'd just ask all these birds to help me."

"You'd talk to the birds?" Peter scoffed. "How could birds help us?"

"They could carry a note to someone," Gwen said with a shrug.

"Spinning straw into gold. Feeling peas under mattresses. Talking to birds. This is all ridiculous." Daniel walked over to Phillip and Marina and kicked the spinning wheel onto its side. "You're a princess because your father is a king. Philip's test has nothing to do with it! Nobody ever expects a prince to go through all of this nonsense. All these silly rules are what got us all thrown in here!"

The two girls stared at Daniel with sour looks on their faces, while James and Peter shuffled from foot to foot by the door.

Phillip walked over to Daniel. "While I appreciate this little lecture on the hypocrisy of our society, it isn't really helping right now. Could you calm down so we can think, please?"

"And none of this chatter is helping either!" Daniel shouted at Phillip, irritation making his face turn red. "We need a plan. A rational plan." Dropping his voice to a whisper, he added, "And you should just tell them both why they failed the test."

"Not the time," Philip hissed through clenched teeth.

"I liked my bird idea," Gwen said with a sniff. "See that little bluebird on the bottom rafter over there? I'd just stick my finger out like this," she said as she held her arm out in front of her. "I'd say 'Mr. Bluebird, come sit on my finger.'"

The bird turned its head toward the girl, unfurled its wings and swooped down from the rafter to land on her extended finger. It sat there chirping and flitting its head back and forth as if awaiting further instruction.

"How did you do that?" Peter rushed to Gwen's side. "Marina, you try."

"Mrs. Owl, can you come here for a second?" Marina called up to a large owl. The owl hooted twice before dropping down to the edge of the large basket in one long dive. It sat staring at the girl, its large yellow eyes unblinking.

"Did you two just talk to birds?" James said with a wide-eyed stare. "You just talked to birds! That is amazing!"

"While this is fascinating," Daniel interrupted the excited chatter, "unless those birds can fight a king and his guards, it doesn't help us much. I need you all to concentrate or King Rupert is going to behead us in the morning."

"Daniel," Phillip said, placing his hand on Daniel's forearm, "they just talked to birds."

"I am aware of that, Phillip, but unless that bluebird can pick me up and fly me out of here then I don't see what—"

"Wait!" Phillip interrupted him with an excited cry. "Oh, Daniel! That's brilliant."

"What?" Daniel shouted.

"Quick, everyone," Phillip ordered the assembled group, "Help me dump all the yarn out of this big basket." He began throwing the skeins of yarn onto the floor. "Once it is empty, we need to tie pieces of this yarn all around the edges of the basket. Then we can all climb inside and Gwen and Marina can ask the birds to grab the yarn in their beaks and just fly us out of here."

"Phillip," Daniel asked, "are you suggesting that we have these birds carry us out of here? Besides the fact that we will probably drop to our death in the process, this is the most ridiculous thing I have heard."

"Really?" Phillip replied, turning to Daniel and placing his hands on his hips. "You just watched two young women talk to birds. A man outside that door wants to behead us because his daughter can't spin straw into gold. My father is in some kind of frozen state because I wouldn't marry a girl my apparently magical stepmother had locked in a tower for eighteen years. You haven't slept in two years because of a fairy curse! Yes, suggesting that birds can carry us out of this tower is clearly the most ridiculous thing in this situation!"

"Well," Daniel mumbled, "I just think that—"

"Are you going to stand there or are you going to help?" Phillip said and stamped his foot. He flung a few more balls of yarn onto the floor. "It just seems to me that in a situation this ridiculous, the most ridiculous answer might be the right one."

Daniel skulked over to the basket and reached in to pull out a handful of yarn. Quickly, the group emptied the basket and began tying lengths of yarn all around its edges. Once the entire perimeter of the basket was covered in strands, James and Peter helped the two young women into the basket. The four men climbed in and they all sat down.

"Oh, birds!" Gwen sang out. "Please be dears and come lift us out of here! Just grab these little strings and away we go!"

Suddenly the tower filled with the sound of hundreds of fluttering wings. Caws and whistles echoed off the stone walls of the tower, as the birds descended and began grabbing the strands.

"Now fly!" Marina called out to the birds.

Slowly the basket began to shift and shake as the birds strained against the weight of the basket's passengers. As the birds began to flap their wings in unison, Daniel could feel the basket lift slightly.

"This is never going to work!" Daniel shouted to Phillip over the deafening fluttering of the bird's wings.

"You just have to believe!" Phillip shouted back. Daniel watched Phillip's smile grow larger and his posture grow taller as the basket shimmied beneath them. "Come on, Daniel, surrender to the ridiculous!"

The basket suddenly jerked hard beneath their backsides and jolted straight up into the air. As the basket rose higher and higher toward the open roof of the tower, Daniel peeked over the edge, to see the floor falling rapidly away. The door was flung open and King Rupert came running into the room, staring in disbelief at the sight of the birds lifting the basket. As he yelled commands at his guards that Daniel couldn't hear over the noise of the birds, the king shook his fist at the sky. Daniel dropped back into the basket and held his breath, as the remnants of the collapsing roof of the tower brushed the sides of the basket. The birds shifted direction and began to fly away from the tower.

Daniel turned to face Phillip. "It's working, Phillip! It is really working!" He pulled the other prince into a long, tight embrace. He could feel Phillip hold his breath and then sink into the warmth of the hug. Daniel pulled back to look into Phillip's blue eyes.

"What?" Phillip said, a look of fear mixed with excitement flashing across his face.

"Oh, nothing," Daniel said with a slight grin, "I'm just surrendering to the ridiculous." As the basket soared into the dark night sky, Daniel pulled Phillip back into his arms, leaned back against the side of the basket and stared at the fluttering birds overhead. As he looked at the twinkling stars far above the flock of birds, Daniel smiled to himself and sighed, "Ridiculous."

# CHAPTER 13

PHILIP WOKE WITH A SHARP GASP AND LIFTED HIS HEAD off Daniel's shoulder as the basket jostled beneath him. He quickly scanned his surroundings as the fog of sleep began to lift. The dark brown straw walls of the basket stretched around him and the blue sky above peeked in and out between the birds carrying the basket.

He could see his traveling companions piled in the corners of the basket. Peter and Marina slept back to back; their heads leaned on the other's shoulder and their mouths were open. In the opposite corner, James leaned against the side of the basket with his head resting on top of Gwen's head and his arms wrapped protectively around her shoulders. Gwen had her head nestled into James's chest, and a trail of drool ran from the corner of her mouth onto the acorns embroidered on his surcoat.

Philip shifted his weight in discomfort; the woven walls scratched at his skin, and he had a sharp pain in his neck from sleeping with his head crooked at an awkward angle. A soft breath against his ear pulled him out of the last bit of sleepy haze, and he became aware of the warm arms wrapped tightly around his waist.

"Good morning, handsome," a voice as warm as a velvet glove purred in his ear. "Silly birds dragged us across the top of a pine tree. I was hoping you'd sleep a little longer."

Phillip shifted to look into Daniel's face. The prince sat smiling at him and reached over to rub his thumb along Phillip's cheek. Phillip leaned his face into the warmth of the man's hand and blinked the sleep out of his eyes. "Daniel," Phillip said with a yawn and a grin, "good morning. I'm sorry I fell asleep against you."

"No problem. Did you sleep well?"

"My neck is killing me, but it felt good to sleep. How did you sleep?"

"Insomnia, remember?" Daniel said with a grin, as he ruffled Phillip's hair.

"Oh, right. Where are we?" Phillip asked, as he sat up and looked around.

"Still up in the air, despite my worst fears. You know, Phillip, I know you don't think you are ready to be a king, but this was a brilliant plan. That's what a king does when he is presented a problem. He figures out a way to solve it and proceeds. If we had followed my thinking, we'd still be stuck in that tower. But you knew what to do. Like a king would."

Phillip blushed and lowered his chin. Looking up at Daniel through his lashes, he sighed, "You think so?"

"I do, Your Majesty," Daniel said with a wink, as he grabbed the edge of the basket. "Now, let's stand up and see if we can see anything. We crossed The Teeth last night so I figure we're somewhere over Lower Lipponia by now."

The basket bobbled beneath them as the two princes stood and rested their arms on the edge. The shaking of the basket woke the other occupants, and Phillip could hear their grunts and groans as each fumbled into the morning. Looking out, Phillip took in the lush green hills and valleys spreading out as far as he could see. Lower Lipponia was so much greener than her sister nation to the north! Small farmhouses with thatched yellow roofs sat atop the hills, surrounded by split rail fences and small gardens.

Sheep grazing along the sides of the hills looked to Phillip like dandelion fluff scattered along the hills by the breath of a child. A short distance in front of the basket, a large stone castle with five turrets and rippling purple flags glistened in the morning sun.

"Look," Phillip said, pointing toward the building, "that must be the castle of the Lower Lipponian king. We should land there and seek his help with Cauchemar. Birds! Can you please take us down in the courtyard of the castle?"

"I don't think they are listening to you." Daniel turned to Marina and asked, "Could you ask the birds to land us over there?"

Marina stepped to the edge of the basket and lifted her hand. "Mr. Bluebird? Can you come down here?" The tiny bird leading the flock dropped the yarn from its beak and flitted down to land on her finger. It sat looking into her face and ruffled its wings. "Could you please take us over there to that pretty castle?" The bird twittered and peeped at the girl. "Yes, I know you're all tired and I'm sorry if we were heavier than you expected, but if you will just set us down in that castle, then you can go about your day."

The bird hopped twice on her finger and then flew up into the flock of birds. The basket jostled its passengers to one side as the birds suddenly changed direction to head toward the castle. The basket began descending rapidly; the bottom scraped across the tile roof of one of the castle's turrets.

"Birds!" Gwen yelled and grasped the side of the basket so hard her knuckles turned white. "Gently, please."

As the basket glided over the center of the castle's courtyard, the birds opened their beaks and released all the threads holding the basket up. It dropped with a loud "thump" and toppled onto its side, dumping the passengers onto the cobblestones in a jumbled pile of arms, legs, crowns and gowns. As Phillip shifted and pulled against the ground to free himself from the pile of bodies, he saw a man running across the courtyard straight for him. The man's thick gray hair fluttered in the breeze, and his deep purple surcoat flapped behind him. As the man drew closer, Phillip noticed he was wearing a silver crown in the shape of ram's horns and recognized the man as his most recent captor.

"Daniel! James! Peter! Get up!" he yelled as he scrambled to his feet. "King Rupert is here! Stand up and attack him with me!"

"By Gingerfair's girdle!" James exclaimed, as he leaped to his feet and reached for the sword at his waist. "Blast, I forgot he took our swords!"

"How did he get here so fast?" Peter interjected, as he slipped behind Gwen and peeked over her shoulder.

Phillip and Daniel squared their shoulders and prepared to face the approaching king. Just as Phillip was preparing to take a swing at the king's head, Marina came rushing past him and raced across the courtyard toward the man. "Uncle Frederick!" the girl cried as she jumped into his open arms. "Boys! Calm down! This is my father's twin brother, King Frederick!"

"Marina, dear!" Phillip heard the old man say, as he spun the girl around before setting her gently back down. "Where have you been hiding away? I haven't laid eyes on you since that horrible Prince Phillip ruined Bianca's and your reputations. If he were here right now, why, I'm not sure I could be trusted not to put his head on a spike. The headache he has created for me—"

"Uncle," Marina interrupted with a little giggle, "but he is here! Look over there!"

"What?" King Frederick stomped across the courtyard toward the assembled group. "Guards! Grab this man and fling him from the highest turret! No! Tie him down in the courtyard and let the birds feast on his liver! No! Even that is too kind. Quick," the king said as he snapped his fingers and then scratched his head, "someone tell me a good punishment I can give to this—"

Peter stepped from behind Gwen and said, "You could cover him in honey and let the ants—"

"Peter!" Phillip yelled, as he turned to the boy with a glare. "Whose side are you on?"

"Sorry," Peter mumbled and stepped back behind Gwen. "I can't help it. I just have good ideas."

"King Frederick," Phillip said, as he turned back to the king and offered a deep bow, "there will be no need to punish me. I have been punished already by the near murder of my father. I've come to seek forgiveness from you and Princess Bianca, and to request your assistance in rescuing my father and bringing his attacker to justice."

"Nice speech," Frederick said. "And while I am sorry your father was attacked, I have problems enough of my own. Problems you created, in fact."

"I'm sure anything I created can be, um, uncreated? I'll gladly do what I can, if you'll just help me."

"Well, you set her on this path. Maybe you can knock her off it as well. Follow me," the king said with a sigh, as he turned to go back into the castle. He held out his hands to his niece and escorted her beside him. "So, Marina, what news do you have of my simple-minded brother?"

"Uncle, he has lost his mind!" Marina said in an excited trill, as she took Frederick's arm. "He is so determined to conquer you, it eats at his every thought. Oh, speaking of eating, can we have some breakfast? I'd love some hot buttered bread and maybe some milk? Oh, and something sweet? Anyway, he is insane with rage! He locked me in a tower and made me do peasant work! Which I was terrible at, by the way. Have you ever tried to spin? It's hard and makes you really hungry! What was I saying? Oh, yes. He was going to kill my new friends and blame it on you. And I didn't tell you the worst part, he let me eat too much and gain this weight and now..."

Phillip watched as the king and his niece disappeared through the large open doors of the castle, the girl's scattered prattle fading with each step they took. Without thinking, Phillip took Daniel's hand and pulled him along inside.

"What problems is he talking about?" Peter asked James.

"At this point, I've stopped trying to guess," James said with a shrug before taking Gwen by the arm and turning to follow the princes.

PHILLIP HELD DANIEL'S HAND IN A TIGHT GRIP AS THEY ENTERED the throne room. As he looked around at the tall marble columns the held up the lapis- and jade-bedecked ceiling and the long wool tapestries that hung along the walls, Phillip realized that what he and his father called a throne room was definitely lacking. The pastoral scenes of shepherds and peasant girls on the tapestries were arranged in a manner that led Phillip's eyes to the far end of the room, where the king's throne sat beneath the family sigil of a ram's head on a purple banner.

The king and Marina stood a few feet in front of the throne, and the king was arguing with a young girl, who sat on the throne and wore a large silver crown. Her high cheekbones and slightly olive skin showed she was of Gloriannan heritage, like Daniel. Her small, bright red mouth was drawn downward in a sour frown as she argued with the king. Seeing the sleek cascade of raven black hair falling over the girl's shoulders from beneath her crown, Phillip instantly knew who she was.

"It's Bianca," he whispered to Daniel, as they approached the throne. "Frederick's daughter."

"Failed your test?" Daniel whispered back.

"Yes. Without any help from me, either. I found her dead to the world in the bed when I came in to say goodnight and offer her my potion. Snoring like an Osterling boar! But I have no idea what she is doing up there." Phillip looked at the girl sitting on the throne and chewed his lip.

"I said, Daddy, that I don't care if it is my birthday fairy herself who is here to see me, I will not be interrupted while Lady Fiona and I are having our breakfast and… well, look who's here! Fee," Bianca said with a sharp laugh, as she turned to a petite blonde woman standing shyly behind the throne, "look who has the nerve to show up in *my* throne room after telling the whole land that I wasn't a real princess. Can you believe he would just waltz right in here?"

The blonde girl—Lady Fiona, as Phillip assumed—giggled and shook her head before ducking behind the throne and peering back at him through the filigree around its edges. She whispered something into Bianca's ear. Bianca cocked her eyebrow and looked back and forth between Phillip and Daniel. "I think you're right, Fee. That does look like the man in the *Kingdom Inquisitor*. You there, are you Prince Daniel?"

"Yes, Bianca, we've met before. Remember? When you came to meet my brother for a possible marriage?"

"Ah, yes. Andrew, that pompous nitwit," Bianca said with a roll of her eyes. "Fee, you remember what I told you about him? The one who couldn't take his eyes off his own reflection long enough to notice me? What a jackass!" Bianca held out her hand to Fiona and led her around to sit on the arm of the throne and then rested her hand on the girl's thigh.

"Yes," Daniel said with a nod, "that would be Andrew."

"Well, Phillip, if this one is anything like his brother, I don't see how you can stand him. But, eh, to each his own, right? If you want to take him as your companion then—"

"Oh! No, no, no," Phillip interrupted her, "Daniel is just my friend. He is helping me on my quest." Phillip felt Daniel drop his hand and step away. Turning to look at the other prince, he saw Daniel staring at him, his mouth agape and disappointment in his eyes. Phillip screwed up his face and said quietly, "Daniel?" The other prince closed his mouth, shook his head and stepped over to stand with James and Gwen. As he turned back to the throne, Phillip saw Fiona whispering into Bianca's ear again.

"Yes, Fee, men are stupid. He'll figure it out eventually. So, Phil, what're you here for?"

Glancing in Daniel's direction, Phillip tried to gather his thoughts, unsure of what his words had just made happen. He stammered, "Um... I was..."

"Spit it out, boy. You can fix things with him later. You're all keeping me and the lady here from a good breakfast."

"Yes," Phillip said, as he shook his head to clear his mind, "I'm here to warn you about an evil sorceress who has placed a spell on my father and who is intent on conquering all the kingdoms. I figured, Princess Bianca—"

"First, I am going to stop you right there. It's Queen Bianca. And second, whatever you are about to ask, I will help you, because you already did me a favor."

"What favor did I do?" Phillip asked as he looked back and forth between Frederick and Bianca. "And queen? But your father is still—"

"See, young man," King Frederick moaned as he threw up his hands, "I told you that your test had made a mess!"

"It's not a mess. It's simple facts, Daddy." Bianca rolled her eyes and shifted on the throne. She smoothed the purple fabric of her gown across her thighs and reached up to adjust the silver crown on her head. "Yes, Phil, you did me a favor with that absurd princess-test of yours. When I left your castle, I wasn't sure what I was going to do. I loved being a princess! If I wasn't a princess, I was going to have to give up my favorite lady-in-waiting, Lady Fee here. Then it dawned on me, I'm *not* a princess."

"Well, Bianca, the test isn't perfect," Phillip offered as he lifted his hands in front of him.

"No!" She silenced him by raising her hand. "You don't understand. I'm not a princess because I am a *queen*! Why should I sit around waiting for this old lump to keel over?" She gestured toward her father. "I'm ready to be queen now. Queen Bee! It even sounds correct!"

"Bianca," the king wailed, approaching the throne, "we've been over this. You cannot be the queen until I step down and until you are married. Those are the rules!"

"Rules?" Bianca threw her head back and stabbed the air with a sharp, single laugh. "Ha!" Her father scurried down from the throne. "Don't you see, Daddy? Phil changed the rules when he decided he could just go around convincing people that we aren't real princesses. I decided that, not only am I ready to be queen, I'm ready to make some new rules. If you don't like it, Daddy, there are several very comfortable cells in the dungeons where you could have quite a home."

"But marriage—" the king whined.

"Oh, I'm getting married."

"To whom?" Marina gasped, ran up to the throne, and grabbed her cousin's hands in excitement. "Did you find a nice prince to marry? Tell me all about him. Maybe over that breakfast?"

"A prince?" Bianca giggled and cocked her eyebrow. "Not quite. You know, I've been shipped all over the kingdoms to meet prince after prince. Gwen's cousin, Robert? All he wanted to do was talk about pastries and farming. Daniel's brother was a jackass. Then Phillip convinced everyone I'm a fraud. Every time they shipped me off it never worked out, and every time I couldn't wait to get back home to tell Lady Fee all about it." Bianca looked at Fiona and winked. "On my way home from Phillip's castle, it all became clear. I didn't want to marry one of those princes. I wanted to spend my time with Fee. Queen Bee and Lady Fee! It just makes sense."

"You're going to marry a woman?" Phillip asked with a gasp. He blinked his eyes as he registered what Bianca was suggesting. Though he had suggested marriage to Daniel in the testing chamber as a way to get his stepmother to leave him alone, this was not something Phillip had ever considered as an actual possibility. "Can you do that?"

"Why not?" Bianca asked with a shrug. "Phillip, what's the point of having power if you can't use it to be happy?" Grabbing Fiona's hand, Bianca placed a small kiss on her palm. "It's funny. When I met you, Phillip, I thought you were the saddest person I'd ever met, but I've found true happiness thanks to your sadness. So, I owe you a favor. Just name it, and I'll do what I can." Bianca stood; the silver crown slipped a bit. She led Lady Fiona down the steps to stand beside Phillip.

"But what about your people? What will they think?" Phillip asked.

"Phil," Bianca said, as she placed her hands on the prince's shoulders, "most people are just trying to live their lives and find their own happiness. And that applies to your people as well as mine. When they first see your choice, they may think it's strange, but eventually they will understand that you want happiness just like they do. They may not realize it now, but your happiness benefits the kingdom, because a happy king is a benevolent king. We're all better off when we just let people be happy." Tightening her grip on Phillip's shoulders, Bianca turned him around to face Daniel and whispered into his ear, "Sometimes happiness is right in front of you. Even if it seems ridiculous, just be happy."

Phillip looked at the group. In the center of the small crowd stood Daniel, staring at the floor with his dark brows angled down. With his arms crossed over the embroidered acorns on his doublet's breast and his foot tapping on the marble floor, Daniel looked more like a petulant child than the brave man Phillip had come to know. *Why is he that angry when I merely spoke the truth?* Watching Daniel fume, he wanted to erase that frown and never be the source of that angry look again. He wanted to be a source of happiness for Daniel, too. Phillip knew he wanted Daniel to come and stand with him, and, if Bianca's words were true, then maybe he could.

"Surrender to the ridiculous?" Phillip whispered with a short laugh.

"Exactly," Bianca whispered back, before turning to address her cousin. "Now, Marina, what're you doing here?"

"Oh, cousin! Phillip and his friends rescued me!" Marina stuttered out. "My father's mind has gone off the edge of the Pearl Mountains! He locked me in a tower, and I really ate too much, and he was going to behead us all and frame your father and try to take over your kingdom, and he's just become awful, and I'm starving."

"Then go home, claim your throne and throw him in the dungeon!" Bianca belted out, scrunching up her nose.

"Oh, I can't do that," Marina said and flipped her strawberry curls over her shoulder. "Especially not on an empty stomach."

Lady Fiona bent to Bianca's ear and whispered something. "You are right, Fee," Bianca said and frowned at her cousin. "I can't have her staying here. I've got to convince my people to accept two queens. Three of us will be just too confusing."

"Well, I don't want to go back to that awful place," Marina pouted and stamped her foot. "You're much stronger than me. Why don't you overthrow him and bring the Lips back together? He has no money and hardly any army. You can have that miserable kingdom, for all I care. Just make sure he pays for putting me in that tower!"

"Fine," Bianca said and nodded her head. "But what will you do?"

"You know," Daniel interrupted as he stepped up to the two women and shot Phillip a dirty glance, "there is a prince in Sylvania who needs a bride. Why don't you come home with me?"

"Daniel?" Phillip gasped. "What are you doing?"

"Andrew. My brother, Andrew?" Daniel said with a roll of his eyes. "What did you think I meant? Me?"

"Well, I—"

"Anyway, why would you care, Phillip? I'm just a friend helping you on a quest, right?" Daniel turned sharply on his heel and began to walk out of the room. "Some of us know what we want."

"What just happened?" Phillip asked, turning to Bianca. His heart sunk into his stomach as heard the other prince's departing footsteps echo around the hall.

"Ouch," Bianca said. "Good luck with that, Phil. Now, we can't have you walking all the way to Sylvania. I'll have my guards get you a carriage and weapons. If there really is a madwoman intent on killing us all, you'll need weapons. Fee? Please ask the guards to arrange that, and ask the cooks to send up some breakfast."

"Finally!" Marina said, clapping her hands.

Phillip watched as Daniel disappeared through the throne room's doors. Though he wasn't exactly sure what he had done wrong, Phillip knew this was something he needed to fix. He needed

Daniel by his side. However, Phillip felt a nagging worry in his stomach that this was something he couldn't undo.

"I've lost my appetite," Phillip said as he turned to follow Daniel out of the room.

# CHAPTER 14

"WHERE'S MY BABY BOY?" QUEEN RHEA FLUNG HER arms wide and motioned Daniel to come into her embrace. The full skirts of her forest green taffeta gown rustled with the movement, but Daniel noticed that her perfectly coiffed hair, dark as his own and pulled back into a tight chignon, did not move an inch. The tasteful emeralds she wore at her neck and ears glistened, but not as brightly as her eyes, which were green like his own. Daniel hurried across the room and flung himself into her embrace, pressing his cheek tight against hers.

"Mother, I'm twenty years old. I haven't been your baby for years."

"Pish," she said with a roll of her eyes, "I don't care if you make it to one hundred, you will always be my baby boy. Now, come," she said and pointed at the overstuffed green velvet seat of the chair beside her, "sit with your old mother and tell me all about your adventures! I've had tea and your favorite cakes sent up from the kitchens. Your brother says you've been making front page news in that horrible *Inquisitor* thing that he seems to think passes for real news. You've followed my advice, right? Not embarrassing the family, I hope."

Daniel waited for his mother to sit before he flopped onto the chair. He was glad she had decided to greet him in the privacy of her room instead of making him share their reunion with Andrew and his new friends in the throne room. The small sitting room off her sleeping chamber had always been one of Daniel's favorite places. On rainy childhood days, she would tuck him into this very chair and read him tales of brave knights and beautiful ladies while they shared his favorite cakes. Over time, the luxurious jade silk covering the tables and windows and the soft velvet of the chair had come to feel like his mother's own embrace.

"No, Mother," Daniel said with a blush, "I think Andrew has greatly over-reported the facts of my activities, as usual. To be honest, I can't believe he noticed a story about me, since it had nothing to do with him. I haven't actually seen that week's paper, but from what I hear, it's just stories about James, our new friends and me being spotted outside a pub where we found lodging for the night. Those absurd sketcherazzi that Andrew adores were there that night and couldn't resist a troop of royals."

"And this red-headed girl they tell me you've brought to meet Andrew? She was there?"

"Oh no, that was in Bellemer. We didn't find… um… I mean meet Marina until we were in Upper Lipponia." Daniel laughed. "You should have seen Andrew when he met Marina! I don't think I've ever seen him be quiet that long! All he could say was 'you're lovely.'"

"Yes," the queen joined in Daniel's laughter. "He definitely inherited your father's gift of gab."

"She's a wonderful girl, mother, if a bit chatty. But that won't bother Andrew, since he never really listens to anyone anyway. I can vouch for her royalty though. I saw her talk to—"

"You know I'm not concerned with such things," the queen said, with a dismissive wave. "And your little sleeping problem?"

"Curse, mother. You can say curse. No. No change there yet. Ironically, it was an attempt to cure it that let me meet Prince

Phillip of Bellemer." Daniel dropped his chin to look at his feet and shuffled them while he grinned to himself.

"Yes," the queen responded with a gentle smile, "Andrew mentioned you had some boy with you. He is the son of Henry and Marie, isn't he? Oh they are delightful people! Your father almost married Marie but Henry scooped her up first! So tell me all about him. Is he, well, your someone special?"

"Mother!" Daniel said with his eyes opened wide. He shifted in his chair and pulled at the collar of his doublet.

"Oh come now, my dear, I may be old, but I am not an old fool. I told you to look for love out there. So, have you found it?"

Daniel chose his words carefully. "He is wonderful, Mother. I don't think I have met a kinder soul in my life. Okay, he started out a little timid, but on this trip I have watched him grow braver and truer. And smart? Oh, Mother, he's so smart. He will make a wonderful king someday."

"And handsome?" the queen asked.

"The handsomest," Daniel sighed. "Look," he said as he pulled the drawing he had snatched from the sketcherazzo from his pocket. He laid the paper on the tea table so that his mother could see. He smoothed the edges of the paper and traced the outline of Phillip's face.

"Ah, yes." The queen leaned over to look at the picture. "He has his mother's looks. I can see why he would—how would I say it—appeal? Yes, appeal to you."

"Doesn't matter, though." Daniel shrugged and pushed the picture away. "He sees me as a friend. He's not interested."

"How could anyone resist my darling baby boy?" the queen asked, as she pinched Daniel's cheek.

"Well, I think he might be interested, but he knows he has to take the throne and that means taking a bride or being alone." Daniel looked at his mother and frowned. "He takes his future role very seriously and, well, that's a path that doesn't really include falling in love with another man."

The queen sat thinking for a minute before she patted Daniel's knee. "Daniel, have I ever told you the story of how your father and I met?"

"No."

"Well, you know he was living incognito in Glorianna to study at our renowned university. Your father was such a smart man! Anyway, every morning, your father would get up and walk out of the house he was living in and turn to the right to walk to his classes. One morning, though, he woke up to discover that a large hay cart had overturned in the street and blocked his usual path. So, he turned to the left to find a different way to the school. The path he took led him past a small café where my ladies-in-waiting and I would go every morning for wonderful little pastries. Oh, I haven't thought of those pastries in years." The queen paused, closed her eyes, and took a deep breath. "I can almost smell them now."

She opened her eyes again and continued, "Anyway, your father passed by and saw me sitting there. He said he fell in love instantly. After class, he came back and paid the owner of that café an exorbitant amount of gold to find out my name and to reserve the table next to mine for the rest of the week. The next morning when I arrived, there he sat with a tray of pastries and his beautiful face. He missed his morning class every day that week. Can you imagine? Every day that week. The rest is, as they say, history."

"That's nice, Mother, but—"

"Don't you see the point, my child?" The queen shook her head and poked Daniel in his arm. "Come now, think about it. If your father had not found a different path that morning, we may have never met."

"Yes but I don't see what—oh!" Daniel saw his mother break into another smile as her meaning dawned on him.

"Sometimes, my dear," she cooed, "to find true love, you have to find a different path."

Daniel sat still and let his mother's words sink in. He studied the lines of Phillip's face in the sketch. The artist had caught Phillip staring at the crowd with a look of complete wonder; the eyes in the drawing, Phillip's beautiful blue eyes, seemed to stare out at Daniel in wonder as well. Daniel had watched those eyes move from tears to fear to quiet strength on their journeys. This was the face that he had seen when he opened his eyes in the testing chamber and that he now anxiously awaited seeing every morning. In the drawing, Phillip's lips were barely parted, as if he were about to say something to Daniel. *What does he want to say? What do I want to say?*

"Daniel?" the queen interrupted his thoughts.

He stood up abruptly. "Mother, you have to excuse me—"

"Go, baby boy. Find him." The queen glanced down at the sketch and then back at Daniel. "You two should take a walk in the Western Woods. They are lovely this time of year."

"Thank you," Daniel spun on his heel and rushed toward the door. Stopping suddenly, he turned back and ran over to the table to pick up the drawing and shove it into his pocket. "Wish me luck!" he said with a grin, as he turned to run out of the room.

"Good luck," the queen called after him. Folding her hands in her lap, she smiled and said, "Find your own path!"

DANIEL'S MOTHER HAD SPOKEN CORRECTLY. THE WESTERN WOOD was just as gorgeous as Daniel had remembered it. Sunlight danced lazily through the thick canopy of leaves and scattered flecks of bright green and yellow across the floor of the forest. As a child, this had been his favorite place to explore with James and Emmaline and every tree, shrub, and path was like an old friend who had been waiting patiently for his return. Even the songbirds in the trees overhead were whistling airs of joy that seemed to say, "Welcome home, boy. Where've you been?" Daniel paused in a small clearing to let the sunlight play across his shoulders and to feel the warm breeze tickle his hair. Breathing in deeply, he could smell the damp air from the recent rain that covered the leaves with a glimmering sheen.

Ahead of him, Phillip stepped carefully over stones and roots in his path as he worked his way toward the stone gazebo. After his mother's chambers, the gazebo was Daniel's favorite childhood hiding place to read or simply lie on his back daydreaming. As soon as his mother had suggested a walk in the woods, Daniel knew he had to share this spot with Phillip. He had rushed to find the other prince and suggested the walk. Knowing Phillip hated the close, leafy embrace of the forest, he had feared he would be met with a "no" but, to Daniel's relief, Phillip had eagerly accepted, and they had set out.

Now, Phillip paused to catch his breath beneath the spreading branches and deep pink flowers of a large frogberry tree. Daniel watched as the prince stretched his arms over his head and took a deep breath; the hem of his doublet rode up slightly and the fabric pulled tight across his firm chest. The sunlight falling through the branches glinted off the strands of gold in Phillip's brown hair, and the sky and the blossoms around his head seemed to be mirrored in the blue of Phillip's eyes and the pink of his lips. *He is the beauty of my woods.* Seeing Phillip surrounded by the woods that until now had been his greatest love, Daniel knew what he wanted. Standing there, he felt like one of the forest's trees, with his feet firmly rooted in the ground, as strength, confidence and courage flowed into his limbs from the dark soil.

"I will tell him."

A stronger wind suddenly blew through the frogberry's branches and sent a shower of bright pink petals falling around the other boy. Phillip threw his head back and his arms out to let the petals fall delicately on his body before laughing and spinning slowly, dancing in the flutters of pink and white.

"I think these woods like you!" Daniel called out to him. "They're offering you a gift." Daniel chuckled as Phillip stopped spinning and looked in his direction; a grin spread across his face before he clumsily tottered on unstable legs and fell gracelessly onto his backside.

"Careful there." Daniel giggled as he walked up to Phillip's side and offered his outstretched hand to the prince.

"Woods are impossible!" Phillip said and then blew his bangs off his forehead with a quick puff of breath. "The sandy shores of Bellemer are much easier to walk on. But the gift is nice," he said as he picked a few pink petals off his shoulder and let them fall to the ground. Phillip took Daniel's hand and let himself be pulled up. The two men stood face to face, holding hands in silence until Phillip said, "Thank you for bringing me here. It's more beautiful than I could've imagined."

"Well," Daniel said, as he brushed a last blossom off Phillip's arm, "I really wanted to share this with you and I thought we could use a little time away from everyone else." Daniel slid his hand down Phillip's arm and took his other hand. "There are some things I want to say."

"Yes. I'm glad you brought me here," Phillip said with a grin, as he squeezed Daniel's hands. "I was worried you were done with me after what I said in Bianca's throne room, and I wanted to explain."

"Phillip, there is no need to explain. She made an assumption," Daniel said with a shrug. "She wasn't the only one in the room making assumptions. I wanted to apologize for storming out. I just want to tell you—"

"Please, let me go first," Phillip interrupted. "There *is* a need to explain. I was caught off guard and I didn't know what to say when she called you my companion."

"Well, it was a bit blunt to say to people she barely knew."

"Yeah, I guess so," Phillip shrugged, "but that's not what I mean. I was caught off guard to hear someone say out loud what I'd been afraid to think. But a part of me…" he stuttered, "knew… well, knew she was right. I really think I knew that night when we escaped King Rupert in the basket. I know I told you I slept through the night, but that isn't exactly true.

"At first, I couldn't fall asleep," Phillip continued, "because I was terrified we would be dropped or crash into the mountains or who knows what. But then I remembered you were there, just like you have been since that first night in my castle. You have been by my side the whole time, with no gain for yourself."

Phillip paused and tugged at the sleeve of his shirt. Daniel's heartbeat quickened as Phillip seemed to search for the right words.

"I was just about to ask you why you stayed when you pulled me close to your chest. I suddenly didn't feel so scared, and for the first time since I can't remember when, I didn't feel alone. Your arms around me were so warm and comforting that I just felt safe. Before I knew it, I was waking up the next morning still in your arms and still safe." Phillip raised his head and gazed into Daniel's eyes. "I thought 'maybe Daniel *is* him.'"

"Him?" Daniel asked with a quirk of his eyebrow, not daring to believe that Phillip meant what Daniel hoped he meant.

"The one who keeps a vigilant watch in the night." Phillip held his breath while he stared into Daniel's eyes. Daniel held his gaze while he felt excitement bubble up from his chest into his face. Before speaking, he took a deep breath, trying to calm his racing mind and heart.

"Phillip," Daniel said, as he shifted his eyes up to the sky and blinked, "that night in the basket meant something to me, too." Daniel lowered his face and locked eyes with Phillip. "You told me to surrender to the ridiculous, but I surrendered to *you*. The courage you showed putting us all in that basket. The absolute faith you put in the magic of that moment. The kindness you have shown Gwen and Marina, and your need to make things right with all the princesses. Your devotion to your father and your kingdom. These are all things I wish I had in myself. But if I can't have them in myself, then I at least need them in my life."

"As that basket sailed quietly over the mountains, I just looked down," Daniel continued, as he cupped Phillip's face in his hands. "I saw this beautiful face sleeping peacefully on my chest, and I thought, 'I will gladly never sleep again if it means I can see this face every night.'"

"Oh, Daniel!" Phillip cried, as he flung his arms around Daniel's shoulders and nuzzled his face into his neck.

"Hold on," Daniel warned and pushed Phillip back. "Nothing has changed here. You still have your duties. You still have to marry and take the throne."

Phillip threw his head back and laughed. "A wise, if somewhat blunt, woman recently changed my mind on that too! Daniel, those rules were written by and for different people. Not us. These are our lives. Why should we not write our own rules for happily ever after?"

"Can we do that?"

"Well, I *am* going to be king you know. Kings get to write the rules."

"Well, you'll be king if someone marries you."

"I've got someone in mind," Phillip replied with a wink.

"The one who keeps a vigilant watch in the night?" Daniel asked, as he tugged Phillip's hands to bring the other man closer. Pulling Phillip into his arms, he whispered into his ear, "I'd like to be him."

"Daniel?" Phillip asked, leaning his head back to look Daniel in the eyes, "can I do something I've wanted to do since I first saw this handsome face pretending to sleep in my bed?"

"Sure," Daniel replied with a sly smirk.

Tilting his head, Phillip leaned his face closer and closer to Daniel's waiting lips. Daniel held his breath as he waited for their lips to touch.

Just as their mouths were about to meet, the sound of someone crashing through the bushes made both men jerk their heads aside.

"Prince Phillip! Prince Daniel!" Peter yelled. He rushed to them before leaning over and grabbing his side in pain. Desperately trying to catch his breath, he panted a few times before blurting out, "You've got to come back to the castle immediately!"

Daniel quickly pulled away from Phillip and grabbed Peter by the shoulders. "What happened?"

"Peter? What is it? Did Cauchemar show up there? Has she attacked Daniel's castle?"

"My mother? Is my mother okay?"

Peter shook his head and gulped a few more breaths of air. "Sorry... I ran the whole way."

"What is it?" Philip cried, his voice cracking in fear.

"Prince Andrew... Princess Marina..." Peter bent at the waist and rested his hands on his knees as he gasped for breath. "Whew, it was a lot farther out here than I expected."

"Peter! Tell us!"

"After going on and on about Marina being the most beautiful creature he had ever seen, Andrew proposed marriage to Marina.

And—though I can't believe it—she accepted! The birthday fairies have shown up to give their blessings!"

Daniel's eyes grew wide. "You mean the fairies are in my family's castle right now?"

"Yes!" Peter crowed. "I thought they might be able to help us find Katerina."

"Daniel," Phillip said, "maybe they will tell you how to end your curse!"

"Forget my curse! They may know how to help your father!" Daniel exclaimed, as he grabbed Phillip's hand and began pulling him along the path back to the castle. "Come on! Let's go!"

"Hang on, Father," Phillip said, as they began to run, "help is on the way!"

# CHAPTER 15

"THIS PARTY IS A BIT MUCH, DON'T YOU THINK?" JAMES said with a grunt as he sat down on the bench beside Gwen. The green velvet ribbons on his chest fluttered, and the heavy gold scabbard he wore around his waist knocked against the bench. The girl grabbed her goblet of wine to keep it from toppling over and shot an irritated look at the knight.

"We've never had this many candles burning in the entire castle in the whole twenty years I lived here. It has to be hotter in this room than in the kitchens, and Queen Rhea made me wear this ridiculous fancy tunic. Had I known Andrew would turn the room into an inferno…" James gestured around the large open hall, where hundreds of candles blazed in large brass candelabra shaped like trees. Three long tables stretched along the opposite wall, each covered with heavy brocade cloths in the Sylvanian colors of brown and green. Two of the tables were overloaded with bowls of fruits, trays of pastries and three roasted pigs. The third table held an enormous cake, decorated with ribbons and bows in Sylvanian green and Lipponian purple.

At the far end of the hall, behind the thrones where Andrew and Marina sat holding hands and gazing longingly at each other, minstrels played dancing tunes on their lutes. The seven birthday fairies sat at a table that spanned the front of the raised throne platform, each bobbing her head along with the music.

"I think it's pretty," Gwen said with a shrug. "An engagement is a special event, so it deserves something special. I still don't know how the cooks managed to make that big cake on such short notice. Honestly, Andrew had only known Marina a few hours when he proposed."

"Well, he clearly finds her attractive. He actually stopped looking at his own reflection long enough to notice her and propose. He even said Daniel was the first to finally find a girl beautiful enough to be his queen."

"Honestly?" Gwen said with a sour face. James rolled his eyes in response. Gwen giggled before slumping and pouting. "I know she's beautiful, but honestly."

"Jealous?" James asked with a gasp of fake surprise.

"Well, I admit I was hoping to have a big party like this someday, but I guess now that I have no title and no kingdom, that isn't going to happen."

"Aw, come on, Gwen," James scoffed. "You'd be bored just sitting around on a throne all the time. Admit it. You've had fun traveling about the kingdoms with us. How could you go back to just performing your little plays for the maids after you've faced down danger with a brave man like me?"

"True," she said before slumping down even farther. "But it still would be nice for someone to think I'm the prettiest girl in the room."

"Maybe someone does," James mumbled, as he shifted on the bench. "Why, I happen to know that right now there is a dashing knight in this very room who is dying to ask you for a dance."

"Honestly?" the girl craned her neck to look around the room. "Where?" Feeling James tap her on the shoulder, she turned to find him grinning broadly and pointing to himself.

"Milady, would you honor me with a dance?"

"Me?" Gwen said as her face brightened into a smile. James nodded his head as he stood and offered her his hand. "Why, Sir James, I'd be honored!"

As the couple stood to move to the center of the room, where other party guests spun in a dizzying array of swirling gowns and surcoats, Gwen stopped and tugged gently on James's hand. Following her nod, James saw two birthday fairies fluttering toward them on tiny wings. The first fairy, clad head to toe in shimmering silver gossamer, glanced at James and said, "Hello, Ewan."

The second fairy, wearing a simple drop-waisted gown in a deep orange velvet, pulled a pipe from her mouth and blew orange smoke into the air before elbowing the silver fairy in the ribs. The first fairy cast a guilty look at her sister, then leaned forward to fly past the knight.

"Sorry, ma'am, I think you're mistaken. My name is James."

"My mistake," the silver fairy said as she sped by.

"You'll have to forgive Marta," the orange fairy said, "she's a little bit of an idiot. Hello, Princess Gwendolyn."

"Hello, Thora," Gwen said and curtsied. "James, this is my birthday fairy, Thora. She watches over all of us who were born on a Thursday. But I guess you're done with me now that you know I'm not a real princess."

Thora landed in front of Gwen and said "My dear, you are as much a princess today as the day you were born. That boy's silly test has nothing to do with it. I'm not supposed to interfere with your affairs, but this has gone on long enough! As a matter of fact, there's something else you should know."

Daniel approached the birthday fairies' table with his hands tucked behind his back and his head bowed slightly. The two fairies seated at the table turned to face him as he stopped in front of them and cleared his throat.

"Daniel," the fairy in a sky blue gown said, as she played with the large sapphire hanging on a chain around her neck, "you're looking well."

"With all respect, Fria, no thanks to you."

"That's my cue to exit this conversation," the fairy in the pink taffeta gown said, as she stood and flitted across the room. "Think I'll go check in on Phillip."

Fria crossed her arms and wrinkled her face. "This is about the insomnia thing, isn't it?"

"Yes!" Daniel hissed. "What on earth were you thinking? I haven't slept in over two years!"

"Yes, but thanks to Saba, you didn't die on your eighteenth birthday either, did you? And from what I've seen, having insomnia has allowed you to learn all kind of things you never could've learned if you were wasting your time sleeping. I think my little curse may have been a blessing in disguise. Plus, your prince over there seems to like you being awake to watch over him."

"That may well be," Daniel said, his voice lowering as his anger faded, "but I haven't dreamed in two years. Do you know what it is like to never dream?"

"I'm a fairy, Daniel. We're the dream makers. We don't dream. Why do you think we watch your daily lives?" Fria held up the sapphire and showed Daniel the image beneath its glimmering surface. He saw an image of Andrew nuzzling Marina's neck. Looking up at the thrones, he could see the same scene happening in front of him.

"You watch our lives? So you've seen all the things I've been through in the last two years? It never occurred to you to step in and offer me some help or advice?"

"That's against the rules, tootsie," the fairy said with a shrug. "We're only allowed to give you blessings and curses and then only on special occasions. We can't interfere with your lives otherwise."

"Fairies have rules?"

"Yes," Fria said with a sigh. "We've been watching your kind for thousands of years, but it got a bit repetitious. Birth, life, death, repeat. So Luna, my oldest sister, decided we should liven things up by giving each of our wards blessings. The funny thing is, you humans are really boring when your lives are going well. So we decided that your birthday fairy would give each child something not so nice, just to keep things interesting. But then it went too far the other way, and awful things that no one wants to see started happening. It just got gruesome. So we reached our current compromise, one curse tempered by the last blessing. It's been this way for thousands of years, Daniel. Those are the rules."

"And you can just play with our lives like that?" Daniel pounded his fist on the table, making the fairy jump. "How is that fair? You have no consequences!"

"Oh, there you're wrong, sweetheart. An unexpected consequence of our magic was that the fairy who placed the curse had to spend the rest of that child's life giving small blessings. Birthdays, weddings, births, engagements. You name it, we have to haul our backsides all the way across the kingdoms to give you a blessing. Even when you lose a tooth!"

"I thought that was the tooth fairy."

"Pish," Fria said with a roll of her eyes, "Tooth fairy. That's a silly old wives tale. It's just us. We don't like some of it any more than you do, Danny. But, as I said, those are the rules."

"Rules, rules, rules!" Daniel raised his voice. "All these silly rules. I'm sick of hearing about the rules!"

Fria began to laugh, and a faint blue light dazzled about her head. "Danny, a rule is what will let you sleep again."

"What?"

"I really would've thought you'd have figured this out by now with all the reading you did. You have a standard sleep-based curse. Only one thing can reverse sleep-based magic."

"Yes?" Daniel said, his impatience making his voice rise an octave.

"Silly boy, it's true love's first kiss. Everyone knows that."

"Oh," Daniel said, as he stood staring blankly at the fairy. "You mean I just have to…" Daniel turned to look across the room, where Phillip and Peter sat talking to the pink fairy. As he turned back to speak to Fria, he heard a shrieked "What!" from across the hall.

PHILLIP WATCHED DANIEL APPROACH THE FAIRY TABLE AND kicked his foot against the leg of the bench he was sitting on. He regretted that he had agreed to let Daniel confront his fairy first, and the entire evening was taking far too long for his taste. First they had had to sit through the seven-course dinner, with each course dedicated to one of the fairies. Then Andrew had made a long-winded speech about the beauty of Marina and the assured beauty of their future children.

Next, Marina had made her speech about the beauty of Andrew and the skills of the Sylvanian chefs who had prepared the evening's meal, describing each course in detail, despite the fact that everyone in the room had just eaten every dish. Finally, Queen Rhea had asked Andrew and Marina's birthday fairies to bestow their blessings on the marriage. After the usual wishes of fertility and long life and happiness were handed out, the royals were finally at liberty to speak to their fairies. Since Daniel was the one who introduced Andrew and Marina, and thus caused the engagement that brought the fairies, Phillip thought it only fair that he talk to his fairy first.

"You are about to shake me off this bench," Peter grumbled, interrupting Phillip's thoughts. "Just go over there and ask her to help us! These fairies can see what you royals are up to no matter where you are. She'll be able to tell us where Cauchemar is and help us find Katerina. If I were a royal—"

"Honey pie, if you were a royal you'd what?" A lilting voice pulled Peter and Phillip's attention from their conversation. They looked up to see a fairy floating a few inches off the floor in front of them. Her voluminous pink skirts shimmered around her feet as her small pink wings rustled the air. A pair of rosy glasses sat on the tip of her nose, and she looked down through them at the boys. "Peter, if you were a royal you'd never have time to write your delightful little stories."

"You know my stories?" Peter said with a look of shock.

"Honey, you've been so close to Phillip all of his life that I have watched your life too. I am Mitta, Phillip's birthday fairy. I appreciate you being such a good friend to him, especially during the sad times. I know the stories you told him cheered him up so much when he was missing his mother." Mitta pulled the charcoal pencil from behind Peter's ear and held it up. "Such wonderful magic you do with your little wand."

"All I do is write stories. I'm not important like a king or brave like a knight," Peter pointed across the room to where James and Gwen were speaking with another fairy.

"Hogwash!" Mitta said and waved the pencil as if shooing away Peter's words. "Generations later, no one knows anything of a king unless someone writes down his deeds. As for knights, well, this pencil can be a mighty weapon, and you can fight many important battles with words. Have you never noticed that 'sword' is just the letters in 'words' rearranged?"

Mitta took her wand from the loop at her waist, waved it around the pencil twice and whispered a few words. The pencil vibrated in her hand and glowed with a faint pink light before she handed it back to Peter. "Yes, there is much magic in your little wand there. Keep a tight hold on it." Mitta winked at Peter and pushed her glasses back up her nose with her index finger. "So, Phillip, it appears you've made a few new friends. One friend in particular."

Phillip blushed and glanced over to see Daniel having a heated discussion with a fairy dressed all in blue. "Yes," he sighed, "I've made several new friends. Some, like Gwen over there, I didn't expect would ever want to speak to me again.

"Ah, yes," Mitta said with a snort of laughter, "you were being quite the naughty boy with that silly tonic and that testing-bed nonsense. Convincing unsuspecting girls that they weren't really royals? Not nice, young man. Not nice at all. Though it appears you've made the most of it. I do have to admit, it provided the girls and me hours of entertainment. Though I can't for the life of me figure out why you let that ridiculous amateur sorceress of a stepmother of yours put you through all that. Really, pulling out something as archaic as a testing bed?"

"Seriously?" Phillip's eyebrows shot up. "It was your curse that set all of that in motion."

"My curse? My curse was that the search for love would make you leave your kingdom behind. Which, I might point out, is exactly what has happened. You have left the kingdom behind, gone on this wonderfully entertaining little adventure, and found a delightful companion thanks to Thora's clever last blessing. The whole affair has been delightfully entertaining. Even more so than I hoped when I said it."

"That is not what you said!" Phillip gasped as he rose from the bench.

"Phillip," Mitta chastised, "I think I know what my own curse was. I said your marriage would be an adventure."

"That's not it either!" Phillip complained, his voice growing louder and shaky.

"Um," Mitta stammered, "I know it had to do with love or marriage. All my curses and blessings do."

"You said a bad marriage would make me lose my kingdom!"

"Don't be absurd, child," Mitta scoffed, "I would never use a curse that... well... now... that does sound sort of familiar now that you say it out loud."

Phillip widened his eyes and kicked the bench. "You play with my life and you can't even remember what you said?"

"Dear, I've had many wards and I'm an old fairy. The generation before you had so many... I can't be expected to—"

"And it never once occurred to you that maybe someone misinterpreted what you meant? Just once you could have stepped in and helped me out of that mess so I wouldn't have to—"

"Phillip! We are not allowed to interfere like that. Just blessings. And I blessed you with many things over the years like—" Mitta jerked her head to the left at the sound of a loud shriek. "What in the name of—"

Phillip looked up to see Gwen storming across the hall toward him with James and two fairies trailing behind her. As the girl's growling scream grew louder, the other party guests began filing over as well.

"You shrimp!" Gwen ran up to Phillip and kneed him in the crotch. "You're no seahorse! You're a spineless jellyfish!"

"Ow!" Phillip bellowed. "What was that for?"

"You knocked me out!"

"What is going on over here?" Daniel asked, as he rushed up to Phillip and put his hands on his shoulders. "Are you hurt?"

"I hope he is in eternal pain. Your darling over there gave me a tonic to make me sleep and fail that test! Staying awake was the test, and he knew he was making me fail!"

Phillip's face turned ashen and he began to stammer, "Gwen, I can explain—" In agony, he dropped back onto the bench.

"Explain? Honestly! Because of you my father is missing, I've lost my kingdom, and I'll never find a prince to marry me. Everyone thinks I am a fraud! I am so mad I could—honestly! You and Dr. Hickenkopf's Miracle Tonic have ruined everything!"

"What?" Luna, the oldest fairy, interrupted. With her yellow wings and gown fluttering behind her, she sped across the room. Her arms were folded across her chest. "You think that simple tonic he gave you made you fail the test? Thora! What nonsense have you been feeding this girl?"

Thora pouted and tossed her orange braid over her shoulder. "I thought it might make this party a little more interesting."

"My dear," Luna said, as she fluttered over and patted Gwen's head, "Dr. Hickenkopf is really Dr. Nincompoop. That tonic is nothing but frogberry juice and well water. Its only power is to induce tumbly tummy. You were in a testing bed, child. That is an ancient and powerful piece of magic. No tonic that Phillip could get his hands on could have made a true princess fall asleep."

"Gwen," Daniel added, "it's true. James gave me that awful tonic once, and it didn't make me sleep at all."

"You mean I failed fair and square?" Gwen whimpered, as her bottom lip began to tremble.

"That or someone with strong magic did something to interfere. Girls," Luna called out to her sisters, "did any of you break the rules and interfere with these girls' tests?"

Each of the fairies shook her head no.

"Then they all failed," Luna said with a shrug. "The only other possibility would be if some sorceress or wizard used something strong like Sleeping Heavenly Peas—"

"Did you say peas?" Phillip rushed over to Gwen. "By Gingerfair's curls, it was the pea, Gwen! Not me! Cauchemar must have done this! She put the peas under the bed. She has powers!"

"Phillip, I don't understand," Gwen said, scrunching up her nose.

"I didn't make you fail the test! She did! The pea must've made you sleep!

"Girls," Luna asked as she turned to the other fairies, "did any of you see this Cauchemar woman do something?"

"Don't be absurd," Mitta said with a wave of her hand. "That woman isn't true royalty. None of us could have seen what she was doing unless a true royal was in the room."

"Oh," Marina cried out as she ran up to Gwen, "isn't that wonderful news! You may still be a princess. You can take your kingdom back from King Robert and find a prince to marry!"

"Yeah. Great," Gwen muttered and looked over at James with a frown. The knight smiled feebly and then turned to walk away, his head bowed.

"Oh no!" Peter yelled. "This is terrible news."

"What?" Daniel said as he turned to Peter. "Phillip didn't hurt the girls. That is wonderful news!"

"No! These fairies can't see Cauchemar. I was hoping they could tell us where to find her, but they can't see her any more than you or I can."

"We have to find her," Phillip said. "So I can save my father!"

"And I have to find Katerina!" Peter cried.

"Katerina?" the silver fairy, Marta, said with a slight gasp. "Why, I can tell you where Katerina is. She is one of my princesses."

"Except," Phillip said with a sigh, "that girl is not the real Katerina. She's just someone Cauchemar was trying to pass off as

Katerina. The real Katerina was killed with the rest of the Canteran royal family."

"That's ridiculous," Marta said and pointed toward James, "she's no more dead than her brother, Ewan, over there."

"Lady, why do you keep calling me that?" James said.

"Marta!" Luna interrupted. "Have all of you girls forgotten the 'do not interfere' rule? Well, the horse is out of the stable now. Tell him."

"Your name is not James. It's Ewan," Marta explained. "You're the crown prince of Cantera. Cauchemar took you and your sister out of your parents' castle the night it was overrun. She cast you aside here and took your sister with her. Since I couldn't interfere with your lives directly, I wasn't allowed to let anyone know who you really are. But I gave you both blessings when I could. I had Queen Rhea find you. I gave you a strong body and a strong will. I gave you skill with a sword."

James stood still with his mouth agape. "I'm a prince?"

"James!" Gwen flung her arms around his shoulders. "You're a royal!"

"But I like being a knight," James muttered as he pushed Gwen back.

"But a royal, honestly!" Gwen gushed.

"Highnesses," Peter said, "can we discuss this later? We need to find Katerina!"

"Yes," James said, as he stepped up to Marta, "help us find my sister, please. Hey! I have a sister!"

"Luna?" Marta turned to the oldest fairy with an imploring look.

"Fine." The fairy threw up her hands. "Show them. Let's fix this mess you've all made."

Marta reached deep into the pocket of her gown and pulled out her large silver hand mirror. Gazing into the glass, she began to chant "Mirror, Mirror, in my hand. Show me the girl, wherever she may stand."

The royals crowded close around the fairy's shoulders to see what the glass would reveal.

# CHAPTER *16*

*C*ANTERA HAD ALWAYS BEEN A LAND OF GREAT WEALTH, DUE TO
*the numerous mines that dotted its landscape. Iron, gold, silver,
gemstones and coal had all been discovered within its borders
and had made its citizens wealthy beyond imagination. Local legend
had it that in ancient times, a tall and handsome man, Thrigor, had
been king of the entire realm of Clarameer and ruled it from a castle
he erected in the center of the kingdom. In his desire to make his castle
the largest and most ornate that anyone had ever seen, he had mined
the resources from each corner of the land and brought them to Cantera.*

*As the other regions lost more and more of their fortunes to the king's
greed, they began to develop other resources—timber in the woodlands
of the east, produce in the plains of the west, wool and livestock in the
northern valleys, and the bounty of the sea to the south. The greedy
king, determined to keep all of Clarameer's riches to himself, grew more
and more terrified that someone would steal his riches. He built vast
dungeons below his castle and imprisoned the citizens of his kingdom
so they could not steal his wealth. In an effort to hide the vast riches
from anyone who sought to claim some for himself, the king began to
bury all his bounty under the soil of Cantera and spent every waking
moment clawing away at the earth to secret away his treasures.*

*With time, his fingernails were hardened into long claws by all the
digging; they scratched at the flesh of his face as he tried to eat, so his*

*body grew thinner from lack of food. His back grew more and more hunched as he crawled about the dark earth, making large holes and covering his treasure within them. The rabid greed that ran rampant through his veins turned his skin green and made his hair grow stringy and greasy. Eventually all of his treasures were buried deep within the Canteran soil, and Thrigor rested on the largest pile with a satisfied sigh.*

*As the withered king slept, he dreamed that a beautiful huntress came to him and kissed his cheek, making him instantly reveal the locations of all his hidden riches. As he awoke screaming in fear of losing his wealth, the king decided that even he could not be trusted to know where the treasures were buried. He took the last of his gold and rubies and made a large crown for himself. He turned the crown in his hands and whispered the locations of each treasure into one of the rubies, quickly forgetting each hiding place as soon as he had told it to the crown. He said, "Ruby, Ruby, red and round, keep my secrets safe and sound." He plopped the crown onto his head, knowing that as long as he wore it, he could ask the crown where his treasures lay.*

*Satisfied that his bounty was safe, Thrigor turned back to his castle. As he walked along the edge of the river, he grew thirsty and stopped to drink from the sparkling blue water. He caught sight of his reflection in the water, seeing a dirty, green troll with scars all over his face. The troll king reeled back in disgust, causing the crown to topple off his head and into the water below. He screamed in horror at the creature his greed had birthed and in anguish at the loss of the crown.*

*Thrigor's screams drew the attention of a young huntress, Gingerfair, who had wandered down from the mountains to gather flowers for her bridal bouquet. As she ran to the source of the screams, she noticed the glimmering gold crown in the river. After pulling it from the water, she placed it upon her head and said, "Ruby, Ruby, red and dear, whisper a secret in my ear!" Instantly, she knew the locations of all of the troll king's treasures. She ran to her beloved, Godrick, and told him of her good fortune.*

*The young lovers ran to the castle to tell the king of her discovery, only to find the withered old troll sitting on the throne and mumbling to himself. When the troll king saw the crown on the young girl's head, he stamped his feet and demanded she return it to him. He stomped so hard, the ground beneath his feet cracked open and swallowed him whole.*

*Gingerfair and Godrick instantly rushed to the dungeons and released all of the citizens of Cantera, with Gingerfair telling each where he could build a mine to retrieve the troll king's riches. Out of gratitude to the young girl, the citizens named her their queen and threw a lavish ball in her honor. Her first act as queen was to divide Clarameer into five kingdoms, split between her four sisters and herself, so that no one person could ever control all of the land's resources again. Clarameer and her five kingdoms were ruled by the five queens in peace and harmony. Her people lived their lives happy, wealthy and free from that day forward, with only one little fear in the back of their minds—someday the troll king could return.*

"Well, I guess he did." Dinah lifted her bound hands to her face and brushed a stray hair from her eyes. "Kitty, you said you'd tell me a story to make me feel better, but that just made me think about the troll king upstairs. You're terrible at this. I bet you'd tell someone with a cough a story about the rain plague."

"I'm sorry." Katerina sighed and leaned her head against the bars between their cells. "That's how Peter ended it. He's better at telling stories than I am. If he were here..." Her words trailed off as she shivered against the cold air of the dungeon. "It's just an old legend anyway. That man upstairs can't be Thrigor. He'd have to be thousands of years old."

"Silly girls," King Edward muttered from his cell. "That legend is based on facts. My ancestor was one of the queens who was given a kingdom. Maybe he *is* back? Who knows? It's him. It's not him. Who cares? Either way, we're still in a dungeon awaiting Godrick knows what." Katerina heard the bars of his cell rattle as he pounded on them. The sound echoed around the empty hallway of the dungeon. "Dinah's right about one thing, though. You're terrible at storytelling. My daughter performs a play version of that legend much better than you do," Edward said gruffly, as he turned from the bars and shuffled to the stone slab in his cell that served as a bed. "Don't know why your aunt thinks you'd be a good wife."

"Kitty!" Dinah said, as she struggled to stand up and wobbled across her cell toward Katerina. "What about your aunt? Maybe she has changed her mind? Maybe she will help us get out of here?"

"No, that won't happen," Katerina said with a frown. "She's very determined. She claims she's the one who brought the troll king back in the first place."

"Why would she do that?" Dinah asked.

"She wanted him to help her get rid of my parents," Katerina explained. "She let him into the castle and helped him take over. She says I am the daughter of King Francis and Queen Evelyn. She showed me the whole thing in a magic mirror. The only reason I survived was because she stole me away."

"You are Katerina?" Edward gasped from across the hallway. "Kitty. Katerina. Yes, you even look like Evelyn. Of course! It all makes sense now. Well, it makes no sense but... by Gingerfair's girdle! If she would do all that... we are doomed." The man groaned and dropped to his knees.

"Kitty," Dinah begged, holding her bound hands in front of her face. "Tell me this isn't true. Surely your aunt won't do anything to hurt us!"

Katerina closed her eyes and took a deep breath. "I'm afraid I can't tell you that. My aunt is not a very nice lady."

"What an unkind thing to say, Katerina," Cauchemar purred, as she walked out of the shadows and up to the cell. She dragged her fingers along the bars, making small blue sparks arc between them. "After all I have done for you. I'm making you a queen. And for the last time," Cauchemar said as she reached through the bars and yanked on the ruffles of Katerina's dress, "These go down here. You really are a dimwit."

"You! Kitty, this is your aunt?" Dinah screamed as she tottered toward the door of her cell. "You're Phillip's stepmother! The one who told everyone I wasn't a princess and ruined my life!"

"Did I?" Cauchemar said with a slight lift of her eyebrow. "From what I have seen, you were happier learning magic than you ever would have been married to Phillip. I believe I did you a favor. You show a real aptitude for it, too."

"Will you teach me?" Dinah asked as she approached the bars. Katerina's jaw dropped as she looked at Dinah in disbelief.

"Oh, child, I'm afraid I cannot have someone in the kingdoms who might someday be as powerful in her magic as I am. I'll have to dispose of you after you've served as Katerina's bridesmaid."

Dinah dropped her head against the bars of her cell and groaned.

"You still think I'm going to marry that troll?" Katerina asked. She glared at her aunt and yanked the sleeves of her dress back up onto her shoulders. "Have I suffered enough down here to prove your point?"

"Well, not really. But I'm afraid there has been a slight change of plans. It seems the guards along the eastern wall have seen four men and a woman approaching."

"Peter?" Katerina gasped.

"Yes. And those meddlesome princes. But we'll deal with them in short order. Then, old man," she said as she turned to the cell behind her, "you'll have a little father-daughter reunion."

"Gwen?" King Edward jumped up from the slab and ran to the bars of his cell. "Don't you dare lay a finger on my daughter."

"Oh, I can take care of her just fine without touching her at all." Cauchemar pointed her finger and shot a bolt of burgundy light at a rat scurrying between the cells. The animal screeched in pain before falling onto its side. The two girls turned away in horror as the animal kicked its feet in the throes of death. Cauchemar watched until the animal lay still and then turned to the girls with a smirk. "Ladies, get some rest. We don't want dark circles under the eyes when the court artist paints your wedding day portrait."

Cauchemar turned quickly and swept out of the hallway with her long train trailing behind her. As she reached the doorway, she turned and snapped her fingers, causing all of the torches in the dungeon to extinguish. "Nighty night!"

"Oh, Gwen," the old man wailed in his cell, "don't come near this place. Please don't!"

"I'm sorry, Dinah," Katerina whimpered, as she stumbled over to her slab and lay down.

"Isn't this just lovely," Dinah grumbled. "I have to be a brides-maid. Again."

"I THINK WE SHOULD LEAVE THE HORSES HERE," JAMES CALLED over his shoulder as he galloped out of the edge of the Western Wood. "We're going to have a hard enough time just getting the five of us over that wall, much less the horses. Gwen and Peter, if you want to stay here, we'll understand. Things might get dangerous."

James pointed to the gigantic structure that blocked the horizon. The wall stood at least a hundred feet tall and glistened in the light of the morning sun. The sides appeared to be made of milky white glass streaked with veins of emerald green and sapphire blue. James walked up to the base of the wall and ran his hand down its side. "I have no idea how we are going to do that, of course. There's no way we can climb something as smooth as this."

Pulling his sword from its sheath, he reared his arms back and swung at the wall with all his force. The sword bounced off the surface of the wall and sent a shower of sparks flying about his shoulders. James inspected the surface where he had hit the wall and said, "It didn't even leave a mark. You two better get out of the way while I try again."

Peter looked at Gwen and frowned. "Why do they think we are useless? He does realize that we have been through everything on this journey that he has, right?"

Gwen shrugged and pulled her horses reins to stop beside Peter. "Honestly. All they see is a girl who play-acts adventure and a boy who writes about it. I know one thing, though. I'm not staying with the horses while they see all the action. Cauchemar is the one who slipped that pea under the mattress and I've got a thing or two to say to her."

"I guess he has a point, though," Peter said and dismounted. "The princes and James have their swords. Even you are good with a dagger or a bow and arrow. All I have is this silly pencil." Peter pulled the pencil from behind his ear and held it up for her to see. "What am I going to do? Write a strongly worded letter?"

"Dear Madam," Gwen said with a giggle as she hopped down beside him, "I would like to lodge a formal complaint."

"Peter," Phillip chastised as he and Daniel trotted up beside the pair, "you're not staying here. You've been with me every step of this journey, and it's time you prove you were right about Cauchemar all along. I'm not leaving you here. You either, Gwen." Phillip dismounted and walked over to Daniel's horse. He smiled up at the other prince and held out his hand to help him down. "You've kept watch in the night, but are you ready to save the day?"

Daniel slid off his horse and down into Phillip's waiting arms. He could see Phillip trying to maintain an air of bravery, but knew the other man's heart had to be pounding with fear as hard as his own was. As Phillip pulled him into a tighter embrace, Daniel cleared his throat. "You know, I've been thinking."

"You were awfully quiet on the ride here," Phillip replied as he leaned back to look at Daniel with concern. "I just figured you're as scared as I am. I'm making jokes, but I'm worried."

"I'm terrified," Daniel said, "but not just of what may be waiting on the other side of that wall."

"I don't understand."

"Phillip, I'm terrified I may lose you."

"Daniel, I know there's a risk, but I have to take it. My father's life depends on it."

"That's not what I meant," Daniel said, as he wrapped his arms around Phillip's waist and pulled him closer. "We'll succeed. I've no doubt about that. Fate, or destiny, or whatever would never have brought us this far just to fail. I know we'll find her and save your father, but what about after?"

"After?"

"When your kingdom needs you. When your duty calls. When all of this is over and we return to life. Will I lose you then?"

Phillip stepped back and crossed his arms on his chest. He cocked his head and stared at Daniel with a bemused look. "Daniel, I know I told you I want to play this game by new rules, but I think there is still room for some of the old ones."

"Such as?"

"The birthday fairies said the princesses all slept because of those magic peas that Cauchemar put under the bed, right? The pea took over the magic of the bed and the girls' own heritage. The magic in that pea was stronger than the very royalty in their blood."

"Yes, but I don't see your point."

"The way I see it, the magic in that pea should have been stronger than your curse. You should've slept, but you didn't."

"That's not what my fairy said. Phillip, I don't think that pea—"

Phillip reached up and placed his finger on Daniel's lips to silence him. "Shh. You passed the test. You didn't sleep. The rules said that the first one to pass the test is the one I should share my life with. So, I think that's one rule we should follow."

"Well, I guess—"

"No guessing. Your future king has spoken," Phillip said, as he winked at Daniel and held out his hand. "Now, let's go figure out a way over that wall."

Daniel took Phillip's hand in his own and twined their fingers together. As the two princes walked toward the shimmering glass wall, Daniel swung their hands back and forth freely between them. He looked down at his hand in Phillip's, seeing their fingers clasped tightly together and he knew that his hand, his heart, and his very life had found their home. The unspoken promise in the other prince's words washed over his skin like warm sunshine pushed by a breeze through the trees. Daniel wasn't sure what his future would bring. Life as the whispered-about secret lover of the king. Life as the uneasily accepted consort of the king. Life ruling upon the throne beside the king and beloved by the citizens. Daniel didn't care, as long as his life included Phillip. Should he lose him in the battle with Cauchemar and Thrigor, Daniel would gladly accept death at the end of the troll king's sword. The fear of the battle ahead and the possible loss of his friends and of his own life faded under the sudden brightness of the light Phillip had brought into his life. Daniel squeezed Phillip's hand and smiled when the other man squeezed back.

"So, James," Phillip called out to the knight, who was staring at the glass wall that stretched above him with his sword dangling from his hands in defeat, "have you figured out a way to get us over?"

James scratched his head and shifted from foot to foot. He took a few steps back and eyed the wall up and down before stepping up to its face and knocking the glass with his knuckles. "As far as I can tell, it's at least a hundred feet high and thick as a troll's skull. Even if we had a rope long enough to reach the top, I have no idea how we'd get it up there."

"Wouldn't matter anyway, silly," Gwen said, as she swatted at a fly that was buzzing about her head, "that's a magic wall. From what I hear, as you near the top it just grows taller." She turned to speak to the young scribe who sat on a boulder behind her. "Peter, you write about magic. How do you think we should get over it? If this was your story, what would you do?"

"Me?" Peter gave a short laugh as he stepped over to the wall and pulled the pencil from behind his ear. "Well, if this were my story, I'd let the writer be the hero for a change. I'd have the handsome but ignored scribe step up to the wall like this and draw a door." Peter put the point of the pencil against the smooth surface and swung his arm in a wide arc over his head, leaving a faint line along the wall's surface.

After drawing a door shape, he quickly sketched a loop on the side for a handle and hinges on the opposite side. "Then I'd have him grab the handle like this..." Peter reached out and placed his hand where he had sketched the handle. "Um... by Gingerfair's ribbons..." he stuttered as the picture of a handle suddenly become real in his hand. With a sharp tug, he pulled on the handle, and the wall swung open along the lines he had drawn. Peter stood with his mouth agape as he looked through the portal to the other side. "What did I do?"

"Peter!" Phillip dropped Daniel's hand and ran to the open passageway. "You did it! Of course! The only way through a magic wall is with a different kind of magic!"

"But I was kidding," Peter said, as he held the pencil up in front of his face and stared at the charcoal point. "I don't know any magic. How did I do that? That fairy of yours! She must've done something to my pencil when she—"

"Who cares!" James pushed Peter into the passageway. "We need to hurry through before it wears off and closes again. And be quiet! We have no idea if there may be guards on the other side! Gwen, give me your hand."

"I can walk fine by myself." She drew her dagger from her belt and rushed past the knight into the portal.

James drew his sword and hurried in behind her, followed by Daniel and Phillip. As Phillip stepped out of the wall onto the dark green grass on the other side, the wall slammed closed behind him with a loud bang.

"Shhh!" James turned around quickly. "I said to be quiet."

"I didn't mean to slam it," Phillip apologized. He stood and looked around in awe. His entire life, he had listened to his mother and Peter tell stories of the beauty of Cantera that the troll king had hidden from the rest of Clarameer by erecting the magic wall. He had heard tales of trees that bloomed sapphires and springs that flowed liquid gold, but as he scanned the horizon he saw only simple yellow brumblefruit trees, purple rumberry bushes and two tawny does running away. Though the land around him looked no different than the Western Woods he had just left, the fact that he was so close to finding Cauchemar and saving his father made it the most beautiful land he had ever seen. He turned to Daniel and said in an excited rush, "We made it! We're over the wall. Oh, Daniel, my father is practically saved! I'm so happy!"

Daniel smiled back at him and chuckled. Phillip placed his hands lovingly on either side of Daniel's face and pulled the other prince closer. Tilting his head slightly and closing his eyes, Phillip placed his lips gently on Daniel's. Phillip felt the other prince lean into the kiss with an amorous moan and wrap his arms around Phillip's waist. As Phillip's heart fluttered at the shock of desire that pulsed through his body, Daniel suddenly became limp in his arms. Pulling back from the kiss, Phillip saw Daniel's eyes were closed and his head drooped on his shoulders. As Phillip struggled to grasp Daniel's falling body, he screamed out in terror, "James, help me!"

"Quiet!" James hissed through clinched teeth, as he rushed over to Phillip's side. When he saw Phillip's struggle with the dead weight of Daniel's body, he helped him ease Daniel onto the ground. "You are going to attract guards! What did you do?"

"I just kissed him!" Phillip said, as he leaned over Daniel's body and shook him by the shoulders. Panic growing in his mind, Phillip slapped Daniel's cheeks lightly and begged, "Daniel? Daniel!"

"Someone's coming!" Gwen said. "We need to hide!"

"We need to go!" Peter yelled as he ran into Gwen from behind. "There are guards coming over the hill!"

"Daniel?" Phillip wailed loudly as he draped himself over the other prince's body. "Oh no, I've killed him. I've killed Daniel!"

# CHAPTER 17

DANIEL WAS SURE HE HAD PROBABLY HAD DREAMS EVERY night of his life, but with the excitement that a day of exploring the castle with James or sneaking into the kitchens with Emmaline would bring, he would forget them within moments of waking. Vague fragments of flying on a dragon's back or climbing the tallest tree in the Western Woods would linger in his mind, but nothing that would not disappear before he closed his eyes the next night. Dreams were something he took for granted until they were gone, and he often wondered what the last dream he had ever had was about. Had he known it was the last, he might have tried harder to remember it.

This dream was different, though. This dream, he would make himself remember. In this dream he had wandered the kingdoms with James at his side. He had seen a king attacked by a madwoman, flown in a basket carried by birds, seen a princess sing in a tavern, and talked with his own birthday fairy. More than that, though, he had seen the face of love. He had opened his eyes in a bed to see the most breathtaking face he could imagine staring back at him, the face of a prince. He had watched this scared young prince grow into a valiant and adventurous king before his very eyes, and felt that king eventually pull him into a tender embrace. He had heard the king profess his love and felt the passionate fire in his chest as the man placed the sweetest of kisses on his lips. Yes, this dream he would make himself remember upon waking, because he knew he must find this man and make the love in this dream his reality. He would find him.

As Daniel's eyes fluttered open, they darted around the room. Dark stone walls and a stone roof hovered above him, and a single flaming lamp swinging from the ceiling sent shadows and light dancing on the walls. He could feel the warmth of someone's legs under his head and smooth fingers brushing hair away from his face. As the fog of sleep lifted, he saw clear blue eyes staring at him in fear and concern. As the face came into focus, Daniel recognized the handsome features of the man from his dream. With a quick intake of breath, he whispered, "Well, that was easy."

"Daniel!" Phillip cried out, as he grabbed the prince's shoulders and pulled him up into an embrace. "You're back!"

"I left?" Daniel said groggily, as he pulled away from Phillip and slid into a sitting position. He looked around at the dark stone walls of the room. The damp, moldy smell of the room made his nose wrinkle, as his eyes struggled to adjust to the flickering lamplight. He could feel the dig of iron bars against his back; his bones ached from the cold, hard stone floor. "Where am I now?"

"The troll king's dungeon," Phillip said, as he shifted up to his knees and flung his arms around Daniel. "The troll king's soldiers captured us. But you're awake! I was so worried that you were gone forever."

"I was asleep?" Daniel shook his head and rubbed his eyes with the heels of his hands. "I'm sorry. I'm confused. I was having the most amazing dream about the most beautiful man, and I wake up to see him here."

Phillip blushed and tightened his embrace. "I thought I killed you."

"What?" Daniel said with a laugh, as he leaned back and stared into Phillip's eyes. "How could you have killed me? The last thing I remember was rushing through the glass wall, celebrating, and then—Oh! Phillip, did you kiss me?"

"Yes," Phillip said with an embarrassed duck of his chin. "I was just so happy to be so close to our goal, and you were standing there looking so handsome with the sunlight glowing behind you and I just couldn't resist. But as soon as I kissed you, you slumped in my arms and I had to drop you to the ground. I thought you were dead and I had lost you forever."

Daniel threw his head back and laughed. "While that was a fantastic kiss, you're not getting rid of me that easily!"

"I don't understand."

"You cured me! Just like the fairy said, 'true love's first kiss.' That's the cure. I didn't realize its effect would be quite that immediate. I knew it would come from you, but I thought I might have a little more warning."

"My kiss cured you? Wait, did you say 'true love'?"

"Yes, my love. Your kiss. True love's kiss."

"Oh, Daniel, do you mean—"

"Well, look who finally decided to wake up!" James interrupted. He bounded over to Daniel's side and knelt beside him. "Your timing was as terrible, as usual."

"How long have I been asleep? And how did we get here?" Daniel asked.

"Well, since there are no windows," Peter said as he joined the group, "I can only guess it has been a day or so. By Godrick's curls, you snored like an Osterling boar."

Daniel pulled his shoulders up around his ears and grinned sheepishly. "Sorry. Did my snoring get us caught?"

"Oh, no," Peter said with a roll of his eyes, "you can thank Prince Killer Lips over here for that. When you collapsed, he started screaming that he had killed you with a kiss. He tried kissing you a few more times to reverse it. When that didn't work, he started wailing again. All that yelling attracted guards, and they came over to capture us and bring us here."

"Peter!" Gwen's voice called out from the next cell. "You are leaving out the most important part! The battle!"

"A battle?" Daniel asked, as he turned to look at Gwen poking her face between the bars. Another woman whose hands were bound in front of her stood beside her glaring at him.

"Well, it wasn't much of a battle," James said. "With you snuffed out like a candle and Phillip wailing over your body and Peter here not being much use with a sword, we were easily captured. I tried to fight them off and I stabbed at least four and Peter stabbed two, but they just kept coming over that hill."

"You are leaving out the best part!" Gwen said with a stamp of her foot. "Daniel, I fought!"

"Oh, yeah," James said with a wide grin, "Gwen took out a few herself."

"What?" Daniel said with a look of disbelief.

"Honestly! You should've seen it!" Gwen said and waved her hands in excitement. "I was sitting beside Phillip trying to wake you up and then I started watching James and Peter sword fighting with some of the guards. As I watched them parry and thrust, I thought 'that looks like the dance my father taught me when I played Brundigar the Battler.' So I pulled your sword out of your sheath and walked right up to one of those nasty guards and started dancing the Brundigar dance. Before I knew it, I had stabbed two guards. Daniel, it wasn't just a dance. I can fight! Honestly! Then I tried Hugor the Warrior's dance and I knocked out three more. I was on fire!"

"That would be thanks to me," a man's voice boomed from across the passageway.

"That's my father, King Edward!" Gwen said. "We found him! He was captured by the guards after he left Dealonia. That stepmother of yours wouldn't let us be in a cell together, though."

"I was coming here to see if I could take out Thrigor and claim Cantera for Gwen," King Edward explained from the cell across the hall. "When she didn't marry Phillip, I knew it was time, and I set out. I let myself get captured in order to get into the castle, but I didn't know that sorceress would be here. I thought I would lead the way for Gwen to come in and conquer. That's why I taught her that dance," the old man said, beaming with pride. "I knew she would lose our little kingdom, so I wanted her to be ready to take over Cantera and have a kingdom of her own. Of course, you aren't supposed to teach a princess how to fight, so I had to find a way to train her without making it obvious. So I encouraged her acting and taught her how to fight as if it were for a dance or a pantomime. What she thought was acting was actually training."

"And I was wonderful!" Gwen crowed. As she danced around the cell and pretended to swing a sword, she bragged, "I was knocking them flat left and right! And I felt so powerful!"

"A lot of good it did you," the woman beside Gwen said, before turning around to walk back over to the other side of the cell. "You're still stuck in here just like the rest of us."

"Well, they were magical guards," Gwen said with a pout. "As soon as you stabbed one, he would split in half and become two guards. Before we realized what was happening, we had doubled the number."

"Hmmph," the girl grunted. "You needed someone magic like me."

"Who's that?" Daniel said as he strained to look around Phillip at the grumpy girl.

"That's Dinah, King Robert's sister," Phillip said with a dismissive wave ."And she's just as much a ray of sunshine as she always was."

"I heard that, you guppy!" Dinah called from the shadows. "If my hands were free, I'd turn you into... well... I'd probably just shoot daisies at you, but still—"

"She's still a little mad at me," Phillip shrugged. "And evidently can do magic now."

"Magic! That's the answer!" Daniel jumped up. "Peter, why don't you draw—"

Peter held up the two halves of his broken pencil. "It didn't survive the battle. Dinah's right. We're stuck here. And what's worse, Cauchemar has Katerina up in the castle. She plans to marry her to the troll! I finally find Kitty, and I am stuck down here helpless!"

"That is my sister and this is my kingdom!" James said, as he swung his arms out around him. "That *thing* up there and that woman stole my throne and my family from me. And I cannot do anything down here."

"That evil woman," Daniel sighed, as he leaned back against the bars behind him. He jumped as a hand reached through the bars and landed on his shoulder.

"What an unkind thing to say about your hostess," Cauchemar snarled, digging her nails into the flesh of Daniel's shoulder. "Not very princely at all."

"Cauchemar," Phillip said, as he stepped over to the bars and grabbed her hand, "someone needs to hang a bell around your neck, you old cow, so you can stop sneaking up on us." He flung her hand off Daniel's shoulder and glared at her through the bars.

"Some people," Cauchemar said, as she withdrew her hand and turned away from the cell. "You do nothing but nice things for them and they never say 'thank you.'"

"Thank you?" Phillip said with a look of disbelief.

"Why, yes." Cauchemar sneered and gestured toward Gwen. "I have reunited father and daughter. I brought the orphaned prince back home. I have arranged a perfectly lovely marriage for Katerina, complete with an audience full of royalty. If you think about it, I'm even responsible for you and your darling prince meeting in the first place." Cauchemar glanced at Daniel and sniffed. "True love's first kiss. Isn't that just precious?"

Daniel reached through the bars, grasping at the woman. Cauchemar pointed her finger at his hands and sent a small orange bolt of light arcing at him. It sparked on his fingers and singed the hair on his arm as Daniel yanked his arm back into the cell.

"Uh, uh, uh," Cauchemar tut-tutted as she shook her finger at Daniel. "I guess all this time groping your little prince has made you forget to keep your hands to yourself. Phillip, you may as well kiss him back to sleep one last time. Having two kings in Bellemer doesn't really fit into my plans."

"Plans?" Phillip asked.

"Yes," Cauchemar said, as her eyes seemed to look into the past, "my mother was right. You royals cannot see past the end of your nose. You're so secure in your present, you never think of the future, living each day and blithely floating along with no care for tomorrow or worry about your place in this world. Not me. I plan. Occasionally the plan has to be altered because of some little bump in the road, but it's still a plan."

Daniel watched as Cauchemar turned and flared her skirts as she began to stalk slowly back and forth in front of the bars of the cell. "When your grandfather died, Phillip, and your aunt shoved my mother and me into that tower out in the woods, I could see the writing on the wall. My mother died of a broken heart, leaving me nothing but the book of spells that had been handed down in our family for years. Mother had always told me that the book had come from the troll king himself." The witch stopped and lifted up her hands, as if reaching for the stars. "I devoured it, learning all the magic I could to secure my future. In the very back of the book I found a spell I couldn't understand, but I recited it anyway. As I finished calling out the words, the ground beneath my feet rumbled and opened and there he stood." Cauchemar gestured to the open air in front of her as if someone were there. She shrugged, dropped her hands and began pacing in front of the cell again.

"Thrigor?" Daniel gasped. "But that cannot be! He's just a myth."

Cauchemar stopped and stared at Daniel with a condescending glare. "I thought so, too. But he was back, and he demanded I take him to his castle so he could reclaim his throne." She began walking again as her mind wandered back to the past. "I pointed out that several thousand years below the ground had left him in no condition to conquer a queen and her army. I nursed him in our tower. He taught me magic and I helped him regain his strength. When a year had passed, I made him a deal. I would help him conquer the castle, and he would help me secure my own kingdom to the south. I could have the royal children and he could have his riches back. Eventually we would merge our two kingdoms and begin conquering all of Clarameer." Cauchemar paused her pacing and took a deep, satisfied breath. She turned to the two princes and snapped her fingers in front of their faces. "So, that night I let him into the castle and he began creating his magical troll army. By the time I had escaped with the children, he had conquered the castle, imprisoned the citizens down here and raised that magic wall."

James stormed up to the bars screaming, "You helped him murder my family!"

"Silly boy," Cauchemar laughed, taking a cautious step away from the cell and turning away, "he would have killed your family with or without my help. I saved your life that day."

"But why not marry him yourself?" Peter asked from the darkened corner of the room. "Why force Katerina?"

"Have you not been listening?" Cauchemar screamed as she spun back to face the group; flames ignited around her shoulders as her eyes flashed with anger. "He is a troll! A man who spent thousands of years underground! I wasn't going to marry something that hideous! Absurd."

"Oh, Kitty," Peter groaned, as he curled up into a ball on the stone slab bed.

"Now," Cauchemar said, as the flames died down, "I expect your best behavior at the wedding. One step out of line and—" Cauchemar flung her hands out in front of her and sent small bolts of lightning shooting through the cells and stinging the skin of each occupant. They all screamed, and the smell of burnt skin and hair filled the room. "Let's just say... that was me holding back."

Daniel pulled Phillip closer and yelled at Cauchemar, "You expect us to stand by silently while you marry Katerina off to some troll and then kill us all?"

"Well," she said with an icy grin, "I expect your silence during the wedding. But when we get to the killing part, I fully expect you to scream." She stood with her hands on her hips and shook her head. "Now you should all rest. We have a big night ahead of us! The guards will bring you up for the ceremony soon." Cauchemar strode toward the stairs leading out of the dungeon. As she stepped onto the first step, she stopped and snapped her fingers over her head. Instantly all of the torches and lamps burning in the dungeon were snuffed out.

Daniel slid down the bars onto the cold stone floor. Phillip flopped down beside him and lifted his arm to blindly drape it around the other prince's shoulders. Pulling Phillip snug to his chest, he nestled his nose into his hair and breathed deep. Over the angry thumping of blood in his ears he could barely hear the other prisoners shuffle around the cells in the darkness. He tried his best to see Phillip's face, to offer a look of reassurance, but could only feel the warmth of the other man's skin against his cheek. Daniel leaned his head back against the bars and fought the tears of fear and anger that were stinging at his eyes.

"Daddy?" Gwen called out into the darkness.

"Be brave, little girl. We shall fight," King Edward called back to her.

"Kitty!" Peter yelled at the top of his lungs.

"Daniel?" Phillip whispered.

"Yes?" Daniel whispered back.

"What's going to happen?"

Daniel closed his eyes and let a few tears slide down his cheek. With his eyes closed, he wished he could return to sleep and the dream world he had been in before waking to this new nightmare. He took a few deep breaths to calm himself, wanting to sound as strong for Phillip as he possibly could. "We're going to get out of here, and you are going to kiss me to sleep every night."

Daniel sat listening to Phillip's shivering breath and the moaning of the others in the cell. His mind raced with thoughts of how to escape and how to protect Phillip, but nothing made sense to him. He heard Phillip take a deep breath and say with a tremor, "I know my kiss already told you, but, Daniel, I love you."

Daniel let the words linger in his ear; a bit of the earlier dream returned. The words calmed the pounding of his heart and gave him the strength to swallow down the last of his fear. He was unsure of how to escape, what the next day might bring, or how he could possibly protect Phillip and his friends, but he would try. He pulled Phillip closer into his arms and said the one thing he was sure of, "I love you, too."

# CHAPTER 18

P HILLIP'S STOMACH ROLLED AGAIN AND HE TASTED VOMIT
at the back of his throat as he looked up at the creature
sitting on the throne. He wasn't sure what he had expected
a troll who had lived underground for thousands of years to look
like, but no imagining could have prepared him for the sight before
him. A decrepit lump of greenish flesh lolled across the throne
with ropey strings of drool dripping from its gaping, wheezing
mouth. The gold and ruby crown of the Canteran royal family
sat askew on the small patches of greasy gray hair that sprouted
from its head. Occasionally, its rheumy left eye would open and
skitter about in the socket to take in the room. As it shifted on
the throne, the jewel-encrusted sword on its waist would clatter
against the wooden throne and break the silence. Above Thrigor's
head hung the tattered remains of the Canteran banner, a red field
emblazoned with an ebony pickaxe.

To the left of the throne, James and King Edward stood with
their heads bowed, staring at the ground; two of the troll king's
magical guards stood behind them with spears pointed at their
backs. On the other side of the throne, Gwen and Dinah stood
holding bunches of wildflowers in their hands as guards held spears
to their backs as well. Beside the throne, Katerina stood holding
a small bouquet of wildflowers. Her head drooped as well, and

tears fell from her cheeks to the bodice of her lacy white gown. A veil made from the yellowed lace curtains that Cauchemar had snatched from the windows in the queen's chambers hung limply down her back.

"Poor Katerina," Phillip whispered to Daniel at his side. "How can Cauchemar marry her to that… thing."

"At least she gets to live," Daniel whispered back. "Why make us watch this? Why not kill us all immediately?"

"Same reason she hasn't bound us," Peter said as he leaned between to the two princes from behind. "She is confident in her magic and Thrigor's guards. Also, her heart is filled with the venom of an Obenland spider."

"Silence!" Cauchemar yelled as she swept from the back of the throne room to stand beside the troll's throne. She took Katerina's right hand and laid it on top of the troll's hand. His long fingernails skittered against the arm of the throne in reaction to her touch. Cauchemar cut her eyes at Phillip and Daniel and pointed her finger at them. "There will be no more interruptions. It is time to begin the wedding. Normally, an event like this would begin with music, but today—" The sound of horns blowing in the distance echoed around the empty hall and interrupted her speech. "What was that?"

"You aren't the only one who can plan." Phillip sneered at his stepmother. "That's all the armies of the other kingdoms. Before we came here, I sent the birthday fairies to carry messages to each king or queen to tell them what was going on. They have gathered their armies around the wall and are prepared to attack. You should surrender now."

"Wall will stand," the troll king gurgled from its throne. "Wall strong magic. Usurpers killed. Throne taken back. Twenty years wall stood. Wall will stand until I fall."

"Then maybe it's time you fall," James said as he spun around and shoved the guard behind him onto the ground. As the other guards stumbled toward him, he jumped onto the throne to straddle the troll king's body. He pulled the sword from the troll's waist and raised it high above his head. "This is for my mother," he said, as he brought the sword down and buried it to the hilt in the troll's chest.

The creature bellowed and writhed beneath James, grasping at the knight's thighs with its long dirty claws. As it thrashed about, the crown tumbled from its head and rolled across the stone floor, coming to rest at Katerina's feet. A bubble of blood formed at Thrigor's lips as the last breath wheezed from his body. Suddenly, the guards disappeared in a puff of yellowish smoke; the spears they had been holding fell with a loud rattle. Phillip covered his ears as the deafening sound of the glass wall shattering into millions of pieces pierced the room and vibrated against his skin. Phillip watched as the troll king's body withered and shriveled, until it disappeared completely.

Katerina stooped to pick up the crown and placed it on her head. "Ruby, Ruby, red and dear, whisper your secrets in my ear." She blinked rapidly as the knowledge within it passed into her mind. Looking at James, she called out to the knight, "Ewan? Is that you?"

As James turned to look at his sister, Cauchemar stepped between the siblings and screamed, "No! What have you done?" Lashing her arms out, she sent flashes of blue light skittering toward the pair. Each was struck in a blinding flash and frozen where they stood.

"Kitty!" Peter pushed his way between Phillip and Daniel and rushed toward the throne. Cauchemar turned with flames dancing about her head and flung another bolt at the boy, freezing him in mid-step. Turning to the other royals gathered around the throne, she began flinging bolts of lightning at each as she screamed in rage. After each was frozen in place, she turned to face Phillip and Daniel, her shoulders rising and falling as she gasped angry breaths. "You!" she wailed as she stepped from the dais down to the throne room floor. "This is all your fault."

"Surrender, Cauchemar," Daniel said as she inched closer to the two princes. "The armies of Clarameer are at your gate. You'll never escape alive."

"That may be, but I will take you out first. If I can't have my throne then this spineless dolt will not have one either!"

"You cannot kill me," Phillip said and puffed out his chest.

Cauchemar paused and stared at the young man. "And just how will you stop me. I have magic! True magic. And only magic can fight magic."

Phillip stared at the woman as the flames around her head died down, until his eyes widened as an idea occurred to him. Looking at Daniel, he reached out his hand to the other prince and smiled. "A friend of mine once spoke some horribly clichéd words, but I see now that they are true." Taking Daniel's hand in his, he pulled the prince closer to his side. "Love is stronger than magic."

"Absurd," Cauchemar said with a snort.

"Daniel," Phillip said, as he turned to the other prince and dropped to one knee, "marry me?"

"What?" Daniel asked as he looked down at Phillip. "Phillip, this is not the time for—"

"Oh, please," Cauchemar scoffed.

"Will you marry me?" Phillip asked again.

"I don't understand what you're—"

"Just answer me now!"

"Yes," Daniel said with a chuckle, "of course I will marry you."

"You will stand with me?" Phillip asked.

"Forever," Daniel said with a gentle smile.

"I've had quite enough of this," Cauchemar huffed as she pulled her arms back and prepared to fling a spell at the two princes. As she brought her arm down, seven loud popping noises split the silent air of the room as the seven birthday fairies materialized between Phillip and his stepmother.

"Oh, Philly!" Mitta exclaimed, as she and Fria hovered to Phillip and Daniel's side. Pulling Phillip up from his kneeling position, she squealed, "I'm so happy for you, my little dumpling! We're here for your engagement blessings!"

The two fairies embraced the boys and kissed their cheeks, leaving small pink and blue lip prints where the kisses landed. Just as Mitta pulled her face away from Phillip's, a bolt of burgundy lightning crackled between their heads.

Jerking her head toward the source of the spell, Mitta exclaimed, "Dagnabbit! Why you ornery old jackass! How dare you try to hurt my little Philly on one of the happiest days of his life! He just got engaged! Have you no respect for love?"

Whipping her wand from its loop on her waist, Mitta blew a forceful puff of air through the silver ring on its tip. A small pink bubble formed and then popped loose and raced across the room toward Cauchemar. As it bobbled along, it grew larger and larger until it met Cauchemar's outstretched arms and engulfed the sorceress within its shiny pink surface.

Phillip stood with his mouth open as he watched Cauchemar beat her fists on the sides of the bubble and open her mouth in a scream that remained trapped with her inside the bubble.

"Some people," Mitta said with a roll of her eyes, as she turned to Fria, "they just can't leave a sweet moment alone."

Phillip walked slowly toward the bubble and watched Cauchemar as she scurried around with a look of terror. As he approached the shimmering surface of the bubble, small rainbows reflected off it and danced about his face. His stepmother stopped scrambling and looked at him, her face drawn downward in defeat.

He took a deep breath and said, "Don't worry, Cauchemar. Once you have reversed the spells on my friends and my father,

I intend to show you the mercy you refused to show anyone else."

"Phillip," Mitta said from behind him, "be careful, doll. My bubbles are rather fragile."

"You talk about plans and power. About who deserves what. Talking. Talking. Talking. But most of all," he continued, "you kept talking about the rules. How things should be and how they shouldn't. What the rules allow. What they don't allow." Phillip ran his finger slowly down the surface of the bubble. "But in all that talk, you forgot the most important rule of all. Your happiness shouldn't deny another's happiness. Don't ever try to deny a person their happily ever after."

As the last word left his mouth, he punctuated the sentence by stabbing his finger into the shimmering surface. The bubble burst with a gush of air that made Phillip's hair flutter back from his face and his eyes water and close against the wind. When he opened them again, there was nothing in front of him but empty air.

"What did I do?" he asked, as he turned to Mitta with a look of shock. "Where did she go?"

"Can't really say?" Mitta said with a shrug.

"Really?" Daniel said from beside the other fairies. "Is this another silly rule?"

"No," Mitta said with a sheepish grin, "I threw that bubble on a reflex without my glasses on. I have no idea what spells I attached to it. So I really *can't* say where she went."

"Oh no!" Phillip wailed as he rushed up to the fairy's side. "But I needed her to reverse the spells on my friends and my father. Mitta, you have to remember where you sent her! You have to bring her back! She has to—"

"Phillip, darling," Daniel said as he grabbed Phillip's shoulder and turned him to face the throne, "look."

Phillip's friends were moving again and smiling at him. One by one, they stepped down to the floor of the grand hall and rushed to Phillip and Daniel.

"Phillip! You did it!" Gwen threw her arms around his neck. "Honestly!"

"I can't believe she is really, finally gone!" Peter crowed, as he slapped his hand on Phillip's back. "Good work, sire!"

Phillip stood silently staring at his gathered friends, unsure of what had just happened. He looked around at their faces and could see the joy in their expressions. He knew they were expecting him to say something, but he had no words for the relief he felt as the weight of his troubles and the toll of the journey lifted from his shoulders. He opened his mouth, but the words his mind scrambled to find just turned into a nervous laugh. Suddenly his knees began to tremble and he felt as though he might drop to the floor where he stood. Phillip stared at his feet to try to steady himself. As his body began to waver, he felt the warmth of Daniel's fingers snaking into his hand and intertwining with his. Phillip glanced down at their hands, then up into Daniel's face. The love and admiration dancing in the other prince's eyes shot through his body like a wave of light and heat, and Phillip felt the strength return to his legs. Daniel squeezed his hand, and Phillip's mind landed on one word Daniel had said—"forever."

As Phillip steadied himself, he caught sight of the seven fairies assembled across the room, all looking at him with peaceful smiles. Mitta floated slightly forward from the group and nodded her head at Phillip. *I should thank her.* Suddenly, he was interrupted by the sound of a horn blaring in the distance. The armies gathered at the Canteran borders would arrive soon to find no army to battle and no foe to vanquish. After he had traveled across all of Clarameer's lands and gathered the kingdoms together, Phillip had been able to conquer the witch with one single poke of his finger. *Was this Mitta's plan all along?* Phillip watched her bobble on a breeze that floated in from the windows. The fairy patted her bouffant hairdo and winked at him. Phillip threw his head back and laughed.

"Phillip? Sweetheart?" Daniel squeezed his hand again. "Are you okay?"

"Yes!" Phillip said as his laughter ebbed. "I'm just happy! It's over. It is finally over!"

James and Katerina walked up behind Daniel arm in arm. James tapped Daniel on the shoulder. "Highness," James said with a nod of his head, "I'd like you to meet my sister."

"James," Daniel beamed, "I mean Ewan, you don't have to call me Highness anymore. You are the king of Cantera now!"

"No," James said as he turned to Katerina, "The crown rolled to her feet. It picked her, so she is the queen. In a strange way, Cauchemar actually trained her for this. I'm better at adventure." James glanced over Daniel's shoulder at Gwen. "I think there is a different adventure ahead of me."

"Daniel!" Phillip turned to the prince, scooped him into his arms, and spun him around. "Her spells have been broken!" Setting Daniel down, Phillip took his hand and began pulling him toward the door of the room. "My father should be free now! We have to hurry home to see him!"

"Phillip, wait."

"Come on, Daniel. Let's go. Home!"

"Wait," Daniel begged as he dug in his heels and pulled back against Phillip's hand. "I have to ask you something first."

"What?" Phillip said and stamped his foot.

"Did you mean what you asked me? Will I marry you?"

"Oh, that?" Phillip said with a grin. "Well, I had to find a way to fight magic with magic. It just occurred to me that the quickest way to get some help would be to get the fairies here."

"So you just did it to get the fairies here? Or did you mean it?" Daniel asked, as he held Phillip's hand and looked into his eyes.

Phillip looked back at Daniel and flashed a mischievous grin.

"Phillip?"

"Well..."

# $E$PILOGUE

I N HER SEAT OF HONOR AT THE RIGHT OF THE KING'S THRONE, Mitta fluttered her tiny pink wings in pride as she looked around the grand hall at the crowds packed along the two sides of the room. Of all the weddings she had attended in the past year, she was sure this was the grandest and best attended of them all. Hundreds of candles blazed in the large chandeliers, even though bright sunlight streamed through the room's tall windows, scattering over the assembled crowd. The walls of the room were bedecked in banner after banner, embroidered with the colors of the kingdoms of Clarameer, while a rainbow of pennants in the birthday fairies' special hues hung across the back wall. Beneath the banners were long tables loaded with trays of pastries, fruits and all the bounty of the five kingdoms. Mitta had been pleased to see that the sketcherazzi were at least four rows deep outside the castle walls and had been scratching away at a furious pace as royal after royal flooded into the castle for the ceremony. She knew this would be front page news in the *Kingdom Inquisitor* for at least a week.

Looking to her right, she saw James, using the name he had chosen to keep, standing with his chest puffed out and his hands on his hips. The leather tunic and breeches he wore showed the wear and dust of his travels among the realms of Clarameer, Glorianna and Osterling. She and the other fairies had enjoyed watching as he and his traveling companion had met adventure after adventure, and she hoped he would find his way into Obenland soon. Glancing to her left, she saw James's companion, Gwendolyn, beaming at the crowd. Though she had discovered the comfortable joy of wearing breeches and a tunic while traipsing about with James this last year, Gwen had let her father convince her that the deep gold velvet gown she wore today would be much more flattering on the pages of the *Inq*.

Gwen's father sat in the second row to the right. Since he had surrendered his kingdom to King Robert, Edward had decided to stay on as an adviser to Queen Katerina, helping her decide which of the many rhymes Cauchemar had taught her were true and which should be cast aside. He had also taught her the same dances he had taught Gwen, just in case. Queen Katerina sat beside him, the ruffles of her Canteran red gown firmly up on her shoulders where she preferred them. The citizens of Cantera adored Queen Katerina for freeing them from the troll king's dungeons. Her husband, King Peter, was equally beloved for having converted the dungeons into a library for all the citizens to enjoy.

Behind Peter sat King Robert, stuffing his face with a pastry he had pilfered from the tables of sweets along the sides of the room. His wife, Queen Emmaline, held her small son, Prince George, on her lap and dangled a golden chain to keep him entertained while they waited for the ceremony to begin.

Across the aisle sat the cousin queens, Marina and Bianca. The very pregnant Marina and her husband, King Andrew, sat staring into each other's eyes, oblivious to the pomp surrounding them. Queen Bianca, having conquered and imprisoned Marina's father and reunited the two halves of Lipponia, was respected by all the kingdom's citizens, but Mitta knew Queen Fiona, Bianca's recent espoused, was the true favorite of the people. Though she hardly said a word, Fiona's hidden wisdom helped her royal wife rule their kingdom well. The two queens sat with their arms intertwined and occasionally leaned their heads together to whisper to each other and laugh.

Mitta's attention was pulled back to the front of the room as King Henry and Queen Rhea stepped from the side of the platform in front of the thrones. King Henry motioned to the trumpeters on either side of the room to play a short fanfare to quiet the murmuring crowd. Both parents beamed at the assembled crowd before King Henry nodded toward the front row. Mitta glanced over to see Princess Monique, or Lady Moon as she had decided to be called, stand up and turn to face the crowd. A quartet of lutes began playing a tune behind her as she held her head high and began to sing the opening lines of "True Love Someday Will Be." As Mitta hummed along with the tune, the entire crowd turned to face the large oak doors at the back of the hall.

The doors opened to reveal Prince Phillip and Prince Daniel standing arm in arm. Prince Phillip wore a tunic of Bellemer blue, except the sleeves were a deep Sylvanian green. Daniel's tunic was of a similar design, but with the colors reversed. Both men had a crest embroidered upon their chest of a seahorse with its tail wrapped around an acorn, which Mitta thought was pretty but an ecological impossibility. Both men wore gold coronets, which glittered in the bright sunlight. As the music swelled, the two men began to walk down the center aisle toward the front of the room.

Mitta looked over at her sister fairy, Fria, and grinned. Her cheeks were beginning to sting from all the smiling she had done that day, but she couldn't stop the reaction. Fria winked at her and pointed toward the front of the room. Mitta glanced down to see Dinah, the sorceress princess, step quickly out into the aisle in front of Phillip and Daniel. Mitta held her breath as she watched the two men stop and stare at the girl, confusion clouding their faces. Dinah stood with a look of annoyance before raising her hands to cast a spell. Mitta slipped forward on her chair, ready to spring into action. Dinah laughed and thrust her hands forward. A shower of rose petals burst forth from her hands and fluttered around the two princes. They laughed and kissed the girl on either cheek before climbing the three steps to the platform. Both men hugged their parents before turning to face each other and hold hands.

Mitta's wings fluttered in delight as she watched a look of love pass between the two young men. Their parents began to recite the words of the wedding ceremony that the royals of Clarameer had used since the days of Gingerfair and Godrick. After thousands of years and countless weddings, Mitta knew the words by heart, so she was caught by surprise when the men added two promises at the end.

"I promise I will be here each morning, to keep a valiant watch over your heart and your soul."

"I promise I will be here each night, to send you to sleep with the kiss of eternal love."

*Mitta, old girl, you done good.* Mitta stretched her toes out in front of her and looked at the amethysts that sparkled there. *Once this ceremony is over, you can have a well-deserved nap. Then it's time to figure out this whole heir-to-the-throne thing. That's going to be a doozy.*

Mitta giggled quietly and scanned the crowd. One face caught her eye. *Luna is going to clip my wings for interfering, but it only seems fair.* Discreetly pulling her wand from her side, she held it up and nipped the tiniest of breaths into the silver ring. A minuscule pink bubble floated away from her wand and out over the crowd toward its intended recipient. It bobbed and bounced along the breezes in the room and over the heads of the royals in the first few rows. When it reached the third row, it made a quick turn, landed on Peter's head and silently burst. Peter shook his head and reached up to scratch where the bubble had landed. As his hand passed his ear, it brushed the pencil tucked away there. Peter grinned. Pulling the pencil out from behind his ear and his pad from his tunic pocket, he began to write.

"Once upon a time, but about six months before that..."

The End

# ᴀ̶CKNOWLEDGMENTS

GETTING THE CHANCE TO WRITE AND PUBLISH THIS BOOK HAS been like a fairy tale come true for me. Therefore, I need to thank all the many fairies, wizards and unicorns that helped to make it possible.

First and foremost, I have to thank the entire IP team for this amazing opportunity. Thanks to Annie, CL and Lex for believing in this story and giving me the chance to get it out of my head finally after twenty years. May the birthday fairies bless you twice this year!

Thanks especially to Annie for making me realize that this story could be more than just "something fun." Also, I thank you for calming my fears when I was scared to let it be more than that. Sneaky feminism forever!

Thanks to Liz and Nicki for helping me iron out the wrinkles, tidy up the grammar and realize that things have to make sense on paper not just in my head.

Thanks to Becky for taking my vague ideas and even vaguer descriptions and turning them into the artwork for the book. How did you create things that are exactly as I envisioned them? Are you sure you're not psychic or do you have a magic wand you're not sharing?

Thanks to Eric Nelson for reading a muddled version of this tale years ago and encouraging me to continue with it after I had grown up enough to tell it. Your teachings and advice have stayed with me long after the classes ended.

Thanks to Knits, Mimsy and Heidi for being willing to listen when I wrote myself into a corner, wanted to humblebrag or just felt like being silly. You are the beautiful birds over my flying basket.

Thanks to Scott R. and Scott H. for the constant friendship, encouragement and occasional art project. Love you, My Lous!

Thanks to Carrie for being my loudest cheerleader, constant reader and swiftest kick in the backside. This book would not exist without your initial push and continued encouragement. Brewbaggery shenanigans forever!

Thanks to my parents for giving me an early love of imagination, reading and storytelling. Your love, understanding and support have made me who I am today. You have always been my greatest listeners. Brewer family motto: The joy you take in telling a story increases the joy others will take in hearing it.

Thanks to Fab for understanding when I disappeared into this other kingdom for days at a time and for waiting on me with open arms when I returned. My greatest joy in life is knowing I get to share the road with you.

Finally, thank you to the many LGBTQ people who have come before me and fought the hard fight for the freedoms I enjoy today. I stand on the shoulders of many far braver than I.

# Questions for Discussion

1. *The Rules of Ever After* takes several traditional fairy tale themes and turns them on their collective ear. What are some of these themes, and how are they used differently in *The Rules* than in their original form?

2. Monique explains that her Happily Ever After wasn't ruined by her unexpected turn of events, but that it gave her a chance at a new beginning. How did the characters in *The Rules of Ever After* redefine "Happily Ever After"?

3. What established rules are imposed on the characters, and how do they find a way to navigate around them?

4. How does losing status cause a chain of events that leads characters from *The Rules of Ever After* to discover something new about themselves? Does being free of expectations open new doors for them?

5. What is the difference between a rule that is meant to protect the kingdom versus a rule that is designed to maintain an established order? Are they the same thing, or different? Are there examples of these in *The Rules?*

6. How does *The Rules of Ever After* illustrate the power of friendship? How can friendship show you a new path that you might not have seen by yourself?

7. The author has said that *The Rules of Ever After* is a book he wished had been available to read when he was young, because fairy tales did not include gay characters. Does the inclusion of a gay character change the essence of a fairy tale?

8. The villain Cauchemar says that she is just trying to get her Happily Ever After, too. Can anyone have a Happily Ever After, even if they deny it to someone else?

9. Fairies use magic to interfere with the lives of other characters in *The Rules*. By granting both blessings and curses, are the fairies striking a balance? What is the role of the adversity that they create?

10. With lives dictated by curses and blessings and rules, how are the characters lives changed when they take an active role in reshaping their lives and their world?

## About the Author

KILLIAN B. BREWER GREW UP IN A FAMILY WHERE THE best way to be heard was to tell a good story, therefore he developed an early love of storytelling, puns and wordplay. He began writing poetry and short fiction at fifteen and continued in college where he earned a BA in English. He does not use this degree in his job in the banking industry. He currently lives in Georgia with his partner of ten years and their dog. Growing up in the South gave him a funny accent and a love of grits. *The Rules of Ever After* is his first novel.

# Say **hello** to

**duet** TM

an imprint of interlude **press**

## Also from
### duet

**COVER NOT FINAL**

**Summer Love** edited by Annie Harper

Summer Love is the first collection of short stories published by
Duet, the young adult imprint from Interlude Press.

These short stories are about the emergence of young love —
of bonfires and beaches, of the magical *in-between* time when
young lives step from one world to another, and about finding
the courage to be who you really are, to follow your heart and
live an authentic life.

The contributing authors have written stories about both roman-
tic and platonic love featuring characters who are gay, lesbian,
bisexual, transgender, pansexual and queer/questioning. The
authors also represent a spectrum of experience, identity and
backgrounds.

**ISBN 978-1-941530-36-8  |  Available June 2015**

# **duet**books.com
the **young adult** imprint of interlude**press**

CPSIA information can be obtained at www.ICGtesting.com
Printed in the USA
LVOW08s2241300715

448332LV00001B/98/P

9 781941 530351